Debra Adelaide is the author of several novels, including *The Household Guide to Dying* (2008), which was sold around the world, *Serpent Dust* (1998) and *The Hotel Albatross* (1995). She is also the editor of several themed collections of fiction and memoirs, including *Acts of Dog* (2003) and the bestselling *Motherlove* series (1996–1998). She has also been a freelance researcher, editor, book reviewer and literary award judge and is now an associate professor at the University of Technology, Sydney, where she teaches creative writing.

Also by Debra Adelaide

Novels
The Hotel Albatross
Serpent Dust
The Household Guide to Dying

Anthologies
Motherlove
Motherlove 2
Cutting the Cord
Acts of Dog

Non-Fiction
A Bright and Fiery Troop (ed)
Australian Women Writers: a Bibliographical Guide
A Window in the Dark (ed)
Bibliography of Australian Women's Literature

Letter to George Clooney

DEBRA ADELAIDE

PICADOR
Pan Macmillan Australia

First published 2013 in Picador by Pan Macmillan Australia Pty Limited
1 Market Street, Sydney

National Library of Australia
Cataloguing-in-Publication data:

Adelaide, Debra, 1958– author.

Letter to George Clooney / Debra Adelaide.

9781742613093 (paperback)

Short stories, Australian.

A823.3

Typeset in 12.5/18 pt Granjon Roman by Post Pre-press Group
Printed in Australia by McPherson's Printing Group
Edited by Julia Stiles.

Papers used by Pan Macmillan Australia Pty Ltd are natural, recyclable
products made from wood grown in sustainable forests. The manufacturing
processes conform to the environmental regulations of the country of origin.

i carry your heart(i carry it in my heart)

— ee cummings

Contents

The Sleepers in that Quiet Earth

Having formed these beings she did not
know what she had done.
— Charlotte Brontë,
Preface to *Wuthering Heights*, 1850

She had planned the story and already written something that could be an opening chapter. From time
to time when ideas came she would write them down in
a book her mother had given her. It was not the sort of
notebook she would have chosen to write in, not stories
anyway, but it happened to be there when she needed it.
A spiral-bound notebook, the paper rough and absor-
bent. The cover was the wrong colour, a fake kind of
purple, a purple trying too hard, a purple that didn't
even fool small children. She wondered if it was meant
to be a children's notebook, if her mother, in her frail
condition, had bought it without thinking. The cardboard cover felt like plastic. Her fountain pen would

not work on the paper. She would write the story on her laptop.

But the purple notebook contained a list of recent contact details, and Dove had brought it into bed with her one evening along with the phone. She reached for the notebook early the next morning. She'd had a restless night and had woken several times, then again before five. For ten minutes or so she lay there, seeing the story in her head, the story she would write, she could write, when she had emptied her mind: that day's work, then the bills and emails that needed attending to, calls she would have to make before the end of the day. Her mother's caseworker had left three messages, of increasing frustration and, she suspected, hostility.

Yet her mind seemed unusually focused on the story already. She wrote down the ideas that had awoken her, then showered and dressed, but she continued to see it unfolding. Unlike in a dream, she could see details of the clothes her character was wearing, the colours of the houses and the lawns she was passing, then the bus she was riding, and where she sat on it, three seats behind two women with rose-tinted hair and string shopping bags. The bus was almost empty.

As she made her breakfast and put a load in the washing machine, she continued to see her character and hear her voice. The cat butted at her ankles, wailing. She bent down to the floor with its bowl. 'Here you go, puss cat.' She rarely used its name. The cat pushed its face into the biscuits and Dove ran her hand along its back. It could eat and purr at the same time, or maybe that was a growl. Dove had little affection for it, but it had had nowhere else to go. The mewling wail barely abated as it chewed its food then sat to lick its chest. But even the cat could not block out the sound of her own story in her ears as she tidied her breakfast things and went to the bathroom.

'See you, puss.' By the time she grabbed her bag and keys and shut the front door, the whole story was clear already, again, clearer than a dream. She even knew the weather that day, could see the sky with its shredded-tissue clouds, on that warm day in the suburbs. It was midmorning, a Tuesday. Her character's name, Ellis, was unusual for a woman.

———◆———

Ellis was visiting her father, in his home in Ashfield. Riding the bus, Ellis thought about the names of these suburbs, on this summer's day when men like her father were busy in their gardens. Ashfield, Haberfield, Strathfield. She thought, as she pushed open the window of the bus to let in more air, how odd a name like Ashfield was, how the negative connotation of the first syllable contrasted with the romantic one of the last. How the place was, in its orderly suburban way, filled with houses and parks, cabbage tree palms and eucalypts and camphor laurels – so unlike an ashy field – but that once it must have been something like a wasteland, to gain the name. On this particular day the air smelled like a field, a great one, of hay perhaps, or wheat, recently mown. As if all its men had conspired to cut their front lawns that morning, infusing the warm air with the smell of freshly sliced grass, which Ellis breathed in as she pushed her face up to the window of the bus. She wondered if the inhabitants of Ashfield, so comfortable and untroubled, ever thought the name Ashfield odd, discordant.

It was a slow journey, but once they had turned off Parramatta Road, she didn't mind. At this time it was a pleasant way to travel, if you were not in a hurry, though at other times the buses could be frustrating. Into town, for instance, where the journey past Railway Square and down George Street was always slow. She had not yet learned to drive, although she thought she would. Vince had urged it, especially now, but she had not been keen for her husband to teach her. She suspected that his amiable nature would change once she slid behind the wheel of his Valiant. Her father, who rarely went out these days but who held strong opinions, thought Annandale, where she and Vince lived, a lowly, seedy suburb with too many migrants and not enough foot- paths, and that if she at least drove she could get away more. But Ellis's father had never gone all the way down to the waterside and seen the gardens, the massive homes on the escarpment, and experienced the grandeur of the place. He equated Annandale with the grimy strip of shops on Parramatta Road, the crowded terraces closer to Glebe, the motor workshop on the main road, where Vince worked. Ellis suspected he had never dwelled on the name, Annandale.

⬦

Dove did not know why her character's name was Ellis, but as she saw her alight that bus, at the stop before the gate of her father's house, she knew without any doubt that this was her name. Lately she had been reading *Wuthering Heights*. It was possible that the name Ellis Bell had stuck in her mind, although every way she examined it, she could find no connection between her character, a young woman in suburban Sydney some time in the late 1960s, and that of the novel or its author or the author's pseudonym. She was only aware that she liked names commencing with E and with the El sound especially. They seemed natural, mellifluous (a mellifluous word itself), and rolled pleasingly across the tongue and out through the lips. Eliza, Ellis, Ellen, Elizabeth, Eleanor. If she were going to have a character in a novel – and it seemed that this might be the case – she would want to utter that character's name over and over, at least in her mind, to roll it around, easy and smooth, a sweet lozenge.

At what point she knew that Ellis had a baby she could not say. But the baby must have been there all along.

Reviewing the scenes she had already visualised – it was like pausing and replaying a film in her head – Dove now saw Ellis well before she reached the bus stop where she would alight. She saw her shifting the baby on her lap. The rose-tinted elderly women had cooed at him as Ellis had boarded and made her way past them to her seat. But after she had passed them, what Ellis did not see, preoccupied with propping the collapsible pram against her seat so it would not roll away, and settling the baby in her lap, was these two women whispering something disapproving about babies needing to wear more than singlets even if the weather was warm. One of them remarked on the absence of his sunhat, but Ellis had removed this and placed it in her shoulder bag before boarding the bus, since he was prone to flinging it off. Her father had given her the hat, and she would place it on the baby's head again before she walked through her father's front gate. It would make him glad to see his grandson wearing it. He was so very happy to have a grandson.

⁂

During her lunch break, Dove phoned her mother's caseworker, then the hospital ward manager, and finally the care facility ten minutes' drive from her home. She had been ringing every day lately.

'Good news,' said the Grange's residential services officer. 'We can take your mother soon. Possibly even next Monday.'

If there are no further hitches, Dove thought. Instead she said, 'Wonderful. I've been waiting for ages. We've been waiting.' Then, in case this was construed as a complaint of sorts, 'It's such a relief. Mum will be so much better off with you.'

She tried not to think about why the room, which last week was only a possibility, was now available.

'And,' he said with finality, 'we won't be able to ... accommodate any other changes. Again.'

'I realise that,' Dove said. She would try to discuss it tonight, though her mother could only speak with great effort, rationing her words out one or two at a time. Her lucid periods were mainly in the early evenings. A month or so ago she had breathed the words, 'Nursing home, Dove. Less trouble,' into her daughter's ear and reached for her hand and pressed it. Dove had spent considerable time at work on the phone, and later at home in the evenings sending emails. Except on the designated day of the move, having taken the morning off work, she had arrived at the hospital to find her mother sitting up in bed, preternaturally alert.

'I'm going back home,' she had declared with unusual clarity.

'Mum, you can't ...'

'Viv will be missing me.'

'But the Grange, they're expecting you. It's all arranged.'

Her mother had stared as if she'd never heard of such a place.

'He needs me,' she said.

Dove had folded her lips together then and not reminded her mother that the cat had not lived there for two months, that her flat was on the second floor, and that managing stairs had long been out of the question. Instead she had sat down and rearranged the reading glasses and tube of hand cream on the bedside table, until her mother lay back on her pillows and closed her eyes. Her mother had spoken three languages and played principal violin with a symphony orchestra. She had given music lessons and translated documents to put her daughter through university. Dove placed her hand on her mother's cheek, kissed her on the nose, and returned to work.

Now as she put down the phone she hoped the new arrangements would not be undone again. Perhaps she should visit straight from work. It would mean not getting home until after seven and by then the cat would be hysterical. It was slight and fussy and had cost her mother a small fortune over the years in vet's fees. How long did Burmese cats live? She had thought about smuggling it into the hospital but had visions of it leaping out of its basket and running through the wards, the kitchens, snarling in some corner of a closet, or worse, an operating theatre, bright and sterile, ready for surgery.

But then, it was possible the cat would snuggle into her mother's neck, as it had every night of its life, and sleep. And her mother might relax, without her medication, sleep more deeply, or for longer. Or forever. Dove wondered if the prospect she had had in her mind from time to time, of the two sleepers together, slipping quietly into death, was such a bad thing. The cat was stricken enough as it was. When she had first grabbed it at her mother's place, it had wailed and scratched her. Her mother had been lying on the kitchen floor since the night before, unable to move. Dove didn't want to think of the cat leaping across her mother's legs and kneading her chest in its anguish. Her mother had still been playing the violin when she bought the cat. She would remark on the cat's peculiar attentiveness. 'If cats could play a musical instrument,' she once said, 'it would be the violin.'

Tonight, they might have a conversation of sorts. Her mother might ask about her writing. But probably Dove would just read to her again. At first she wasn't sure if her mother was paying attention, or even enjoying being read to, but she never complained and was always quiet. Sometimes she lay there awake, saying nothing at all, and Dove would put the book down, say goodbye and leave as her mother stared into a distance no one else could see. And sometimes she simply closed her eyes and drifted into sleep.

Dove was surprised to discover her character was so stable and dependable. Ellis had developed into a good wife, a fond mother, a devoted daughter. There was no evidence of the sadness of her early years, of the great hole in her life. At sixteen, she had returned to Ashfield from boarding school, and gone to secretarial college. It was when she had commenced working in the garage on Parramatta Road, typing invoices and managing orders, that she had met Vince. She took another stenography course at night school and had just completed it when she became pregnant. Dove suspected Ellis was a little too dependable, and wondered if she was even boring or unexciting. But then she knew about Ellis's deep and terrible fears. Sometimes these fears manifested themselves in dreams so strong they woke Ellis, and she would sit up in bed sweating and clutching her chest. Or worse, so strong that she did not wake even though she struggled violently to do so. Many of these dreams were about entrapment. Ellis would cry with all the might of her chest to be let out of some dark and stifling place, but her cries were mute, her struggles impotent. Though if Vince had woken and watched her as she slept beside him dreaming these terrifying dreams, he would have thought her sleep was benign, as peaceful as the slumbers of the dead in the quiet earth.

One of these recurring dreams involved Ellis on a hospital bed in an operating theatre. She was anaesthetised to the point where she was incapable of making a sound or a movement and yet her mind was awake and alert and she knew that the operation about to be performed was all wrong, that her organs were perfectly healthy, and that the doctors had to stop. Stop, stop, stop. She always tried to yell this, tried to claw her way through the fog of the anaesthetic, but there were no exclamation marks in her speech. She mouthed the words, and there was no noise. She tried to lift her arms and form fists but could only look at her hands lying useless and heavy like sandbags on either side of her body. Although she was surrounded by lights and covered in sheets she felt as if she had been nailed into a coffin and lowered into the ground. She wept dry, unformed tears as she realised how she was going to sink back into the fate of being sliced open and violated, and how no one would hear her, and no one would ever know. The unfairness of it. And they would never know how hard she had fought, to stay alive.

<hr />

Dove sat upright in bed as she held her hands out to Ellis and lifted her free of the dream, just in time. She herself was sweating, almost gasping with the effort. The cat was pinning down the bedcovers. She nudged it aside and got out of bed. It was the early morning, when dreams were at their most powerful. She had never felt more connected to someone, more concerned on their behalf, and yet Ellis was only a character, in a story that had barely begun to be written. The cat followed her as she went down to the kitchen for a glass of water. Standing at the sink, she felt a strange urge to get dressed and drive to the hospital. At four am no one would notice or care if she slipped in. She could perhaps take the cat. If her mother was asleep she could just sit there and read.

They had chosen *Wuthering Heights* because it was shorter than *Jane Eyre*. She had read the novel, several times, but as Dove had sat beside her mother's hospital bed in the evenings or on a Sunday afternoon, she had begun to entertain doubts about this. The story was far more complex and surprising than she had imagined. She was not sure if her mother had taken any of it in, but she had lain there for a half or an entire hour, day after day, as Dove read, neither objecting nor expressing interest in the story. Sometimes she fell asleep, and Dove would keep reading aloud until the end of a chapter. On the following visit, her mother would murmur assent if Dove offered to read and, if she suggested something else, would just shake her head and almost smile.

As she thought about it more, she became aware that she had not so much dreamed this character with the curious name Ellis, as rescued her from the soil of her imagination. Ellis Bell – the name ringing, alive with possibilities – was on the 1847 facsimile title page of the novel, reproduced in her Penguin English Library edition. It was there in the biographical notice by the author's sister Charlotte, also included in her paperback edition and marked in her own hand, proof that she had indeed read it, and read it attentively, even though she seemed to remember a different novel altogether. And the more she considered it, the more she felt she had read the name Ellis often enough so that it had lodged in her mind like a speck of grit, eventually turning into something hard and polished.

Except her character was nothing like a pearl, waiting to be plucked from its shell. Ellis was unformed, limp. She was more like an abandoned creature that Dove had found somewhere, beside a remote road, leading nowhere. Sometimes she would lie half awake in the early mornings, feeling the cold autumn air, listening to the clock's gentle pip pip pipping, the alarm set for six-thirty, and think of this character whom she may have dreamed up, or who may have been someone she knew, from her past, but had forgotten, or had met once, on a bus or in a shop, or was somehow connected with a novel written over a hundred and fifty years ago.

She dragged this mute creature back into being, and it was a physical effort, as hard as pulling oneself awake when one knows one is not yet there at the crack of wakefulness. It was like dragging her out of the ground itself, the soil clinging to her, damp and cold. She sat her there, in a ditch, and watched the rise and fall of her chest, and knew she would live. It was half light, barely dawn. Why had she been beside the road? Had she fallen, or been pushed from a vehicle? There was nothing else about, no cars, no people, no buildings. There was not even a sound, or any trees. The road emerged from a scrubby background and curved to the same drab vanishing point. Ellis was clad in ordinary clothes, pedal pushers and a boat-neck knit sweater, striped orange and cream. Her hair was half across her face, tangled and dirty, but recognisable as a pageboy style. It was reddish brown. But her body was half coated in black soil and her legs were oddly straight from being dragged into the light, her bare feet – her shoes were lost – pointing back towards the ditch, and rolling beyond that, the landscape disappearing in a black-green cloud.

But even as Dove dragged her from the oblivion of unconsciousness, as she heaved and struggled and swore for those last crucial metres in order to get the limp form away from where the cold earth and the dark scrub conspired to hold Ellis back, she was also seeing Ellis, in the story in her mind, in another place altogether. In the suburbs, in fact, in Ashfield, juggling her baby and stroller on that bus. It was re-running in her mind but it was not the same scene replayed, rather the same scene viewed from a different angle, and she noted new things: Ellis holding out a coin, the driver jerking the bus away from the stop, Ellis careful not to

14

fall, sliding into the red seat halfway along, on the left, the baby on her lap. He was called Charlie. The women three seats in front, having discussed the absence of his sunhat with muted disapproval, were now holding their heads up high, gazing this way and that in the anxious manner of old people, looking out for their stop at the corner store.

Then Ellis was walking down that street in Ashfield. It was wide, lined with cabbage tree palms. She was walking along the warm concrete footpath, smelling again the scent of grass, and of dust, of boiled onion and meat dinners, from the houses she passed. Brick homes, most of them, neat, silent and unwelcoming, their front gardens fenced, with hydrangeas, lassiandra and plumbago – why were the flowers all blue and purple? – her father's place no exception.

She had reached the front gate, she was through it, and had then turned to push it shut, listening for the latch's oiled snick on the green wire gate, before walking up the path, when Dove realised Ellis had forgotten to replace Charlie's sunhat, as she had meant to before she met her father, and there was nothing she could do about it.

❖

The images in her head refused to emerge from the pages. Cathy racing barefoot across the moors. Heathcliff beside her, both yelling with delight. *Wuthering Heights* was not about wild free childhood at all. It was barely even Cathy's story. Instead it was the story of a servant, the housekeeper, the only one of her generation to survive. It was orderly, controlled, quiet. The novel had been swept and folded and locked. All the interesting, passionate characters were dead and buried before their time.

How had this happened? How had its author, Emily Jane Brontë – Ellis Bell – so independent and stubborn, let this maddening, self-righteous housekeeper, this character who pretended to be much older than she was, steal the narrative like that? Dove recalled wisps of stories about the author of *Wuthering Heights*. Her potent imaginary world. How she refused social obligations. The visions she saw on the moors behind the parsonage at Haworth. How she once took a poker from the fire and scorched the bite of a rabid dog on her forearm. Her refusal to accept medical attention, until the hour before her death. *You can send for a doctor if you like*. How she then turned her face to the wall and closed her eyes forever.

As Dove read the final chapter, where a woman sat in the kitchen sewing while her young charges played with words in books, she marvelled at its author. Emily Brontë had been brave as well as stubborn. She had permitted her story to be rewritten. She had abandoned it to the control of its readers. Although she conceived it, wrote it, published it – with a dodgy publisher, against the advice of her sister Charlotte – she had then let it go, entirely. It was no longer her story. She had created a magnificent illusion. Dove thought about why she had never realised this before, and why her reading of the novel was now so different.

'"...and wondered," Dove read, "how anyone could ever imagine unquiet slumbers, for the sleepers in that quiet earth."'

She closed the book and stared at her mother, whose eyes were shut. It was so simple, but it did not occur to her until she was placing the book in her bag to take home. It was not just that she had read the novel at the bedside of her dying mother. She had, for the first time, read the words aloud.

———◆———

When she abandoned the purple notebook and began to steal a half-hour in the morning before work, or ate instant noodles at the computer in the evening, she wrote with a sense of compulsion, almost peril. She dreaded interruption. The phone would ring. Someone might knock on the door. She feared the story would slither off and disappear like a snake into the bush. Or that she might just grab it by its tail and pick it up, only to see it transform into something quite unlike the story that had brought her awake those weeks back, awake with such clarity and urgency that she had reached for the notebook and scribbled pages of draft scenes before getting out of bed.

As her mother began to be less agitated, more compliant, the phone calls, the meetings, the arrangements, began to dwindle. Dove rang the Grange for the last time.

'I'm sorry,' and even as she said it she wondered why she was apologising. 'But my mother won't be leaving the neurological ward.'

The residential services officer cancelled the booking with cool efficiency. 'We can refund your interim deposit,' he said, making it seem like a very special favour when Dove knew the waiting list was long. 'But you'll need to invoice us.'

Back in the hospital, the staff began answering her questions with increasing vagueness. The evening nurse smiled and said, 'Your mother isn't suffering. Don't worry, we're monitoring her every day.'

Dove asked the resident outright, 'Will she die soon?'

The resident cocked her head and shifted her folder to another arm.

'The important thing is that she's remaining stable. And we're doing all we can to keep her comfortable.'

And Dove had to concur. Her mother was at peace, lying back on clean linen, her white hair, her white skin, smoothed and thin, exposing the bones of her face. Sometimes she would accept a few mouthfuls of soup or ice cream, a cup of tea. Other times she wanted nothing, waved her daughter away, her hand stiff like a dry leaf.

Dove had by then written enough of her story to begin revising it, and so she sat beside her mother's bed with her laptop. A structure emerged. As she worked she learned to block out the noises of the hospital. And she began to understand how to suspend work, quickly if necessary, hitting the save key and closing the computer if her mother called out, or if one of the nurses came by. She began to trust that the story would stay with her, and that her character, if she were strong enough, would remain in her imagination. And it was true that just as Ellis had lain on the earth choking for air, her breathing becoming less ragged, more regular, and as she had survived the ordeal of the nightmare operation, she would survive being tucked into a corner of Dove's life as she waited at the bedside of her dying mother.

Now that Ellis continued to live in the story that was still being written, Dove wondered at her fluidity, how she could be there in the ditch in the growing dawn, gasping and leaning on her elbows, struggling to sit up, crushed and exhausted yet clearly, undeniably, alive, and yet at the same time be walking to her father's house. Her mother coughed softly beside her.

As she saw Ellis at that gate, Dove wondered why she was even making this visit at all, but having watched her place Charlie on the path where he would take his first unassisted baby steps and then hold her hand out and take him further up to the front door which was now being opened by her father – who was

19

saying 'Hi-dee-hi' as he had for as long as Ellis could remember – she knew why Ellis was here, on the same day each week that she always visited. She knew that knowing this could be painful, and that she would have to be brave with her story just as Emily Brontë had been brave, and follow it where it had to go and then let it run ahead of her, alone. Ellis was here because her own mother was not and had not been for a long time, not since she was a baby. Dove finally understood this, and she typed this in between paragraphs, just a note in case she forgot, as her mother began to cough slightly again, a noise more like a groan. And now that Ellis was a parent, she came to prepare meals and clean the house for her father, with his only grandson. Charlie was beaming, arms out, tightrope walking, wobbling as he stepped forward, once, twice, three times, as Ellis laughed, reached out and grabbed him just in time before he fell, and swung him up to her delighted father on the front step. Dove's mother coughed once more. She wished she had brought the cat in after all.

If You See Something, Say Something

There were two ads in the *London Review of Books* personals that attracted me that morning. Felix Green at a hotmail address wanted a clever mistress for very light duties, mostly conversation and drinking coffee. It was the name that intrigued me most, as I believed I could handle much heavier duties than that. But the idea of an amusing, interested, attractive and wealthy-enough man called Felix Green, aged 56, was promising. Only problem was, he lived in London and I was here, in carriage two on the 8.50 to Sydney's Central Station.

Rail Clearways – untangling our complex railways.

Did you know that a sick passenger on a train at Berowra can affect trains to Penrith?

Or that delays at Sydenham affect trains at Parramatta?

Ralph, no surname, however, was seeking a companion for an overland journey through South America the following September, and was after someone with wit and resourcefulness, including the ability to mend a Kombi van with a hairpin and duct tape. The companion was not stipulated as female, but the hairpin made it clear.

I always liked the name Ralph. It was the name of the first boy I was in love with, back when I was twelve years old and in my last year of primary school. Ralph had caramel hair, brown eyes, tanned skin and the most dazzling smile in the entire western suburbs. I believe I am still in love with him. He lived in a white fibro house down the hill, screened by pampas grass, which we would drive past on our weekly trips to the shops. There and back, I would slyly twist my neck and slide my eyeballs as far as they would go, to stare at Ralph's house without letting my mother know I was staring. I am sure she always knew. I would wonder which of the flyscreened windows represented his room. Speculate on how, in the thick of the night, I would sneak from my house, at the top of the hill, and come to his window. I dreamed of fighting my way through the pampas grass and standing there until he opened the screens and leaned out, either to gather me up into his bedroom, or to leap out and join me in the steamy summer night. There we would exchange our first kisses, gently sliding our tongues together to taste each other's passion – just as the magazine stories said. I for one would lick his glorious shiny teeth. He would almost burst at the tender warmth of my full lips.

This was all sheer fantasy, as Ralph barely knew I existed, let alone cared about me. Had I appeared under his bedroom window late at night, he would have told me to piss off. Nevertheless, for years I secretly yearned for Ralph and his brilliant white smile, mourning the final day of term when he went off to a private boys' school and I entered the local State high school. I would be tormented forever by the thought of him bestowing those splendid teeth upon other girls.

———◆———

Shop Here: Ladies Children Babies
Sleepwear Outerwear All Sizes
Fines Apply
Skateboards Prohibited

Over a year of travelling on the Illawarra line and I had come to take more notice of the signs. For a chronic reader, signs are vital. When I forgot my reading matter, which was rare, I could only read what was spelled out on the walls and hoardings and carriages surrounding me. It is no great leap from merely reading the signs to interpreting them, and then only a small step to start seeing in them something of profound significance.

Sometimes the signs speak directly to you. Sometimes it is as if the signs were made for you alone. Hundreds of thousands of commuters every day go up and down the line, but a sign will be there for only one purpose: to speak to you. As I began to see and understand more in the signs surrounding me, I realised that the ads I was reading in the *London Review of Books* were becoming more fragmented. The personals were dissolving. People's lives were disintegrating by the month. The ads were more desperate, fanciful, audacious, unlikely.

Man, 45, seeks female, preferably under 40, for companionship. Dinners, movies, concerts, drives in the country. Okay, I want sex as well.

Amid the plaintive and comically anguished offers or requests for vague relationships, Ralph's ad struck me with its note of purpose, its promise of tangible adventures.

I had never driven a Kombi van, let alone attempted makeshift repairs on one. But I had operated my old Corolla with a metal nailfile, and I felt that counted. In fact it was something I was proud of, as it involved ingenuity, persistence, a tricky manipulation of locks and contacts every time I wanted to open the door or switch on the ignition. With my nailfile skills, I felt I more than met Ralph's requirements, even without the duct tape. But with duct tape I was a virtuoso. It was duct tape that was still holding my downlight together over my reading chair. Duct tape that kept my vacuum cleaner going; duct tape that ensured the noise from my muffler was kept to a minimum, and duct tape that meant the radiator continued to function. Friends and acquaintances (all male) had explained that duct tape was not designed to withstand heat. So the downlight would break apart again, the muffler would let fly with a growl sooner or later and the radiator hose would sizzle and explode. But in all instances they were wrong. Yes, I qualified for Ralph.

Dear Ralph

I read your advertisement in the *LRB* personals. I kept my old Toyota Corolla going with a nailfile (on reflection, a hairpin would have done the job nicely). However you are in the UK and I am in Australia. And next September I am not free. Plus I don't have a passport. So why have I replied to your advertisement? I just thought you should know that there is at least one woman in the world who is resourceful with vehicle repairs.

While waiting for a response, I received the next issue of the *LRB*. The neuroses seemed to have cranked up a notch. A professional M, 38, of Basingstoke at Box 19/12 wanted a girlfriend who could make his mother cry – a heartless common slut who would eject his mother from her two-year complacency. A female meteorologist, age not given, announced herself devoid of all pleasure since 12 June 2008. She did not specify what she wanted, merely what she was. Some of the correspondents were assertively punctilious about their requirements. For instance, a man, 37, sought a psychoanalyst/tailor/stevedore. Another man wanted a woman no older than 50 who was familiar with failure and beards, and whose taste in music was restricted to Belgian jazz. Ralph's request for a resourceful driving companion was looking quite tame by comparison. Though he was yet to email me back, I did not regret contacting him.

———◆———

Sometimes the signs contain useful information. People stick up those photocopied messages, advertising bargain computer packages for sale, or rooms to rent in houses nearby, Chippendale or Redfern. Messages sticky-taped to poles and pillars with optimistic little tear-off flags at the bottom, telephone numbers that remain fluttering in the wind.

Units to Let 8994 3001

Sunny room in house with private courtyard. No animals.

Meanwhile a physicist (M, 45) with a big dirt bike and swim fins was after a female pillionist to explore molecular gastronomy in Auckland, New Zealand.

A workmate of mine was planning to set off to New Zealand. She was the adventurous type so I emailed her the details in case she fancied the idea.

———◆———

Ralph seemed disinclined to reply. As the months passed, the *LRB* personals became increasingly lengthy and narrative-driven, much of them desperate. It was still the forum for obscure neuroses and wittily inflated egos, but concision was becoming sacrificed in favour of something more complex. Ralph's little message regarding hairpin repairs and South America was a mere prologue, barely an opening chapter, amid a score of ads that became less like ads and more like stories. Entire novels. Ones that spoke passionately of lives lost, careers forsaken, relationships curdled. Rancour was the dominant emotion. Pseudo-comic relief was tempered with self-deprecation and revenge fantasies. The columns seemed full of pathetic, impotent men and cold, bored but occasionally glam women in their fifties.

One ad ran for more than twenty lines, detailing the progress of the proposed affair once it was met with a reply, and concluding with the request that respondents just cut to the chase and send a post-relationship Christmas card, preferably along with a gift. This was in the issue that ran an ad for the *LRB* Personals Singles Night, which of course I would never attend, headed with one of its more famous ads:

I've been taller than this. And left handed. And once had all my body parts. So you won't be the biggest compromise I have had to make. Sensitive F, 43.

There was also an announcement: the *LRB* was proud to let readers know that the first divorce had occurred resulting from a marriage that had begun in its columns: 'What was once a desert is now but a wasteland. Don't say we didn't warn you.' Along with the bottle of champagne awarded each issue to the best message, the whole personal ads thing was beginning to look like a carefully contrived narrative.

———◆◆———

Within the carriage, the signs were generally far less ambiguous.

Stand clear of moving doors

Do not place feet on the seats

At night travel in the guard's carriage marked with a blue light.

Was that an invitation? Or an instruction?

———◆◆———

When I had given up on Ralph, almost forgotten him, a reply came. Rather terse, with no apology or explanation for the lateness.

If you can fix a Corolla with a nailfile you ought to be able to fake a passport with an old ration book and a rubber printing set. By the way, do you think it is true that the novel is a moribund literary form? Someone who reads the *LRB* should be able to answer a question like that as well as mend cars.

Regards

Ralph

Unexpected though it was, the question was pertinent. What was I even doing reading a publication like the *LRB* if I couldn't offer an opinion on current literary matters? I knew enough about these to know that there was some debate as to whether or not the novel was dead. Indeed, only the previous week I'd read a weekend literary supplement in which a journalist claimed to have proved it. And yet I noticed on the trains that the novel was by far the favoured choice of reading matter. After free newspapers, of course. The novel was generally the latest vampire fantasy, or something by John Grisham, but still a novel.

I replied thoughtfully, citing the reading habits of commuters on the Illawarra line as evidence. Then I mentioned that I thought the real reason the debate even existed was not because the novel was moribund (except I used the word 'dead'), but because other forms – like memoir, biography or even travel – were more lively and popular these days because they were being written more like novels. I wondered if Ralph was a secret novelist. Or a travel writer. Of course, *that* would be why he was planning a trip to South America: to write his next travel book. His question had been some sort of sly test. Perhaps even his initial ad was a test. But a quick search on the net revealed no information about an author in the UK called Ralph Poole. There was a Ralph Poole in Cumberland who was a car dealer and hire-car agent, with his own modest website. That made sense, though the dealership seemed to be restricted to those very small makes of vehicles that the English favour, none of which were familiar to me. And no Kombis were listed.

Meanwhile I did worry about Ralph's use of the word 'moribund' when 'dead' would have been adequate. Would a writer use that word, or just someone with pretensions to writing? I also reminded Ralph that in Australia we'd barely had rationing, besides which, it had been discontinued long before I was born. And that I was more of the Letraset generation, not likely to use a rubber printing set.

Ralph's next email was a bit disconcerting. It arrived so swiftly, considering the months I had waited for the first reply. And it was long, with photographs attached. He also seemed to have drawn a tight line between my lack of a passport and my interest in the contemporary novel. He asked what novel reading (or writing) crime I had committed to deserve having had my passport taken away. He also advanced very strong views about the impropriety of drawing upon real life – one's own or others – to construct fictions.

At that moment the prospect of a long trip through a foreign country in a dodgy Kombi with someone holding such ideas seemed unattractive. Imagine crossing the Amazon and having to listen to the righteous indignation of a person incapable of seeing the grey areas between life and art. Someone who used words like 'moribund'. Suddenly I was glad I had no passport.

The worst crime, I replied to Ralph, was not confusing real life and fiction but bad writing. Boring writing. I could also have said pompous diction but at this stage was not prepared to give up on the relationship, if that's what it was.

━━◆◆◆━━

Desert Rose (35) wanting to meet dusky lover for sandstorm romance, poetry reading and wine. In other words, let's drink too much and have tent sex. Omar Khayyam enthusiasts welcome.

Ralph had also mentioned his wife. Disaffected, he called her. But wife all the same. So why was he advertising for a companion on a trip to South America? And why was he also emailing photographs of his trusty Kombi? One of them was of the engine, which I found almost offensive in its intimacy. Nearly 17,000 kilometres separated us and this was only the second email: I was not ready to peer into the engine of Ralph's vehicle. Especially not with a wife lurking close by, disaffected or otherwise. And Kombi engines are so compressed. I could not spot the place where he invited me to consider placing a hairpin, should my hairpin/nailfile repair skills ever be called upon. Nor could I see any evidence of duct tape. It was likely that Ralph's *LRB* ad was wishful thinking, that he'd never been with the sort of woman who could effect repairs with personal grooming items, or with duct tape, or with anything at all. The photograph was of an unequivocally male vehicle. Right down to the dull interior. He promised to paint it letterbox red before the trip – but wouldn't that attract guerillas and drug runners? Or would its original mustard colour be worse, suggesting a military vehicle? Maybe he should consider inoffensive banana yellow or safe clinical white. Perhaps I would suggest as much in my next email.

It seemed likely that, despite his philosophical objections, Ralph was quite creatively fictionalising his own life. Certainly he was plotting it. His ad in the *LRB* personals was nothing short of evidence of that. Surely, like me, he'd also read Desert Rose's ad? Why didn't he contact her? He could invite her to travel through the sands of Africa instead.

As I corresponded with Ralph, sedition laws were being passed in this country that would mean writers could be thrown into jail for expressing their opinions. And there were other signs that had recently sprung up. *If you see something, say something*, the posters on the platforms urged us. But if you said something in writing then the consequences could be grave. Incitement to a terrorist act. Obviously it depended on what you saw, what you said, and to whom you said it.

There are security cameras all along the Devonshire Street tunnel and City Rail officers patrolling each end. Sometimes the officers stand at the turnstiles, tall and intimidating in their dark uniforms, fondling their truncheons. Even the women officers are forbidding, packing muscles and gazing out through dark glasses at the buskers.

Sometimes I wondered about people like the blind woman draped in robes who stood halfway along the tunnel singing 'Waltzing Matilda'. It is well known that this is one of the most subversive songs ever written, possibly even unpatriotic. I wanted to explain all this to Ralph until the thought struck me that he could be implicated. South America could have been a kind of code. And if it wasn't, at the very least it was a continent with a significant number of unstable governments and volatile political leaders. My passport wouldn't matter (since it didn't exist), but Ralph could well have his confiscated and I should warn him.

But after I emailed Ralph, I almost fainted with the implications of what I had done. Cyberspace was the least private space of all. I may as well have closed my office, burned my belongings, cut and dyed my hair and fled to Tasmania.

Ajax Spurway Fasteners Ltd

Est. 1956

Way Out Buses

Fancy Some Horseplay?

Erskineville

Fresh Seafood. Gourmet Sandwich.

On the Illawarra line the signs eventually vanish, for after Erskineville you enter the tunnel and from there, past Redfern and into Central, the only signs are the ones in your mind, and the ones written within the carriages.

Do not travel between doors.

Please vacate this seat for older or disabled passengers.

⊸◆⊷

Ralph emailed again, so he was obviously still safe. And yet he did not mention South America, Kombi vans, duct tape or even the contemporary novel. He merely elaborated on the rubber printing set. It was a must for any enterprising child of the postwar era, who could fashion for himself all sorts of documents – from collections of poems to give to unsuspecting relatives at Christmas, to stern if rather wobbly notes directed to a teacher. He provided an example of the former:

My rabbit has a lovely nose
Pink and wet and shiny
But it is never slimy.
by Ralph Poole, aged 7

And the latter:

Ralph is to be ekcused from rugby practise and
Arithmatic today due to a bad head cold. Yrs affec-
tionnately, Mrs V. Poole (Mother)

He also explained that he was an electrician by trade but
at heart a philosopher. Which was why he was bound to
pose provocative ideas, such as isn't the novel dead? (Or
moribund?) But I knew better. It was clear what a man
who had been faking letters and writing poetry from
the age of seven really was, and I wanted nothing more
to do with writers. How the Kombi or South America
fitted into this profile, I didn't care. I had failed to read
the signs. And the signs were everywhere, planted
in places as unlikely as the *LRB* personals, which I
reserved exclusively for my train reading. I should have
heeded them. I would vacate this column for younger
or more desirable correspondents.

Semiotician (F, 39) seeks meaning of life. Or of
anything.

The Form of Solemnisation of Matrimony

At first Lucille was reluctant to tell her parents. They had never really liked the boy at the time, thinking him fey and shiftless – which he was – and they were not the type to forgive easily or change their hearts. But her mother surprised her.

'Of course you're going to get married. Three daughters, and all these years I've never got a single wedding out of it. It's the least you can do for me.' She even offered to make the cake.

Her older sister would fix the flowers, and her younger sister agreed to play the cello. There was an aisle, but she did not want her father to lead her down it, not now, not after all these years, although she knew he would have done it, had she asked. The wedding would take place in the shop, which was only appropriate. She would open up the back room and there would be ample space. Five years earlier, Lucille had taken an extended lease on the old church. A retrenchment payout. The terms were long enough to take a risk, not so large that the business didn't have to pay its way, in the end. She had spent the first year removing birds' nests and stripping floors, the second travelling the world in search of stock.

Early on in the day, it began to rain. She got up when it was still dark and set to work down the long aisle to the former porch and vestibule, to finish clearing away the goods and displays and set out the chairs and tables. She had borrowed folding chairs from the woodcraft factory in the next town. There would not be enough for all the guests to sit down, but the idea was they should mingle. And the service as such would be brief.

She placed the bolts of raw silk and hanks of vegetable dyed wool in boxes, hung the felted coats and embroidered jackets and skirts behind curtains. The scrolls and wall hangings and musical wind chimes, the rice paper kites, the enormous feathers, some dyed, some not, the scarves and woollen hats and berets and plaited belts and bandannas, the purses and pouches and wallets. She packed them all in cardboard boxes and stacked them out of sight behind the curtains. As she worked she thought that the church grew lighter, despite the clouds outside, the increasing rain. And it seemed to her that everything around her was brown. All the natural dyes and native pigments of the things she touched. Muddy, dark, depressing. Tertiary colours, all of them. Brown coats, beige moccasins. The earthenware pottery, the oatmeal raw silks and wools. But brown, brown, brown.

She cleared the shop counter, placing the cash register underneath, and beside it stacking the baskets of small things – beaded balls, quills and pens handcrafted from wood, Guatemalan worry dolls. Lacquered pill-boxes. Natural fibre greeting cards, illustrated by a local artist. Vegetable oil soaps, rough cut, resembling dried tofu. Bare, freshly polished with Mr Sheen, the counter gleamed. It was a single slice of red gum. But still brown. How had this happened? She hated the colour for herself, never wore it. Had never worn it since school, in fact, as it was the colour of her uniform, and she hated school. Whichever way you looked at it, whatever shade the fashionistas called it – Chocolate Drop or Raisin or Brown Sugar or Cinnamon; brown was sellable if edible – brown was the colour of mud, of shit, of sludge and scum.

Now, with all the handcrafts and fabrics packed away, the church was clearer. The light inside seemed blue. She looked out the windows to the west, where the hills rose sharply, bony flanks smothered in dark green. So much rain in the last few months. There was no wind, the rain fell straight as a waterfall. A single, vast wet sheet drawn across the landscape. But if it had not been raining, she knew the light in the church would be green, or gold, or both. The church faced the street; opposite was Bean There, the new cafe, the post office and newsagency, and Cowbells, the organic bakery and dairy. Diagonally across was the better of the town's two pubs. But the arched windows along the sides allowed a clear view. To the east, she could see past the straggle of little shops, a plant nursery, and a row of low cottages, the garage and petrol station, until the town evaporated. It was a good position, though not as good as the Catholic church farther up the hill, on the highest point of the town.

Last time, it was going to be a Catholic church. She tried to remember why. Perhaps his parents? She had been eighteen, a mix of stubbornness and carelessness, and hadn't given a toss if the wedding took place in an RSL club or a cathedral or a garden shed. It was fortunate that he had come to her, swallowing too hard, looking at the floor, before they had made final arrangements. She had not felt it in her heart, as she might have expected, but lower, in her abdomen, her bowels. It was as if she'd been kicked in the stomach. She felt ill for days. Years. He had had the grace to disappear completely, which meant she was spared that other pain. Hope. Hopeless hope. If she'd ever seen him around, at parties – there were many mutual friends – at university, in bars and clubs, she would have felt worse. By the time she came down here, he rarely brushed past her mind, but if she had thought about him much she would have known that here, hours away from the city where they met, after all these years, thirty of them, she'd never see him.

———◆———

'Lucille! Such rain!' Her mother was at the door, shaking off her umbrella. She placed it in the corner and walked to the counter, producing a white box from out of a shopping bag.

'Can I have a look?'

Margaret raised the lid. They both leaned over and peered inside.

'Oh.' Lucille held her mother around the shoulders. 'It's beautiful. Perfect.' The cake was a simple one, a single round layer, iced in pale pink. The cerise iced roses on the top had silver cachous fixed to resemble raindrops. As they looked, a real drop slid from Margaret's face onto the surface. They both drew back. Her mother blotted it with a tissue.

'I'll find a safe place for it. Where's Dad?'

'He dropped me off. He's gone to fetch Cassie and her cello from the station.'

Lucille took the cake to the kitchen bench and placed it on a raised platter. Not brown. A white ceramic one with lace-like holes around the edge. She had an old silver carving knife which she'd already polished and decorated with a ribbon. Margaret unpacked jars of babaganoush and olives and began prising crackers out of their packets. She had brought six different types of cheese. Lucille's father had already stacked beer in a bar fridge he had borrowed for the occasion. A box of red wine was waiting beside glasses that Margaret had washed and polished by hand. There were trays of antipasto, covered in clingwrap, bowls of roasted nuts, multihued bread rolls from Cowbells – spelt, rye, sourdough, all brown – an entire ham waiting to be unshrouded and sliced. Her father would doubtless do that too. Lucille wondered if anyone would come.

As her mother hummed and sliced salami and fruit, Lucille packed away the last of the felted slippers, the leather belts and the embroidered handtowels. Possibly her guests would think she didn't trust them. But she preferred the place to be tidy, as unshoplike as possible. Even though the rows of pews had long been removed, the altar now stacked with prints and screens, vases and garden pots, hand-thrown, most of them, unglazed, brown, and there was not a prayer book in sight, the church looked more like a church again. Above the altar hung dozens of dream-catchers, crystal beads, silk-ribboned curtains, artificial butterflies on strings of fishing line. They would all dance in the breeze, but she couldn't risk opening the window up high behind the altar, for the rain would rush in. She pushed the last box against the wall, drew back the curtain and arranged a nest of chairs, a coffee table, smoothed over a lawn cloth and set out a candle. She lit the candle and blew out the match.

'Early for that?' Margaret was wearing one of the Red Centre Women's Collective aprons, covered in a design of bush tomatoes. They were brown too.

Lucille looked at her watch. 'Another half-hour,' she said. 'Anyway, they're eight-hour candles. I might light them all.'

As she did, weaving her way through the church, pausing at the few little tables, the shelves, the counter at the front, bending, striking, then blowing the matches out, her sister Julia arrived with the flowers. Together they placed sprays of miniature roses and maidenhair fern on the tables next to the candles. They had placed the last spray on the bench next to the cake when Julia lifted a final bouquet, creamy pink, out of the box.

'Peonies! But aren't they out of season?'

'You have no idea how hard it was to get them.' But Julia's twisted smile showed how pleased she was. She held the bunch, tied simply with green raffia, cradling the droopy heads against her chest for a moment, before looking up and handing them over. Lucille instinctively raised them to her face, but remembered peonies had no scent. She cradled their heads too, to show her appreciation, then placed them on the table next to where the celebrant would stand. She tidied away the box of remaining candles and took off her own apron. It was time to get dressed.

⟹·◆·⟸

But she did see him. Several months back, she was at the rear of the church late one afternoon. She had been about to close early, it had been so quiet, when she'd heard the bell. In the doorway, he was bending over, tapping something, grass cuttings, off the soles of his boots, and the late light threw shadows. Even when he stood upright and stared back at her, as she walked towards him, up the centre of the shop where the aisle between the pews once was, his figure still twig thin, she did not recognise him, nor he her. Her hair was longer than it had ever been, her figure fuller. Deep lines scored his face, his cheeks were stubbly, the chin sharp. His eyes seemed sunken, darker than ever. As the last of the afternoon light dropped on him he seemed both lucid and tenebrous. A devil blessed by the last touch of heaven. Who had been first to realise?

'David.' She could not remember the last time she had spoken his name aloud. He held out one arm and walked towards her, and she wondered how the years could drop away so quickly, like a satin gown that, untied, just slithered to the floor. By the time he touched her, or she touched him, all her rancour was underfoot – she kicked it back and stepped up to greet him. Before he had even said sorry she knew that she had always loved him, always would. And even as she smiled, and he smiled, and they both laughed, and embraced, holding back and staring into each other's faces, then embracing again, as long-lost lovers do, she hated him for that.

—➤➤—

In the tiny bathroom, really just a closed-off end of the rear porch, Lucille took down the frock she had hung there and slipped it over her shoulders. She gazed at herself in the mirror behind the door. The frock was a simple one, creamy pink silk. Her red gold hair, reaching to her waist, had frizzed considerably with the rain. Margaret poked her head around the door. She was starting to look worried.

'Dad and Cassie are here. And someone's just pulled up out the front, Aunty Lucy and Norman, I think. Thank god the rain seems to be letting up.' She paused, not mentioning the obvious. 'Can you open this?' She held out a jar of Persian fetta, marinated. Lucille took it and turned away to deflect the unasked question. Just don't, she said to herself, don't.

Holding the jar out from her dress she twisted the lid. It didn't budge. She turned the basin tap on and ran it under hot water for a few seconds. The lid loosened on the second try, coming away with a soft gulp of air. A few drops of green virgin olive oil speckled with pepper slid into the basin and Lucille stepped back by instinct, looked down, and sighed in relief. Her dress was unmarked.

'Aren't you going to wear some make-up?'

'I have.' She handed back the jar, wiped her hands and picked up the pink gloss she was applying to her lips.

'And fix your hair? What about some of those decorated combs from Morocco? One on either side would look nice.'

But Lucille was already scooping it back up into a loose bunch, which she tied with a ribbon that matched that of the wedding cake knife.

'This will do,' she said. 'I only need it to be out of the way.'

Holding the jar out before her with both hands, like it was a gift of the Magi, Margaret disappeared inside. Lucille felt the reproach of the deliberate action, the stiff straight back. Her arms dropped from her hair. She would not glance at her watch. Nor check her phone. And whatever was her mother thinking? The rain was not easing off at all. Only the sky seemed less grey.

She picked up the stockings and eased them on, then the low heels, in cream to match. Lucille had chosen the frock from the third dress shop she had entered, on a visit to the city specifically for the purpose. David had accompanied her, and they both began to feel ill less than an hour into the shopping expedition. They stood at the entrances to at least ten places, then stepped back knowing better. All the shops played music that made her spine shudder. The assistants were aged about twelve.

'Only people under twenty-five buy clothes,' she said. 'Let's go back.'

But David took her to a lane that featured boutique shops and stalls that spread into the cobbled road, with coffee and wine bars. He knew someone, a wife of a friend of a friend, who made individual garments and didn't care about the youth trade. The woman had matched purples with reds, emerald greens with blacks and golds. The interior of the shop was like an Amazon forest, lush and bold. But at the back was a rack of dresses in softer colours. Lucille held one up. Shot silk, it was pink one way, silvery another, cream in a different light. It had a crossover front and reached to the calves which emphasised the curves her body had developed in recent years. As she zipped the side she felt that it was exactly the right dress and when she came out of the dressing room both David and the woman nodded.

'I only finished that last week. I must have known you were coming,' she said.

<hr />

The day before, she had removed the dividing screens between the shop and the middle room, where there was a galley kitchen to one side, an open living area on the other, and between the middle room and the rear, where she slept. Now the whole church was open from front porch to back. A long high lozenge of cool air amid the pouring rain. Her personal belongings were tidied away, there were two thin lounges with cushions – red and purple, she was suddenly relieved to realise, not brown – and the bed was now a divan, covered in a striped Mexican blanket. Some of the guests were looking around pointedly. Exclaiming at the charm of the place, the ingeniousness of the living arrangements combined with her business. In small eddies they came, three here, five there, dumping their wet things on the porch and pretending the rain didn't matter. Pretending to be sociable, casing around for people they'd not seen for years, relatives, old school mates. Really, they were all eyeing the door, and wondering why Lucille was waiting down there by the kitchen bench.

She felt her intestines tighten. The celebrant was already here, chatting to her father who was fixing him a whisky and soda. He was an out-of-work actor and children's party juggler. He had another func- tion later that afternoon, in a town an hour's drive away, but had agreed as a favour to David, whom he knew somehow. Lucille forced herself into the knots of guests, with hellos and air kisses, accepted presents and pointed out where to hang coats, all the while his absence chewing at her stomach. Despite herself, she checked her phone. No message, no missed calls. A few mouthfuls of champagne helped for ten minutes.

After that she began to feel queasy. Thanks to her parents, the food and drinks were plentiful. She took another of the champagne bottles from where her father had placed them in a wooden – brown – barrel of ice and took a wooden bowl of nuts to give her other hand something to do. They were brown too. Then there was a platter of babaganoush and teriyaki rice crackers. Julia was handing that around. Why couldn't her mother have brought something colourful, cherry tomatoes or Sicilian olives?

Seated on one side of the former altar, Cassie was staring at the rafters playing a flaccid version of Pachelbel's *Canon*, which she had first resisted. So clichéd, she had complained when they'd discussed the program the week before. But Lucille had not wanted music with too much personality. Cassie could keep her esoteric chamber music and be thankful that Lucille had at least not asked for a cello version of 'The Wind Beneath My Wings'.

She circled around refilling glasses and chatting to the guests, spending thirty seconds, a minute, with each before moving on, all the while trying not to think and therefore thinking too hard on it. Standing over by the red gum counter, her great-aunt Lucy, for whom she was named, raised her eyebrows meaningfully. Lucille had hugged her and pecked Norman on the check when they'd arrived then artfully moved the conversation on. Aunty Lucy's diabetes. Norman's golf. How lovely it was they came so far south for the wedding. Her father was giving the celebrant a second whisky.

Another group arrived, recent friends, reading and drinking buddies from neighbouring towns, laughing and stamping their feet out on the porch, all of them, even the men, wearing colourful gumboots. Why hadn't she thought of that? Her cream shoes were already feeling damp, soiled. (Why wasn't he here?) She might change her shoes. She had to do something. (*Why?*)

'Champagne and snacks that way,' she pointed towards the trestle table where her father was standing, bottles aloft, head cocked to hear orders above the growing hum of conversation, the laughs, the plaintive call of the cello. She took their raincoats, umbrellas, and tossed them in a corner of the vestibule, where a puddle was forming. She turned her back on it and faced the room, looked all the way down past the counter, Aunty Lucy, the tables glowing with candles, the platform where Cassie was turning sheet music on her stand, a Navajo dream-catcher just inches from her head, her mother to one side still slicing something, a massive watermelon, bright pink – thank god – the whole length of her shop, her home. The rain would never stop.

She could do something. Margaret looked up as Lucille walked past, dodging sympathetic glances and offers of more drink, then she continued slicing, raising droplets as the knife slammed through the last of the watermelon. Lucille knelt at the bed. She whipped off the Mexican blanket, pulled it out from the wall and yanked the handle that turned it into a double bed. Underneath she had stored new white sheets and the doona. The week before she'd washed and dried the sheets outside, pressed them smooth with the steam iron and aired the doona of its ducky smell. She spread the bottom sheet out and drew it tight over the corners of the mattress. Margaret appeared at her side, knife dripping.

'What are you doing?' She glanced back at the guests collected at the front of the church like obedient sheep, trying to look like everything was normal. Wasn't it?

'Marking time.' She brought the top sheet up and folded it back exactly twenty-five centimetres, as if this were rehearsed.

'But the bed?' Her mother glanced back again. 'Everyone's watching!' She hissed this, like it was a dirty secret.

'Yes,' Lucille whispered back. 'But I still need it made up. May as well do it while I wait.'

Her mother muttered something that could have been 'crazy'.

'Yes,' Lucille whispered again, agreeing, whatever. They could all think her crazy. They all did anyway, deciding again to marry, at the age of forty-eight, a man who had already let her down.

As she rose from smoothing the doona it seemed to her that the light was lighter. By the time she pulled the slips onto the pillows and placed the gold brocade tablecloth across the foot of the doona – she had already decided it would do for a bedspread – she was sure. She looked out the window then. A break in the clouds to the west, an arch of light, a soft glow across the smooth white bed. She did not care what happened now. The guests could continue to drink, to party. Maybe the celebrant could juggle for them. She walked over and opened the back door of the church. Like all the windows and doors it was arched. Damp had made the timber warp and she tugged hard, releasing fine drops of water that settled on her hair and her dress. She felt like one of her mother's African violets, which Margaret tended with a spray nozzle. Her hair would be like fairy floss by now. She patted it down, congratulated herself on not wasting time at the salon. If she'd had the henna treatment – brown, anyway – that the hairdresser had offered she might by now have been dripping dye onto her pearly dress.

The back porch was soaked, its wooden steps down to the yard black and slick. The view across the vacant land next to her was unimpeded all the way to the hills, where the sky was white and faintly glowing, like an opaque window grudgingly admitting the light. Perhaps her mother had been right. The clouds were definitely thinning, the rain might stop altogether. It was now drizzling, not pouring. Standing next to a potted palm were her zebra-striped gumboots. She kicked off her shoes and stepped into them, then went down the steps and followed the path until she reached the corner of the church. Without turning around she knew that someone had come to the back door, was watching her. Julia. Her mother. Aunty Lucy. She didn't care.

⸺◆⸺

He was bookish and musical, which was why she supposed she had fallen for him at eighteen. Now he could be considered foolish, tuning pianos for a living – as if anyone had pianos these days – and working in a second-hand bookshop, like an eternal student. She had visited it a couple of times. It was a converted barn on a property up the mountain that was once sliced by a highway but was now neglected due to a freeway bypass. The owners operated it from Melbourne, online orders and internet marketing, and David was left to wrap orders and usher the occasional buyer through the pallets of books from deceased estates, where they were allowed to forage for themselves. In the office was a display of glass-fronted cabinets housing nineteenth-century hardcovers, which from boredom he had organised by colour, and which for amusement she had once inspected. Blue, red and green. *Boys' Book of Adventures* next to Trollope's *Barchester Towers*. A row of black Bibles, missals and copy after copy of *The Book of Common Prayer*.

'You should take one of these,' he had said, and she'd thought she might, seeing as her little church had been stripped of all its books long before. She'd insisted on paying the five dollars, handing over the note with mock gravity.

'Where will you put it?'

There was a barely used cash box in one of the office drawers, but instead David opened another copy of *The Book of Common Prayer* and placed the five-dollar note in the middle of the book, between the pages of the Form of Solemnisation of Matrimony. There the note remained, pressed against the sacred words, *With this ring I thee wed, with my body I thee worship, and with all my worldly goods I thee endow*, back with the remaining black volumes in the glass cabinet.

⟨⟩

Where had she put her copy? Standing on the sloping vacant lot next to the church, she realised she needed to find it, urgently. She would find it and – what? Throw it in the bin? Make a fire and burn it? Take each page – there were many of them, thinner than tissue, thinner than skin – and peel them out, like layers of sunburn, and feed them to the flames. Page by page. Every one, beginning to end. From Concerning the Service of the Church, to the Articles of Religion, all thirty-fucking-nine of them. It would take time. The guests would leave. They could sit there and watch for all she cared, if it took hours. She would do it. But where had she placed it in all the cleaning and packing away?

She picked her way down the hill across the slick grass and walked up the path, back round the side of the church and up the steps, purpose putting boldness into her stride. Not bothering to kick off the gumboots, she walked through the arch of the open door, the guests arrayed along the church, and her family holding their heads at odd angles, trying, she knew, to watch the front door and yet not appear to be doing anything of the sort. People must be getting bored by now. There was no sign of the celebrant. She thought the book was in the sideboard drawer. Cassie was playing the opening of Vivaldi's *Four Seasons* for the second time, her head tilted away from the cello, her feet shifting on the floor. Lucille would ask her father to get the pot-bellied stove going. He was holding champagne in one hand, red wine in another, asking, rather too loudly, if people required topping up. No, it was in a box up under the red gum counter. Aunty Lucy and Norman eyed the zebra boots as she stomped towards them. Pushing past them, conscious the party buzz behind her was now just an awkward hum, dozens of eyes on her, she ducked down behind the counter and was feeling around for the prayer book, it was only the size of a sandwich, when she heard her aunt's throaty voice, 'Lucille. Lucille.' She found the book, stood up, conscious the church was now dead quiet. Across the vestibule, a shadow blocked the open front door.

She had never seen anyone so wet. He might have been standing under a waterfall for the past hour. His hair was a tight helmet, a black basin. His clothes clung to him like a grieving mother. Water trickled off his nose and chin and the puddle at his feet blossomed steadily, his figure reflecting before him in a sudden light that broke through the clouds in perverse splendour. The rain had finally stopped.

A sigh, of amazement, relief then joy, rushed from the guests. Glasses tinkled. Laughter erupted. Someone cheered. Cassie resumed playing Pachelbel's *Canon* again, but much livelier this time. Julia came up to her sister bearing towels.

Underneath the water David's shirt was green. Lucille helped him peel it off, exposing his pale but delicately muscled torso, his fine fan of chest hair. The wedding guests obligingly looked away, poked their noses into their drinks. She loved that chest hair, which was not too abundant, not too sparse. Slicked wet, it reminded her of the first time they had made love a thousand years ago in the humidity of a January night. While he stripped away the rest of his clothes and emptied his boots, she found him a loose shirt and a pair of hemp drawstring trousers from the goods she'd packed away. Moccasins, a tooled leather belt. Everything brown.

'I prefer blue, or green. But we'll cope.' His eyes seemed bluer, brighter from the pinched, damp cut of his face. Someone brought him a glass of red wine. His nose still dripped like a melting ice block, and as she leaned forward to kiss the chilly tip she noticed his hair was so wet the grey had disappeared. Suddenly she felt that love she'd felt when she was eighteen and he was awkward, sensitive and fallible. When she heard him playing piano scales from a room deep inside his house, as she waited at the front, and when he tripped on the hall runner as he opened the door, sorry he had not heard her knocking sooner. That creative awkwardness her parents had despised – why wasn't he studying engineering or working in a bar, doing something useful? – but which trapped her heart.

How had they all forgotten there was no bus service out from the mountain on a Saturday afternoon? He'd waited there in the rain for half an hour before deciding to walk. After ten minutes his umbrella had turned to a skeleton then blown away. As he walked he passed no one, either coming or going. And of course, there had been no phone reception. The wind dropped but the rain increased. He had walked through water to get to their wedding. He was only an hour and a quarter late.

'Shall we continue?' Margaret was at Lucille's side. She was so relieved she hugged her almost-son-in-law tightly through her dislike.

'Yes!' He finished his wine and raised his glass for more, one arm reaching for Lucille, but she had shaken him off, and run out the door, down the front steps and across the churchyard, splattering mud up her boots and onto the silk dress, just in time to catch the celebrant at the door of his car. 'We're ready,' she said, and handed him *The Book of Common Prayer.*

Virgin Bones

This early, the morning queue at the tap is not so long and when I get back Mrs D is setting out breakfast. She still does everything nice, even though we've got the move on. Bread crust mash, bacon rinds fried crisp just as I like them. The kids are already eating, Rusty sitting on top of Our Flower in Heaven, kicking his heels against the side panel. I chase him off. Kid has no respect.

'But Mum's packed up the cushions already,' he says. So she has.

'Mrs D, I know we have to get everything ready fast, but where do we sit for our breakfast today?' She just shrugs, scraping the last of the mash onto my plate.

'Sit on the step. It's swept clean, all ready for that sluicing down now you got us that water.' I sit on the step with Mirabelle.

'Coffee?' I say.

'No coffee, hon,' she says. 'You know that.'

Always hopeful, that's me. I was sure she'd have saved a bit, especially for today.

'Anyway, I used the saucepan for the mash. Can't do both.'

I bet she has got some coffee grounds squirrelled away there. Mrs D is the best wife a man could hope for, always has things super-clean, always puts a meal together out of next to nothing. Our kids might have no shoes and wear charity box clothes, but they are the neatest clothes you will ever see, on the cleanest kids ever. She cuts Rusty's hair with the kitchen scissors I got from a swap. Mirabelle's braids are always sleek and tight. Last night she set the two of them in the tub, washed them head to toe, one after the other in an inch of water practically, while I sat on top of Grandfather Benedict and held Emanuel, which she'd done first, him being so little. All over in minutes, the kids even dusted down with a tin of talcum powder she produced from god knows where, then put into clean shorts and T-shirts, all by dark and ready for today. She could have done a man a cup of coffee. Lester's wife was up the cafe only last week emptying out the knock-box. She generally gives Mrs D some.

'I'll have some of that water for these breakfast things,' she says, which is her way of getting me to eat faster, reminding me that we've still got lots to do.

I hand her my plate and she washes it, dries it and packs it into the milk crate, the blue one. The red one is for my cleaning cloths, trowels and spray bottles, plus I keep an electric cord there, just in case, and a set of screwdrivers which are rusted but still do the job. In the blue crate she keeps her saucepan, our plates and cups, her steel knife and wooden spoon, and underneath a packet of rice or corn or sometimes lentils, a packet of dried chillies, god knows why, no one but her likes them, plus a plastic box of salt. She always has salt, no matter what. And some coffee, twisted in a bit of foil, I'm sure. If you boil it long enough then let it settle, it tastes nearly as good as first brew. Always better with sugar though.

The rest of our stuff fits into three striped bags, and it's lucky Rusty is big enough now to carry one on his own. Mirabelle sets to washing down the steps.

'Don't you get dirty, mind,' says Mrs D, then to me, 'Now we have to clear off all this stuff. I wish I could leave the gas ring, it's so heavy.'

'Sure,' I say. 'And come back and find some low-life's made off with it? Besides, the Family won't like that.'

'I suppose,' she says. She knows I'm right.

First we do Grandfather Benedict. We take off the cotton blankets, shake them outside in the fresh air, and fold them neat. Mrs D stows them in the bottom of one bag while I whack the pillows to flatten them as much as I can. Then the mattress. Or that's what she calls it. More like another blanket, but better than nothing. Then we do Our Flower in Heaven, where the kids sleep. Sleeping bags, blanket, Mirabelle's knitted caterpillar which she's promised to hand on to Emanuel. Mrs D's already got the clothes and other things stacked and ready to go. Mirabelle hands me the empty bucket and Rusty wipes the steps with a cloth, so they'll dry faster. The marble is grey and pink, nicely seamed. Some folks here have all black marble. Yes, it's sober and respectful, but I don't like it. And Mrs D says it shows every speck of dirt, even the dust, and there's a lot of that. Next-doors are forever cleaning their place, plus I reckon it's hotter in there in summer, colder in winter. Our place is just right.

Last night when I was sitting down in the Roses of Remembrance Garden having a smoke with Lester and some of the other men, Mrs D swept the place out. She would have done it twice, in the dark, just to be sure. When I got back she was sitting on the top step, the broom tucked under her chin. She's not a tall woman, my Mrs D, but she still has to bend low to sweep. Lucky it's not the size of a real house, the vault.

'Remember when we moved here?' she said.

As if I could forget. Lester had run all the way up to town to say he'd found us a spot, but we had to be quick. Mrs D needed some persuading, even though it was her own sister who'd just gone and got herself shot. 'You want to stay here in the slum forever,' I said, 'and get us all killed too?'

'Well?' Lester said, still panting. 'The Family won't be there much longer.'

'You run back and ask them to wait. We'll be there,' I said, giving Mrs D the look. Then I told Rusty to run and get those bags from round the corner. Connie wouldn't be needing them any more. But then I went and held Mrs D because it was her sister.

'It'll be so much better there,' I said. 'Fresh air too. None of these crowds, people packed in like sardines. Think of it!'

'But the dead,' she said, crying onto my chest. 'Living among the dead.'

'Better than dying among the living.' Which I thought was quite poetic. It was the violence that got Connie, just a random shot but that's all it takes. She mopped her eyes and got Mirabelle and started putting our things into the bags.

The Family was about to leave but Lester had kept them there until we turned up, talking about this place and that place, showing them the work he'd been doing on the Avenue of Peace. Careful there, Lester, I thought, too much boasting and they'll sell their place and buy another, a better one. Like the vaults in the Avenue, which were all marked out, with a sort of community garden thing happening already. Roses, of course.

There are always roses, though at that time of the year they were just bare sticks in the ground. And lilies. The clients always want white lilies. Some developer was building a multistorey complex with cleaning, maintenance and gardening amenities that all the residents, or their relatives, could use. Sort of like an apartment block, except quieter. And no washing on the balconies. No disputes.

I liked the Family straight off. Father and Mother were good people, I could see that. They travelled two hours each way every other weekend to pay their respects. They were also rich. I already knew that by the pink marble and the brass plates. Father wore a Rolex, and they had arrived in an Audi, with tinted windows. Like so many rich women, Mother wore a well-cut but conservative suit, which I bet cost thousands, though I knew Mrs D wouldn't have given you ten dollars for it. I made my offer straight up.

'Me and my family, we'll see things are right, you can count on that. I've worked here for the last six years, cleaning and such. It would be an honour to look after your folks.'

'There'll be more to come,' Mother said, fixing me with a steely look. 'Great-Aunt's ashes. We're going to relocate them from the Mortdale Centre.'

'Good idea, ma'am,' I said ('ma'am' – where did that come from!). 'Mortdale is no place for a respectable family.' Which was true. We'd had to put Connie there just the week before, but there's no choice for folks like us. Lester used to work there. According to him it's always been full of ferals. And not just people. Some of the cats there, he says, are bigger than dogs. The places are always vandalised. People rip newly planted coffins out of the ground the minute the mourners leave, toss the bodies in the dump and resell the coffins. Connie'll be safe. No one bothers with people like us. She shares a shelf in a wall of five hundred. You need a ladder to get to her and lucky Lester lends us his folding aluminium one, otherwise there'd be no cleaning, no flowers.

'And Father's own Grandmother Sweetapple. She's ailing right now. It won't be much longer before she'll be joining the other residents.'

I'd noticed an empty niche, on the wall directly above Grandfather Benedict. That was one of the lovely features of the Family's place. It had ground-level facilities, space for six residents in all, and then spaces on two walls above. Not too crowded, nice and roomy. Two whole shelves for urns. Classy.

I didn't mention that I'd been eyeing their place on and off for ages. When Lester had first put the idea to me, months before Connie was killed, I'd even thought about moving in without the formalities. But two things stopped me. One being that the Family could appear at any time. You get lots of ratbags squatting in places out here, but the rules are strict. If you're caught, the Trust has the right to confiscate all your belongings and take you to the dump out west, which makes the slum look like a paradise, it's that overcrowded. The other being Mrs D herself.

Mother and Father conferred back beside the Audi while we waited next to the Family vault. Mirabelle and Rusty had run off to the Wishing Well.

Lester leaned close to me and muttered, 'Catholics. Best landlords you could hope for, you know.'

'I know.'

'They might be uptight, but you can always count on them for doing the right thing, financially speaking, I mean. Flowers, fresh *and* plastic. Brasso, as much as you want. And if you play your cards right they might even pay you something for saying a few prayers.'

Lester was right. Not a penny spared when it came to looking after the dead, your Catholics. Down where I work, in General and Non-denominational, it is nothing short of disgraceful. If you ask me, the people living there should be paid by their families to live on those sites. I wouldn't even call them tombs. Rusty is friends with a kid from The Meadows, a misnomer if ever there was one. Kid lives in a tumbledown hovel of old bricks and broken sandstone. It's a hazard. The whole place is like that. And it's the farthest from the facilities.

The Family came up to us.

'We'll need the place to be vacant every year on the Day of the Dead.'

'Of course. We'll move out, no problem.'

'And we mean vacant, don't we, Father?' Father nodded. 'None of your stuff, as we will be staying all night through.'

'You won't need to worry there, ma'am. And we'll make sure we have the place all spotless and cosy for you, come the last day of October.' I could feel Mrs D looking at me, thinking where on earth we'd be moving to, all of us with our stuff.

'And one last thing,' Mother said. 'We'd like you to polish the bones.'

Now I felt Mrs D stiffen, hard as. I nudged her to stay quiet.

'No problem. No problem at all.' I wasn't going to let this place go. Whatever polishing the bones involved, we'd be doing it to secure this place if it killed me. I'd heard of it. Lester would know the details.

'Not Grandfather Benedict,' put in Father. First time he spoke all meeting. 'No need for that. Just Our Flower in Heaven. We want her kept nice and clean.'

Then Mother took out her hanky and sniffed and turned away and Mrs D, who has the softest heart in the world, patted her on the shoulder and they went and talked women's talk, Mother sitting on the step of the vault, Mrs D respectful beside her, while Father and I scuffed our feet and looked at the sky and wondered about rain. He fished out the key from his top pocket and handed it over, looking even sadder. It transpired that Our Flower in Heaven was only twenty-one when she died, and a virgin.

In the end I reckon Mrs D was even looking forward to it. She had that look in her eye, mentally adjusting the fixtures and fittings. How to make the best of the light. Where to place the striped mat she's had forever and puts out in all the places we've lived.

'I could make sure the flowers are always fresh,' she said. 'Every day, I'll fix that. And I'll get some proper vases, not pickle jars or anything. Nice glass ones, or silver.'

'Not gladioli,' said Mother. 'She'd hate them.'

'No ma'am.'

'Or carnations. Old ladies' flowers. That's what she'd say. Nice gerberas, or something fresh. Girlish.'

'Gerberas. You got it.'

When they left I poked her in the side. 'Where the hell we gonna get silver vases from?'

Mrs D poked me back. 'Or flowers.'

<hr />

I dig out the Brasso and do Grandfather Benedict while Mrs D takes care of Our Flower in Heaven. The plates are already clean but we both like to make an extra effort. Then I stand on the crate and do Grandmother Sweetapple. Her plate is a lot bigger than the other two even though it contains less wording, just two lines, but Mrs D says that's because by then Mother and Father must have been even richer. Or they didn't love her as much, I reckon, but feel guilty for it. By the time we finish they're so shiny they look like silver, not brass, and Mrs D always makes sure to wash the residue off the marble. There are never any green outlines on our brass plates. I lift the urns down and wipe the shelves clean while she polishes Great-Aunt and another fella we've forgotten the name of. There're two empty urns, waiting for whoever, and Mrs D gives them another clean and wipe dry just in case the Family think to look inside. We hardly ever use them but sometimes at night you can't go dragging kids all the way off to the facilities. Especially in winter. Then it's time for the bones. Shifting the slab is the worst. And I don't just mean the weight, but that first wave of stale musty air. Mrs D retires behind her apron while I fan the air a bit. But Our Flower in Heaven is a sweet thing, and it doesn't linger too long, the smell.

I'm bending over my crate for the trowel and the hand broom when Mrs D shrieks.

'Oh my god, Dempster, oh my god. Look at this!'

And there in Our Flower in Heaven's coffin is the weirdest of sights. The poor girl is missing one leg, knee down. A vacant pink ballet slipper sits like an abandoned puppy next to its mate.

Mrs D instinctively bends down and looks underneath, not that there is any underneath to the whole slab, which is cemented onto the floor of the vault. She looks around, up, as if the shinbone might have lodged itself on the shelf next to the urn with Great-Aunt, or be stuck to the ceiling.

'How could this be?' She whispers now, looking around, careful no one hears of this dreadful mishap. This calamity. It could be the end of us.

'What are we gonna do?' she demands. 'Dempster. Say something.'

I shake my head. Lift my cap then scratch it. Shake it again. Mrs D crosses herself. She's not even a Catholic but I understand. It's that kind of moment.

'I need a smoke.' I sit on the top step and get out my zip-lock bag. I've only got five butts left but I pull all the shreds out and roll them into one good thick smoke for a change. I need it. Mrs D pushes me off.

'Go away. I've cleaned in here, you know. Don't want you stinking up the place.'

I walk round the block, past the Angel of Death and the row of broken pillars and the flat-roofed vaults where people have erected tents and annexes. I always watch myself here, these folks are prone to throwing out a bowl of dirty water, or worse, without bothering to see if anyone's passing by. But it's all quiet. Most have already left for the day, or they left last night. By the time I return I've got the solution.

'Are you crazy?' Mrs D says. 'She's always worn that miniskirt. Where would you get a long gown from anyway? And even if you could they'd poke around and feel her. They'd know.'

She's right on all counts. And they'll be here in less than an hour. Now she starts muttering about Rusty, saying she'll tan his hide if she discovers it's him who took it, even if it was only for a joke. I don't know about that. Rusty couldn't move the slab on his own, it's almost too heavy for the both of us. Then there's the question of motive. And where he'd put it. But if it's not Rusty, then who? And why?

'All right,' I say. 'How about this? You start the polishing. We've done the rest of the place anyway. And I'll go find us another bone. It won't matter if it's not attached. They fall to bits anyway.'

'Dempster. Are you planning to rob another corpse of its legs?' She has her hands on her hips.

'Leg. And only half. Just the shin.'

———⋯◆⋯———

Mirabelle is across the way sitting on her favourite slab, the one with a picture of a pair of arms reaching out from a cloud down to a child dressed in robes. Emanuel is sitting on the grass beside her. He's a placid baby. Just about ready to walk, but I don't think we'll have to watch ourselves like we did with the others. Rusty was born a runner. Used to dart here and there so fast it wore Mrs D out so much she swore she'd never have another. She must have forgot. Emanuel was conceived right on top of Our Flower in Heaven. Born right on top of Grandfather Benedict, after we shifted beds.

I like to think he's got his peaceful nature from those lovely folks, themselves at peace.

First I go to the facilities. Good place for thinking, apart from a man's basic need. In the cubicle there's even paper today. Someone must have done a train run recently because there's a pile of *Dailies* and a few *Examiners* left, which I prefer as the cheap paper is softer.

Problem is, folks here guard their bones closely. Which is why it's such a mystery how that shin's gone missing. Folks here have been jealous of us for some time, I know that. Firstly because some of the longer term residents had eyed our vault for a while. Reckoned they had prior claims. Then they got suspicious when they heard about Connie. A random shot, was all, poor girl. But people think gangs, drugs, the usual, just because we come from the slum. And then when I found that gas ring at the dump and brought it home, next-doors stopped talking to us. Said we were getting above ourselves. Even though Mrs D offered to heat cans for them, if they wanted. She even gave them a lid of bacon rinds, cooked to perfection. Sent Mirabelle over with a nice message which they just ignored, sending the poor kid back. Mrs D tossed them away, a whole lid full. Which she'd only obtained after hanging around the Concourse all morning until everyone else got bored or had better things to do, and when the kitchen hand came out and threw the scraps in the skip she grabbed them straight away, so they were as clean and fresh as.

On my way out of the facilities I bump into Ranger Sykes. He's okay. So long as you mind yourself.

'Morning, Ranger.'

'Hey Dempster. Nice day for it. And night. Be clear all through, I reckon.'

'You're right there. Bet you got your hands full.' It being the busiest day of the year for him, though Mothers' and Fathers' Day come close.

'You folks all ready?' Officially, he has no business with my place since we got a private arrangement, the Family and us, but like everyone in uniform he takes it too seriously. But I always humour him, it wouldn't pay not to.

'Just about. Place has never looked cleaner. You want to come by and inspect?' Though I sure as hell hope not. What if he looks into Our Flower in Heaven?

He pats me on the shoulder. 'Nah, I know you're good for it, Dempster. Not everyone abides by the rules like you. If they did I'd hardly have a job, would I?' He laughs. I laugh.

I start to walk off when he calls me back. 'Say, Dempster?'

'Yes, Ranger?'

'We're implementing a Client Satisfaction Survey. A form for the families to fill out. Come by my office later and collect one. You give it to your family before they leave. Then you have to read their comments and thumbprint it if you agree. So it's all fair, like.'

'Will do, Ranger.'

'Give my regards to Mrs D.' I watch him walk away. His stomach is getting bigger, straining against his belt.

The thin edge of the wedge. This is the third or fourth bit of paperwork this year. *You have to read their comments*. Meaning, we have to ask them to read them out to us. I know what he's doing. Trying to weed out the illiterates. He won't catch me there. Already I've got Rusty doing his alphabet and numbers with Lester's eldest, who once went to school for a whole year. Then what we do, before dark some nights, is trace over the biggest letters on the plates, all of us reading them out. Mrs D sprinkles the talc on top of Grandfather Benedict, and the kids form their letters with their fingers, then spread it clean, over and over. I reckon by the time of Ranger Sykes's next bit of paper we'll all be able to read it, bar Emanuel of course. In fact my plan is that by the next form he dreams up I'll be signing my full name, with my very own pen too. No more thumbprints. Looking forward to the shock on his face then.

⸺◈⸺

On my way to find Lester I pass the Townies. A whole row of them jam-packed just like they are up in the town where they come from, and honestly I don't know why they bother, except the air here's cleaner. But if you're going to live five families to a place and string your washing across the lane and squabble late into the night over the one TV connection, you may as well have stayed in the slum. One of them yells at me as I pass, young Fingersmith, I think it is.

'Hey Dempster, any more home improvements up your place lately?' Then laughter. I look into the tiny window, basically just a missing brick in the columbarium wall. Three of them, all sitting in the dark around an upturned Frytol tin with a pack of cards.

'Puttin up some shadecloth?' he says.

'Maybe a nice teak deck?' says another. More laughter.

'Nice day, boys,' I say as friendly as I can. Nothing irks them more, I'm sure. Then my king-hit. 'Don't see you moving out for your families today.' Which is true, and I know despite everything they're jealous of folks like us, who have a Family to visit regularly, religiously. Residents of the Townies never get visitors. It's pretty sad. No wonder these boys are as they are.

Funny, though. I was thinking of putting up a bit of cloth, just for the hottest months. I've been keeping an eye out at the dump for a piece of sailcloth or netting that would do.

Lester'll be working down in the Avenue, which is kind of his baby after all these years. He's very particular about his edges. I swear the line where his lawn meets the white marble is so sharp and straight you could cut your fingers on it. I find him sweeping leaves with a broom he's specially designed so it doesn't dislodge the fine white gravel of the path. A bundle of cloth rags he's tied and shredded and trimmed so it gets into every corner. He gets down on his knees to do this, even though the gravel cuts them. He and Mrs D make a good pair, they're both that fussy.

When I tell him the problem he shakes his head.

'No stores left.' He speaks low, in case someone's nearby. 'I've heard there's been a lot of pilfering lately, especially of the young residents. Yours isn't the only instance, Dempster.'

'But why? What do they want with shinbones?'

'It's not only legs. I've heard forearms are taken too. Sometimes whole hips. I've heard . . .'

'What?' We're practically whispering now. He keeps moving his broom as we walk so it looks like he's working. 'What have you heard?'

He looks this way and that. 'Trade. They sell em for medicine.'

'Bones! Who'd want a leg bone?'

'Shh, will you. Come over here.' We walk around the south side of the last block on the Avenue, and lean against the wall. It's cool still, the marble not yet warmed by the sun. No one can spot us here.

'Your girl, she's a virgin, isn't she?'

'I believe so.' Mother and Father have said it often enough.

'There you go, then. People think they've got extra powers, your virgin bones. And they like them nice and dried out, hence your girl. She'd be what, seventeen, eighteen years dead?'

'Twenty.'

'Right, perfect. And they're clean.'

'Cleanest in the whole cemetery.' We're proud of that, me and Mrs D. In fact last time, Mother and Father hinted they'd be amenable to writing us a reference, if we ever wanted. Not that we did. We being happy there. They being happy for us to stay. And so on. But if we ever . . .

'That's it then,' Lester is saying. 'They slip the bone out, take it off to be processed, no cleaning or drying needed, just grinding and packaging in zip-locks, then off to the distributor. Quality guaranteed. I tell you, Dempster, out on the street that stuff could fetch thousands.'

I'm still comprehending all this, wondering what special powers you get from these virgin bones and do you inject it or eat it or what, when he hits me with it, looking at me meaningfully.

'I've heard up at the Mortdale Centre it's getting worse. They're taking fresh bones, so long as they're young and virgin, drying them out artificially. There's such a demand. You might want to warn Mrs D.'

Connie! I'm going to have to get her out of there. Connie all on her own, no one to protect her bones from vandals, it doesn't bear thinking about. I've got to tell Mrs D but then Rusty comes belting out of nowhere and runs right into me, clutching me round the legs.

'Dad, I've been looking for you everywhere! It's Jamie. You gotta come fast.'

Turns out Jamie down in The Meadows has gone and got stuck playing on top of one of the slabs. His mum doesn't know what to do and his dad's already gone to work.

'This is why I'm always warning you about that place, son.' I pick him up, he's so out of breath, and walk as fast as I can. The Family'll be here in fifteen. They're always super punctual.

Jamie's mum is moaning and wringing her hands with about fifty kids hanging off her, grizzling. Jamie himself is sitting on the edge of a double slab that has cracked all the way across, and half collapsed in on itself. The kid is taking it well, not crying at all, though his left leg is at a bit of an angle.

'What were you doing?' I say as I assess the damage. There's a fresh crack right where his ankle is jammed.

'Just jumping from side to side. I missed. Rusty always wins.'

Rusty looks sheepish. I've told him a million times not to play this game.

'All right, well Rusty has to come here and hold you nice and firm.' I glare at him. 'Then I'm gonna prise this slab aside okay? You're gonna be all right. It'll be over in a jiffy.' He nods. I go and grab his mother's broom which is resting against the side of their place, not that it looks like it's used much.

'Okay. Ready now.' By now Jamie's only just holding back the tears. Rusty holds him steady around the middle and I prise the broom handle under one edge of the broken slab. 'When I say, just pull him straight back Rusty, nice and easy. Make sure his foot's free. One, two, three.'

It goes like clockwork. The bit of broken slab's not as heavy as I thought. Next thing, Jamie's out and his mother's fussing over him and all the kids are cheering and crying and I'm holding the slab thinking how best to reposition it when I look down, right down, and that's when I spot it, directly below. Perfect. 'Hey, Rusty. I need you for a second.'

<hr />

We're sitting on the bottom step, our legs spread out onto the lawn, and Mrs D has found some coffee grounds after all and it's never tasted better. We're exhausted. The kids are all asleep early, even Rusty. The Family left a bit of a mess this time, candle wax everywhere and flower petals squashed on the floor of the vault. But I don't mind because they also left a whole lot of rollies with real tobacco – Grandfather Benedict loved his tobacco – and some broken sugar skulls for the kids. Like Lester says, Catholics don't stint. They also gave us two more tins of Brasso. They were very happy with the place, and even remarked on the quality of our polishing. Our Flower in Heaven's bone fitted nicely and if they noticed it was a shade darker they didn't say.

This time I chose the railway terminus on the south line, which is less crowded and has the advantage of the kids being able to run along the shore all day. Mirabelle even found a scallop shell, cracked, but still a shell. Mrs D sat there enjoying the breeze through the waiting room window while I took Emanuel off her for a while. We'll go back there next Day of the Dead to wait it out. Ideally we should have been attending to Connie, but just the idea of staying in the Mortdale Centre all day and night is impossible, with the types you get there. And you wouldn't be able to move an inch in her section. Best time is the day after. It'll be filthy, but at least no crowds. Tomorrow we'll have to get her out somehow.

As if reading my mind, Mrs D says, 'Dempster, I'd really like to bring Connie down here, you know.'

'Mrs D,' I say, 'you deserve that. You surely do.'

I get out my zip-lock bag thinking, I'll have to find a way somehow. Maybe she could rest temporarily in the niche next to Grandmother Sweetapple. We'd have to take her with us of course, every year, so the Family won't know.

'Do you really reckon it could be done?' Her eyes are shining.

'I'm your man,' I say, lighting my smoke and drawing her close. 'I'm your man.'

The Harp Society

One night there was a musical event at a grand house set in such large gardens the driveway disappeared among the shrubs well before the house appeared. The house was invisible from the street. It was a winter evening, with a light drizzle of rain. Lights set low in the garden guided the guests all along the driveway to their destination, though there were few pedestrian visitors. Flora Lindsay arrived just on time, before the doors to the reception room were shut. The friend she was meeting was even later. Either that or she had gone in ahead, although Flora couldn't see her among the rows of chairs. The function was unexpectedly crowded and afterwards she walked back down the drive to wait by the front gates for the taxi she had ordered. Soon it

became apparent that no taxi was coming. In the cold
and dark, looking down towards the street then back
towards the house, no one, she realised, had passed her
by, though several cars were still parked in the long
curving driveway. It was not that it was the time before
mobile phones, just that Flora Lindsay did not carry one.
She walked back to the house where she found a caterer
stacking wineglasses into a station wagon. He took her
into the house by a side door and showed her the hall
phone, where she dialled the taxi company.

The musical evening had been a recital by a harp
ensemble. As Flora hung up, she saw the tall young
woman who had been one of the soloists wheeling
her enormous harp out of the room where the performance had been held. The woman had changed from
her recital skirt into a pair of trousers, and her long
hair, which had been held up with a tortoiseshell clasp
as she leaned over her harp during the performance,
was now tied into a simple ponytail. She was wearing
a small backpack. In its black case, the instrument was
a monstrous thing. Solid timber in frame and sound-
board, it was heavy and unwieldy. Yet the woman
handled it as if it were a cargo of meringues, guiding it
down the steps and towards her van with the same deli-
cate yet strong touch Flora had observed in her earlier,
plucking and stroking the strings. Now she coaxed the
instrument, top-heavy, on ridiculously small wheels, to
the door of her van, where she tilted a ramp down to the

ground, pushed the harp up, at the same time turning the instrument to lie sideways, replaced the ramp, then shut and bolted the doors. And then she got into the driver's seat, turned the engine over and slowly drove off. The van coughed in the cold. Flora heard it puttering a long way down the drive.

It only occurred to her then that she might have asked the woman for help, a lift back into town or somewhere. It also occurred to her that the second taxi she had rung for would probably not arrive either. She pulled her coat tighter and walked back down the driveway to wait. By then it was raining properly, and she wished she had remained at the house under the front porch. She walked close to the fence railings under the branches of a large Moreton Bay fig. The footpath was covered in squashed fruits, foliage and bat droppings, which she stepped around, ducking drips from the leaves and avoiding the worst of the mess underfoot. And yet despite all this she did not feel morose, or lonely, or even uncomfortable. Her spirit was instead buoyant. The program had included unfamiliar pieces – she had never even heard of some of the composers – and yet she had felt that she knew the music very well.

The image of the woman ushering her instrument away lingered. She would be taking it home, Flora assumed. What sort of home would have room for an instrument of that size? And professional musicians had more than just one instrument. Perhaps harps required more than one room, perhaps the harpist's home was given over to her instruments. Coming from a background that had no musical talent and only an amateurish appreciation for music, Flora wondered what it would be like to live surrounded by musical instruments. And that harp, so big, so awkward to manage, what commitment such a musician would need to have. The passion for it, the devotion. What the instrument would be worth, she could not even estimate. More than a first-class fare to London? Less than a car? And then there were the many years of lessons, the hours of daily practice, the preparation for just one performance, such as tonight's recital. How long had the ensemble practised for this one appearance? Several nights a week, for months? And they had not received any payment. There had been a table outside selling the ensemble's latest CD. She regretted not buying one.

At the end of the driveway, nearly at the exit to the street, Flora noticed a small dark blue car with its interior light on. She was not sure if it had been parked there against the kerb when she first walked down to wait for the taxi. The windows were fogged and someone was sitting in the driver's seat. The door opened as she approached and a voice she knew called out. It was her friend Stephanie Lee, who was the publicist of the Harp Society, which had held the performance. She had not appeared all night, even though she was the reason Flora had attended in the first place.

'What happened?'

'My car broke down on the way, twice. And now it won't start at all.'

Flora got in the car to escape the rain. The car smelled damp, and it was cold inside. Stephanie carried a mobile phone and had already rung the NRMA.

'I arrived so late, but the usher let me sneak in the back, so I caught the last half of the performance. Then I came back to see if I could get it started again.'

Stephanie had driven the blue Golf for as long as Flora could remember. Three, four times over the years it had been their strange misfortune to have broken down together, and each time they'd waited patiently for the NRMA to rescue them. Just off the Harbour Bridge, another rainy night. On the way home from camping in Kangaroo Valley. At Broadway carpark. That time the NRMA man arrived within fifteen minutes.

She turned the ignition and it whined disagreeably. 'I'll have a flat battery as well if I keep trying,' she said.

'I thought you were coming with Frank?'

Frank's car was reliable. He was a luthier and carted harps all over the place for his customers.

She sighed again. 'Yeah, well. Frank.' She paused. 'What did I miss? Anything special?'

'Did you hear what the compere said at the end?'

Stephanie shook her head. 'I'd slipped out by then.'

The concert had been a charity event, raising funds for a refugee children's organisation. There was an inflammation of the long war in Afghanistan, and just the day before the news had reported that a contingent of international media had been attacked. Two Australians were unaccounted for, whether killed or captured it was still not known. It was said that the insurgents who had mounted the attack were teenage rebels, led by a boy who was only fourteen but who already had two wives.

At the end of the performances, the compere had thanked the audience for their attendance and their generosity.

'I am sure you all agree that the harp is a particularly beautiful instrument. That the music played upon a harp has the power to bring a special joy to the heart of every listener.'

Then she asked them to consider something.

'Imagine,' she said, 'if every child in the world who at the moment holds a weapon in their hands held a musical instrument instead.'

Along with every other member of the audience, Flora Lindsay breathed the words 'oh, yes' to join a sigh of longing and hope that rippled throughout the room and lingered after everyone had gathered their bags and coats and left their seats.

In the dark foggy car, Stephanie Lee was looking ahead. She was not really listening to Flora, who felt a fat drop of rain crawl down her scalp from where it must have landed in her parting.

'Did you know who that pedal harpist was?'

Stephanie shook her head again. 'Actually, I didn't know any of them.'

———◆◆———

The harpist would perhaps be home by now. In the rain and the dark, would she leave the harp in the van to bring it inside the next morning, Flora wondered. No, of course she would not. She would repeat the process in reverse and usher it inside the house, where she would unfasten the cover and set the instrument back in its place, in front of a music stand, or beside a piano. Maybe, as late as the hour was, she would sit there and run those long supple fingers over the strings again, and play a quiet tune while the kettle boiled for a cup of tea. 'Danny Boy'. Or a Bach suite. Or maybe Flora imagined the harpist and her instrument completely wrongly. Instead, she might have been at that very minute hauling the instrument into a noisy nightclub, all dim lights and cigarette smoke, to join a trio playing quirky numbers to an enthusiastic crowd of jazz-folk lovers. Maybe the harpist was downing a glass of red wine and laughing at the sober charity audience, their pearl necklaces and cravats and sensible shoes, relieved to be free of compositions by Peggy Glanville-Hicks and Barry Conyngham, to be playing improvised riffs instead.

But however wild or inaccurate or stereotyped these fancies were, this young woman, this harpist with the shimmering long hair and the strong hands, would not be inflicting any violence upon the world.

Flora did not find it possible to imagine a world without war or weapons, but was it possible to imagine a world where music could smother or even eradicate conflict?

'Where Frank comes from in Germany,' Stephanie said, as if reading her mind, 'everyone in the town was in a choir or a band or an orchestra.'

'Everyone?' Flora asked. 'Really everyone?'

'Everyone, apparently. Except for some old people, and the sick.' She paused. 'Of course not everyone was committed. But everyone started learning to play something in early primary school, and kept it up for the rest of their lives. Or so he says.'

Then she talked about her thesis. Her supervisor, Hannah, who held the musical education of Australia pretty much in contempt, had advised Stephanie to complete her postgraduate degree in Norway. She went to a place on the coast north of Bergen, facing the Faroe Islands across the Atlantic Sea. She had interviewed teachers and clergymen, spoken with families, attended concerts, from informal sitting room performances to town hall events and radio station appearances, and had discovered that not only did all the citizens of Gramsund, Norway, indeed play or sing or perform, the town had minimal levels of violence and the crime rate was remarkably low. In the summer months, nonexistent. But curiously, Gramsund, like every town across the country, was required to maintain a regular army corps, comprised of both conscripts and volunteers, part-time or full-time, who served for a minimum of two years. All these army personnel were armed. It seemed, therefore, that every citizen over the age of eighteen had held and handled, and at some stage even owned and operated, a weapon.

'The thing was, though,' Stephanie said, 'when they happened, the crimes were really weird.'

There was a flash of light in the rear-view mirror.

'I think it's our NRMA man,' Flora said.

They got out of the car as he opened his rear door and grabbed a coil of cable. In the white-blue of the NRMA light, his smooth brown hair shone, and when he said, 'Evening ladies,' neither of them flinched.

'What seems to be the trouble?' His smile revealed large straight teeth. With his thick hair shining on his forehead and his luminous smile, he looked almost superhuman, like a Kennedy. The JFK of the repair fleet come to their rescue. Flora's world brightened a bit.

Over the years of breakdowns, they had come to have a great regard for the NRMA man, whoever he was. Each time when the NRMA man arrived their relief and gratitude were almost erotic. The man who could appear in the dark, and the rain, and hook up long snaking leads to cars and tap parts and screw caps to revive the engines that had let them down, that man, whoever he was, was beyond value.

———◆◆◆———

'You were going to tell me about Frank,' Flora said. They settled back under the shelter of a tree. It would have been impolite to wait it out in the car while the NRMA man got wet.

Stephanie took out a cigarette and a lighter. 'It never stopped raining in Gramsund,' she said instead. 'And it was so cold. You have no idea. Even though it's on the coast, it's miserably cold.' She lit up. 'I think that's why they all played music. Especially in winter, they can't even go outside. I was there for six months and all we did was sit around and sing and play. And drink, of course.'

'You brought me back that duty-free vodka.'

'So I did. Do you still have it? After this I'll run you home and we should drink it.'

She ground her cigarette out and reached for another. The NRMA man was now trying the ignition.

'Is it that bad?' Flora asked.

'Worse. He's gone off with Hannah.'

The engine cleared its throat once, twice, then hummed into life.

'I think you're all good now, ladies,' said the NRMA man, slamming down the hood. Once more his splendid teeth illuminated the night.

———◆◆◆———

Flora Lindsay could not say that she was surprised. Hannah had introduced Stephanie to Frank, and Hannah tended to assert her prior claims. The friendship, professional or closer, was buried back in the mists of their shared European past, which was equally misty as far as Flora could tell. It seemed to her that there was an odd symbiosis between Stephanie's former supervisor, now patron of the Harp Society, and her luthier boyfriend. One summer the three had spent several weeks together when Hannah had agreed to tour the folk music circuit. She had insisted she needed a back-up harp and harpist and on-tap harp maintenance, which Frank provided in one person. Stephanie did publicity.

The previous year, although she had been unsurprised when Stephanie announced that Hannah would be accompanying herself and Frank when they went on holidays to New Zealand, Flora had still expressed some doubt. Stephanie had just shrugged. 'There are two islands,' she had said, implying there was enough room for escape, though for her, or for Hannah, or indeed for Frank, Flora couldn't say.

Although her own playing was amateurish, it was Stephanie's passion for the harp that had led her to Frank. She had in fact abandoned the ethnographic thesis based on Gramsund and returned to research the artisan manufacture of musical instruments in Australia. It was clear that Hannah had never forgiven this, though at the time she pretended to be supportive.

<hr />

It was all over a folk harp, fashioned in the land of the harp. It transpired that the interior designer of the Lodge and of Government House – Mrs Ruth Lane Poole – had commissioned it from a Dublin instrument maker, at the same time that she had ordered embroidered fire screens and silk bedspreads from the art workshop where she had once taught. Within a short time the fire screens had become obsolete while the bedspreads, bought for the visit of a duke and duchess back in 1927, were later auctioned for a charity. The first prime minister resident in the Lodge had no interest in harp music. Musical events in the house were restricted to performances upon the sitting room's baby grand piano, made by Beale's in Melbourne. The harp remained ignored by subsequent prime ministers and, while their families occasionally used the instrument for fun, it remained neglected and eventually fell into disrepair.

Curved and scrolled in the Celtic style, it stood chest high. Its design matched that of the simple carver chairs of the house's sitting rooms, made of Tasmanian black-wood and featuring lyre-shaped backs, most of which were also long banished from the house. When the place no longer housed families of prime ministers, when many of the grander public rooms were shut up and it was operating on a fraction of its staff, Stephanie Lee had applied to the department that ran the Lodge to investigate the storage rooms, the basement, the attics. No one had known about the harp, until she read through Mrs Lane Poole's notes and sketches in the National Library and decided to go searching. Come with me, she'd said to Flora. You're the interior designer, it will be fun.

It was in the second attic. Stacked behind sets of old golf sticks, dusty wooden clotheshorses, wicker picnic baskets and tea chests filled with mismatched crockery, broken lampshades, old bedside clocks and other discarded items of general household use, it was an unlikely member of this collection, the leftover belongings of passing generations of prime ministerial families. Pushing aside a chest full of ice-skates, football boots and tennis racquets, Stephanie had seen an odd-shaped brown case with rusted clasps in a dim corner next to three faded beach umbrellas. When she had pulled it out into the light and flipped the clasps, both of them gasped aloud when the case opened to reveal the instrument of the angels. Stephanie extended a hand and plucked the strings, still taut though dull and flat.

Looking around, at the old sporting equipment, the broken fishing rods, the umbrellas, Flora understood why it had been banished to the furthest corner of this house. Outside activities. These were what most of this house's occupants had been interested in. The old racquets and skates and clubs would only have been replaced with newer ones, as occupants one after the other pursued their tennis, cricket or football. Of all the pastimes this collection represented, music was absent. No broken guitars or forgotten flutes or violins. Not even any recorders. Decades of prime ministerial recreation, and all of it sporting. Among the broken, obsolete items of general household use, there was not a gramophone, record player or even radio in sight. There was no collection of old records, or cassette tapes. No wonder the harp was shrouded in its case, hidden in the corner. It was a small miracle that it had not been sent away, sold to a dealer, or simply discarded like most of the original furniture.

'Let's get it out of here,' Stephanie said.

They gathered it in their arms and dragged it to the top of the steps. It was as if Stephanie had just rescued someone from a wilderness. Found a traveller lost in the desert. It was like seeing Ludwig Leichhardt standing at dusk on a dried-up riverbed way beyond the Darling Downs. Robinson Crusoe on his beach. She held the harp close while from the steps Flora called out to the housekeeper to help them down.

Stephanie asked Hannah if she knew a good luthier, for the restoration.

The harp was to feature in the first of a series of cultural events to take place in the Lodge, organised by Stephanie and styled by Flora. The formal sitting room was a place of inadequate furniture and gilt-framed portraits and was, in Flora's opinion, far too chintzy and yellow. A previous prime minister or his spouse had been overly fond of yellow and gold, she thought. The house was full of it. Wattle-blossom yellow feature walls, polished brass bathroom fittings, wallpaper in gold suede and satin stripes, and the worst horror of all in this room, a lounge suite upholstered in cream linen splashed with yellow and gold cabbage roses. She didn't think anyone used cabbage rose designs for furnishings these days. She didn't even think yellow cabbage roses existed. No wonder the room was little used. She pushed aside the slub silk curtains (burnished gold, but still yellow when you thought about it) and opened the window.

'What do you think?' she was saying to Stephanie when a man appeared at the door. 'Good enough for recitals and soirees?'

'Well, it is a decent sized room, but not too big for intimate recitals.' He walked to the centre of the room and shook hands, first with her, then with Stephanie. 'Frank, from Sutton Forest. I've come for the harp.' Then he moved closer to the wall opposite the windows to inspect the portraits of previous prime ministers in their thick gilt frames. 'Perhaps you should remove these. I doubt anyone could play with all these eyebrows. So negative.'

Flora agreed. The faces of Menzies, Whitlam, Hawke and Howard, this close to each other, were collectively forbidding. No one could feel comfortable under their scrutiny. Even the ironically arched brows of Whitlam, while far from hostile, exerted a fierce superciliousness that she was not sure a soiree could resist. And as for Menzies and Howard, bookended along the row by a sheer accident of space, from a distance they seemed all eyebrow now. All resistance and judgment and implacable self-confidence. She marvelled at the vanity of such people, all of them, Holt and Fraser too, with their massive, monstrous eyebrows. Men who would allow their portraits to be painted, to be put on show. Unattractive, most of them. A handful, like Holt or Keating, tolerable at best. To be remarked upon, admired. Were they meant to be intimidating? She would have them taken down if possible. They could be displayed elsewhere in the house. One would not wish to show disrespect, of course, but still, none of these men had ever demonstrated any interest in the musical arts. Perhaps just one. And he would have taken his Mahler collection when he left.

'It's a pity Mrs Lane Poole's original ideas won't work now,' she said.

'Who is she?'

'The designer of this house. All of it, from the crockery to the cornices. Most of her furniture is gone now, but the sketches are still around.'

'And why can't you follow her designs if they're still around?'

She shrugged. 'Well, they're a bit . . . stiff. Cold. Not warm and sensual enough, not for the harp.'

Meanwhile, Stephanie was watching Frank.

'You've come for the harp?'

'That's right. Hannah mentioned you needed a luthier?'

'Ah, Hannah,' she said.

━━◆━━

The harp was apparently the first instrument invented. The earliest were made from hunters' bows, the twanging of the weapon having inspired the idea of music. Stephanie had done the research, though Flora privately disputed the originality of the harp. She imagined that clap sticks or even drums were the first musical instruments. She suspected music historians meant the first civilised, white, western musical instrument when they made their claims for the harp, but were too afraid to say so.

In the sitting room, the heavy furniture had been covered in plain silk blankets for the soiree, while enormous cushions were thrown around the floors and piled in corners. The comfortable seats were low, soft. Flora had had the walls painted in deep jewel-like shades, with a paint that shimmered in the lamplight. And she had replaced the overhead lights with low hanging stained-glass lanterns. With the timber panelling around the large windows, the window seats with their velvet tasselled cushions, the deep dark colours, the room looked more exotic than Stephanie had envisaged. The prime ministers' eyebrows had been removed.

'Frank is on his way,' Stephanie told her and just the way she breathed the name Flora knew it was already a relationship.

'It's more dramatic than I expected,' Stephanie said.

'Red and purples will go best with the harp music. Trust me.'

'Really?' But she agreed it was certainly better than yellow and beige.

'Wait until you see it at night. The place will glow.'

When Frank entered early that evening the room did indeed glow. The sun had almost gone and they were just turning on the first of the lamps. He had rubbed back and re-waxed the maple sounding board and replaced the gut strings with carbon fibre. The satinwood inlay panel shimmered with new life. And the strings sang again with the sweet divine sound that suggested a gathering of the heavenly host. When Stephanie first sat before the instrument, as was her right, she felt like she was reaching out and embracing a cherished member of her family. She would ask Hannah to teach her again.

That night, Hannah was their first performer. The light touched the harp's warm burnished timbers and the glistening strings, and whether they agreed or not that it was the first instrument known to humans, they had all agreed that it was what the angels would play.

⇒•◦•⇐

But not teenage insurgents in Afghanistan. Or any combatants, in any country. Flora was still thinking of the recital in the grand house back up the drive.

Since that night in the prime minister's Lodge, the Harp Society had organised performances, many of them featuring Hannah, all over the country, in stately show homes like the one tonight. Frank had looked after all the harps, and Stephanie had worked on every event, for little or no money, for the love of the instrument, which she couldn't even play.

They got back in the car, where the engine was still humming. As Stephanie engaged the gears and released the brake, Flora Lindsay thought again of the young woman and the great harp, her fingers brushing its strings somewhere, in a bar or cafe, or more likely at home, alone. Stephanie glanced out her window at the rescue van, where the blue light was now extinguished and its owner was in the front seat, writing up his report.

'I love the NRMA man,' she said quietly, pulling out from the kerb.

Glory in the Flower

Bill swayed and clutched the dashboard as the festival director abruptly turned the Toyota Echo – could a more basic car be possible? – into the gravel driveway.

'Sorry,' he said. 'Nearly missed the turn-off.'

It was an old farmhouse and looked it. A corpse of a vehicle of indeterminate make surrounded by long grass sat by the front fence. Other rusted items dotted the long front yard – it could not be called a lawn – where someone had recently mown between rocky garden beds and red-brown clumps of junk that looked like nineteenth-century plumbing or agricultural parts. Or perhaps they were sculptures? The place was meant to be some sort of cultural facility.

Bill unpacked his legs from the front seat. They were already stiff from the flight and did not come willingly. Eventually he hauled himself out of the preposterous vehicle and stood still for a few moments, discreetly flexing them back into life. He didn't want his first real experience of Australian soil to be undignified. He slowly walked up the driveway as Cameron opened the boot and heaved out bags. How long had it been? Forty, fifty hours since he'd left home? He didn't want to add them up. It felt like an eternity. Two connecting flights. The flight from Heathrow had been delayed by bad weather. Then the long wait in Singapore because of engine trouble. They were meant to have been sent to a local hotel but instead stayed in the terminal where he tried to sleep and not think of the opening night reading he would now not be giving. Meeting him at the Riverside airport, which proved to be a tin shed in a vast brown field, Cameron had been almost surly, as if it were his fault. Bill was beyond fatigue. He felt numb, disembodied. His head was elsewhere, nowhere, floating off into the sere air. He wished it were back home with Dot, resting against the antimacassar as she stroked his temples. His body was twitching like a ventriloquist's doll. He felt stiff in joints he didn't realise he had. Even his elbows ached, and he'd never once considered his elbows, ever. They were the least interesting parts of him. They were not poetic, elbows. No one would ever be inspired to write about the elbow.

Bill had been surprised when they'd passed through the town and Cameron had pointed out the new municipal library where the festival was taking place. Nearby was a decent-looking hotel, and Cameron was boasting about the bars and cafes that had been opening up recently. But he kept driving, through the town's outskirts, past an industrial estate, then a racecourse, until there was nothing but road and fields, mostly brown.

'Where are we going, exactly?' Bill had said, his head turning back involuntarily where the town disappeared along with all suggestion of hot baths, strong drinks and soft beds, which by then he craved in any order.

'It was in your notes. Used to be a farmhouse but it's a cultural centre now. It's used for all sorts of things, workshops, meetings. Perfect for the masterclass. Lucky you made it in time for that.'

It was intended, Bill thought, to be a criticism. Cameron dumped the suitcases on the verandah and felt about in his pocket. Bill shivered. The difference in the temperature now and when he had landed at the tin-shed airport, a good hour or so before, was discernible. The light was fading. It was not yet six pm and already the place was in shadow. Cameron found the key and was now trying the lock, turning the key one way then the other with no result. Bill stamped his feet and looked around. On the verandah was a barrel-shaped tin with a toilet seat on the top. Inside it was a spiky potted plant. He concluded this was intended as amusing, perhaps ironic. Next to it was an old sofa, grey with mould. He breathed in deeply of the clean country air, which brought a sharp stab to his chest. It was even colder now!

Cameron thumped the door with his boot and it finally opened. The house was dark and he groped around for a light switch in the hall. What seemed to be a twenty-five watt bulb dangled glumly from the ceiling. There was no lampshade. There was a strange smell, of stale cold dinners, long past.

'In here.' Cameron led him down to a sitting room, switching on more lights as he went, lights that half-heartedly flickered into being. The house seemed to be in two parts, separated by a wide T-shaped hall: bedrooms off to one side and another sitting or living room past the central sitting room which merged into a kitchen, with an island bench of orange laminate.

'Sunroom over there,' Cameron said.

Sun? There were presumably windows behind the thick drapes and blinds drawn low.

'And out the back's the workshop shed.' He gestured to the back door. 'For tomorrow.'

Bill had not factored in a shed. Something book- and Turkish rug-lined was more in his mind. When the whole masterclass thing was proposed he naturally imagined it would be in an antipodean version of his own study – okay, without the pipe, he could cope with that – with a real fire and low tables stacked with books

and writing materials. Maybe a tray of glasses and something in a decanter. At least a bottle of decent red.

He would address the shed situation tomorrow.
Meanwhile the thought of red wine prompted him to
poke around in the kitchen. The fridge contained a
plastic litre bottle of two per cent milk, orange juice,
bacon, eggs, cheese. Cheese was promising. He examined the packet. Sliced Lo-Fat Tasty. He put it back. He
opened the cupboard above the kettle. Teabags, instant
coffee, sugar and Equal. Another cupboard yielded
sweet biscuits and breakfast cereal. There was a sliced
loaf in a plastic bag on the bench and a set of instructions
for operating the gas heater in the sitting room. By the
time Cameron came back from putting his bags in his
bedroom, Bill had looked into every possible corner of
the kitchen and even the sitting room sideboard, which
contained several board games and a stack of *National
Geographic*s which he knew without looking would be
twenty years old. They always were. Not a single drop
of alcohol.

The house was freezing.

'They told me the weather would be mild this time
of the year.'

'Oh,' Cameron said, 'the days have been perfect. Just
brilliant. But as soon as the sun goes . . .'

If he'd known, Bill would have brought his greatcoat,
the one he wore out walking, which even in the English
winters sufficed. He would have packed his woollen

hat, and a pair of gloves. And a proper scarf, not the white silk one he'd optimistically brought, thinking it suitable for elegant literary dinners.

Speaking of which, Cameron was talking about dinner, at a Lebanese restaurant. 'I'm sure there'll be someone who can drive you back here,' he said, sounding vague.

Bill was so bone-stiff, so weary, so cold, the thought of eating *and* having to play the part of the distinguished British poet was almost nauseating. He told Cameron he would pass on the dinner, that he'd make do with something from the fridge, though he doubted he would even bother cooking the bacon and eggs. Maybe some toast and jam. A cup of tea. It would not be as nice as Dot's teas. She had a way of producing hot scones, pikelets, little ham and mustard sandwiches, as if it were as easy as opening a packet of Digestives.

'Look, I have to go.' Cameron glanced at his watch. 'I've got the keynote speaker waiting for me.'

Bill gaped. The *keynote* speaker? Then what did that make him? Had these people even read his CV? Did they not know about the awards, the honours, the rumour he was a shoe-in for Poet Laureate? Which he'd probably decline due to his republican views. He wished desperately for a drink. Brandy would have been perfect.

'Oh, I nearly forgot. Here's your festival kit. And the others will be along later.'

Cameron rushed out and Bill heard the thud of the front door, then the Echo crunching down the driveway. He sat in the gloom of the sitting room and looked through the calico bag. It was stamped with a purple logo featuring what appeared to be a river that flowed from the nib of a quill pen. *Riverside Literary Festival*, it said. He had not noticed a single stretch of water since he had landed. It was going to be a very dry few days.

And what was that about the others? Or had he misheard Cameron in his fatigue?

❧

Dot had come into his study with the letter.

'They're offering twelve hundred dollars if you stay on and do a masterclass.'

'What's that in real money?'

'About six hundred pounds, give or take.' It seemed decent, for an extra day or two. 'They say it will be informal, no more than half a dozen people.'

'I don't think so.' It was a concession, he felt, to actually fly all the way out there just to give one of his readings.

'Bill, we could do with the extra cash. Plus, it'd be good for you. You need to get away. And you love travelling.'

'I love walking tours. Not flying. Don't they have any famous poets of their own?'

Dot just stood there, folding the letter. She was wearing her pink checked apron. Poking out of its pocket was a pair of cotton gloves, grey from use. Bill felt a flush of shame. She'd probably been cleaning the downstairs fireplace grate when the post arrived. And here he was spending the entire morning trying to nail down a visionary gleam, or at least a glimmer.

'So long as I don't have to read any of their work.'

It wouldn't have been fair to her, apart from anything else. And she was right: they needed the money. Since grants were rare these days he had to take what he could. He wasn't much use at anything else. Other people in his position had something to fall back on. Sam had his allowance from the Wedgwoods. Robert, it seemed, could write anything for money: essays, reviews, biographies, knocking them off with enviable ease. His own legacy from Raisley was fast going – he couldn't believe the cost of the basics these days, like fuel and bread and pork chops – and he doubted he should have put so much of it into his superannuation, as he'd been advised. Wouldn't be able to get his hands on that for years now. He was not the most brilliant proofreader but managed to get some work here and there – corporate stuff, usually, nothing literary – not that the pay was anything like it should be, for such work. Wore his eyes out. And he could only do that sort of thing in the best light, which always curtailed walking excursions or cloud-watching, all the

activities he liked to reserve for when the weather was
at its kindest.

———◆———

He was eating Just Right with the two per cent milk
when he heard the door. Fumbling and talking, more
fumbling, then thumping. He pushed the blanket
aside – he had not managed to follow the gas-heater
lighting instructions – and made his way down the
hallway back to the front door. Yanking it open, he was
hit with a fistful of fresh cold air, making him gasp. Two
women stood on the porch, dressed in padded jackets
and knitted beanies.

'Come in. Quick. Before the cold.' He whipped
behind them and slammed the door shut. The hallway
still smelled stale and dusty.

They were Sharon Someone and Louise Something.
When they appeared in the sitting room he realised
they were both carrying backpacks.

'Are you all settled?' Sharon or Louise said. 'We'll
choose our bedrooms then.'

What did that mean? He might have been cold and
miserable but at least he was cold and miserable on his
own. And there were other bedrooms? He'd gone into
his own room, where Cameron had left his bags, but
had quickly withdrawn when he'd seen how cheer-
less it was. The entire house looked like it had been
furnished by a charity store. Nothing matched, and

everything was threadbare, or just plain bare. His bed sported a pink chenille bedspread – something he had never known existed until now – and the bathroom's only product was a minuscule cake of soap, previously used. Expecting the usual bath gel, conditioner, complimentary razor, provided for distinguished authors at hotels, he had not packed products. He especially liked the little sachets containing a sponge and shoe cleaner. And he always took the soaps home for Dot.

The lavatory was unspeakable. He was not that fastidious, having made do with an outside one for most of his life, but this was disgusting. He had tried to scrub it with the brush behind the bowl, but the porcelain remained dark brown. And the littlest room in the house was the coldest. A small louvre window remained stubbornly fixed in the open position.

Sharon and Louise bustled back from locating their rooms. They did not seem bothered by the cold. They flicked the kettle on and clanged about with cups and spoons. He didn't suppose they'd thought to bring a bottle of something.

'Cup of tea, Bill?'

'No. Wait, yes, I will. Please.' He tried to keep the chill out of his voice but it was really all too much. What were these people doing here?

Almost on cue, Louise or Sharon said, 'I don't think the others will be here until tomorrow. They're local. But how wonderful the masterclass was residential.

It's such a good idea, isn't it? Us getting so much of your attention, all weekend.'

He grunted. So that was the idea. But if any of them thought he'd be polishing their imagery or tweaking their metres before breakfast, they were mistaken. He wondered how much of all this Dot had known, and not passed on.

They'd sent some notes on the workshop partici-pants. He gathered they'd all been vetted by the festival director or some committee. He knew none of the names of course. Seven women, one man. He imagined they were all old, or middle-aged, young writers rarely being able to afford this sort of thing. He'd stuffed the folder in his bag to read on the flight out and had almost forgotten about them. Flicking through the submis-sions, he pretty much confirmed there were no mute inglorious Miltons amongst them. The notes had come with samples of their work and despite himself he read a poem, then another, his heart descending into the pit of his stomach. By then, according to the blue worm on the screen in front of him, they were over the Tanami Desert. Too late to turn back.

Now he grabbed his calico festival bag and his tea and retired to his room. His bones still ached but he wouldn't risk the bath. It might have been cleaner than the lavatory bowl but he held no hopes of the hot water supply. There was no desk in the room, no chair. He unpacked his pyjamas and climbed into bed with his folders. The festival bag contained brochures for horseriding, canoeing and gold fossicking, along with vouchers for a pizza place, drycleaning, a local bookshop and a folk museum. The festival guide included his own photo and bio, along with a dozen or so others, none of whom he had ever heard of. There was a journalist, two filmmakers, some children's authors, a literary blogger and several authors of something called speculative fiction. The keynote speaker appeared to have written one short novel that had been an international success on numerous electronic platforms via crowdfunding. He was turning it into an interactive app for locative media. Bill sighed and tossed the bag aside. The bedside light did not work. He got out of bed, switched off the overhead light, tripped on his suitcase strap in the sudden complete dark, and fell onto the bed. He crawled up and under the covers and shivered there for a few minutes, then got out, groped for his coat, spread it over the bed and pulled the sheets up over his head.

⪼◆⪻

He was sitting up in bed with all the covers pulled up to his neck, reading over his notes for the session later that morning. Surprisingly, he had slept, not waking until morning, though having forgotten to adjust his watch he had no idea of the time. By the time he had hopped about on the freezing lavatory floor – he had not thought to pack slippers – the warmth he'd generated during the night had evaporated. Poking about in the wardrobe, he had discovered a small fan heater, which he'd perched on the end of the bed, its cord stretched as far as it could from the one power point on the other side of the room. The windows had curtains that looked like they'd been made of a child's old bedsheets, but he'd pulled the miserable strips of pastel, clown-patterned cloth together anyway to create an illusion of cosiness. Underneath the blankets he was wearing two pairs of socks and his coat and he was still freezing.

There was a knock on the door and, without waiting for his reply, Sharon poked her head in. She was fully dressed and wearing dark red lipstick.

'Bill. Can I have a word?' She came in and shut the door behind her.

'Of course, Sharon.' Where would she sit?

'Louise.'

'Sorry, Louise.' She looked grave. 'What can I do for you?' He had refreshed his mind with notes on his students – should he even call them that? – and now recalled that Louise was the one whose portfolio included three short poems all in rhyming couplets on the topics of washing up, pruning roses and a barbecue. She had rhymed 'sausages' with 'partridges'. Somehow he knew that Louise was always going to be married to the imperfect rhyme. Indeed to the rhyme, which every poet of any worth had got out of his system by now.

'I've had a bit of a rethink. I feel my work won't be suited to this masterclass.'

'Really?'

'Yes, and I have to tell you, Bill, I've already got someone interested in publishing me.' (Perhaps in her parish newsletter?) 'I had a look through your collection last night.' (He'd left a copy of the *Ballads* in the sitting room.) 'And I feel you and I have different styles.'

'Different? I suppose so . . .'

'Yes, completely, well, incompatible. So I phoned Cameron first thing, he's giving me a refund.'

'Right.'

'So I'll be off.'

'Right,' he said again. It seemed the only appropriate word to hand. He was not sure whether to be pleased or insulted.

By the time he faced the others it was clearly late in the morning, later than the masterclass was scheduled to start.

'Aren't we meant to be in the shed?' one of them said.

They all trooped out the back door and found the shed. Its original purpose was clearly agricultural, but now it contained several trestle tables, an easel with butchers' paper and half a dozen metal chairs. It was vast and arctic.

'We'll use the sitting room,' he said. 'Can someone light the heater?'

By lunchtime he had a headache from the unflued gas heater. Someone suggested they open a window, but behind the curtains, behind the holland blinds, the windows refused to open. After lunch, which he stretched out as long as possible, he opened all the doors to the sitting room and the back door to let in some fresh air. There was not a single cloud in the sky and the sun shone like crystal. He could not work it out. It got far colder than this at home, but he was always cosy inside. What did they make their houses from? The walls must have been thinner than plywood. When the class ended at five he decided to go for a walk. Now that he realised how fast the night fell here, he would have to be quick.

He crunched his way down the drive, and turned west on the road, walking in the centre as there was no fear of traffic. Not a single vehicle had come past as far as he was aware. It was clear he was not going to be able to take part in any of the festival, that he would be earning every penny of the six hundred pound fee (unless Dot had misled him about that too?) listening to his class read their terrible poetry. The last one, just before he called a stop, had produced a simile likening motherly love to a long hand-knitted scarf. They all wanted approval, not constructive criticism. They hadn't a clue what it meant to be a poet. None of them demonstrated a skerrick of spontaneous overflow of powerful feeling. Of any feeling. He had once written on what it meant to be a poet. What is a Poet? he had asked, and answered simply and plainly: a man speaking to men (though Dot had chided him for not including women), a man of sensibility, enthusiasm and tenderness. Above all a man with passions, able to rejoice. He had detected no passion or joy within this lot and their dreary verses. The one man in the class was writing about bushwalking. That was promising, he'd thought, until the monologue he had commenced reading after lunch took them almost to afternoon tea, and as far as Bill could determine it was only about a man sitting in a dingy office thinking of going on a walk. And its metre was enough to cure insomnia.

Tomorrow he would change the rules, get tough. He'd heard of one workshop teacher, somewhere in America, who used to demand his students stand up to read their work, then he'd yell out 'Stop!' when he got bored, tell them to sit down, then point at the next victim, without giving a single word of feedback. Some would be commanded to stop before they finished their first sentences. Only those with the greatest fortitude survived, the rest fled sobbing or cursing, and never returned. This was a masterclass. Bill would show them he was the master.

The road turned a bend and the tarmac turned into gravel. He kept walking, enjoying the feeling under his soles. There was nothing on either side of the road, the bare fields, the odd tree. Another bend brought him to what seemed to be a meadow. In the distance was a clump of trees, atop a hill. He turned off the road, stepped over a ditch and wandered across the grass towards the hill, careful of cow pats or other hazards. On the hill a wind developed and he pulled his coat tighter, sticking his hands in the pockets. He turned around and saw the house where he was staying, which he could see now had two chimneys. So why on earth didn't it have a fire, some decent heat?

He turned back and wandered past the stand of trees, down the other side of the hill. There was a pleasing sight: a little pond or dam at the foot of the slope, with willow trees. Five cows were walking away towards a fence, and in the distance beyond it he spotted a smudge of dark green, and a wisp of smoke curling into the evening sky. The sun was very low by now and he shaded his eyes, but it seemed that there was another house, or a cottage, where the cows were returning to be milked. Someone was home. He made his way towards the pond and there at his feet he discovered a clump of flowers, early spring blooms gently dancing in the cold breeze. He leaned down and cupped one. It was radiant, fresh, a tiny golden spot of glory.

—⊷◆⊶—

The still, sad music of humanity clanged in his ears all through the long day following. They were doing eight-line exercises, reading key texts by famous authors – luckily he'd thought to bring copies as the house's only book was an old Webster's dictionary – reading out each other's work, closing their eyes and visualising, staring at a collection of objects he'd quickly gathered from around the place – a feather, a sandshoe, the mean sliver of soap from the bathroom – then writing a response in three minutes before he called time and took away their pens. Then he got them to write about body parts. Ears, knees, the nose. Elbows. All the despicable writing class tricks he'd picked up from others in the game, tricks he would have been ashamed to use himself, but which he now clung to like life rafts. He walked around and made them follow him: around the house, out the house, along the road, across to the hill, past the pond, around the cows that stared with indifferent eyes, and then back the other way. Forcing movement, forcing rhythm, finding a line, a phrase, an image. And finding, eventually, warmth. By the end of the day they were all exhausted but at least he was no longer cold. And the spark of joy that had somehow been ignited burst into a small flame when Cameron arrived at five-thirty with two six-packs and a stack of pizzas.

'Bill, this has been the best masterclass ever,' said the one man, whose name, Bill now bothered to recall, was Michael. Mike.

'Yeah,' Sharon said. 'For a while there I thought you'd didn't like us. Weren't that interested. But today's been great.' She took another slice of the ham and pineapple.

'And when you gave us that daffodil and said we had to write about that,' Mike said, 'well, it was brilliant.'

'Cheers,' they all said, clicking beers.

'Have you all filled out your survey sheets?' Cameron said.

<hr />

At the boarding gate he discovered the festival committee had upgraded him to business class. He could stretch out as far as he liked. He could order food and drinks whenever he liked. He could sleep! There was no one beside him, no one near him. He settled back in his seat, took off his boots and stretched his legs as far forward as possible. A glass of champagne was presented to him, which he accepted with a smile.

Before he stowed his coat away, he took his leather wallet out of the inside pocket and pulled out the one bloom he had picked from the host of golden daffodils by the pond. It was now flattened. The philosophic mind was hard won, Bill reflected, and life was too short. He would put Riverside and its literary festival behind him and get on with it. He would marry Mary after all. Dot would understand. Dotty would *appreciate* it. His sister had been nagging him about it for years. He would present her with the daffodil, when he got back, and then perhaps after tea he would read her the little poem he'd drafted out the night he'd got back from his lonely wander and was in his bed again, huddled against the cold and the threat of banal poetry. He would write more new work on the trip back. The flight was long enough. He could already feel something forming in the back of his mind. It was fresh, like a waking dream, something about immortality and joy and finding glory in the flower. They would laugh like children when he told her all about Riverside cultural life, about the cold dreary farmhouse, the bare liquor cupboard, the two per cent milk. They would talk long into the night, he with his brandy, she with a sherry. Fifteen minutes into the flight, he was asleep.

Chance

She watched him as he set off early for the bakery. Despite the rain having stopped, the flat roads, deserted on a Sunday, the lack of any local police, and the utter unlikeliness of mishap, he snapped the helmet fastener into place under his chin and applied his riding gloves. Mock saluting her, he pedalled off.

When he returned twenty minutes later with two wholegrain rolls the size of bath bombs, Gretel discovered she could neither be dismayed nor amused. Instead her feelings hovered somewhere in between, in a new place they had not previously reached in this relationship. It was like shifting into another gear. Or worse: into neutral. She quite honestly didn't know what to think of a man who made all that effort and took such precautions to retrieve exactly one bread roll each. Was it parsimony, or precision? Thoughtlessness (what were they to eat for lunch anyway?) or intense devotion to the cause, to the moment, to the small sacramental act of their breakfast?

Of course Lance could not be parsimonious. The thought was not possible. He had brought a side of smoked salmon in his esky. She wore his gold chain bracelet, an extravagant present for such a short relationship. He was not a mean man, he was far from ungenerous. And yet there were the rolls, occupying a modest space on the platter, which Gretel quickly filled with a tub of butter, the remaining banana, napkins, knives, anything – too much clutter and condiments for just two bread rolls. She took the platter out to the verandah, steamy and rinsed clean from the rain earlier, placed it down on the wet plastic table, and returned for a towel to wipe the chairs dry.

And then there was the helmet, which Lance was now wiping inside with a handtowel (surely he hadn't sprayed it, surely that wasn't disinfectant?) and placing on the shelf in the living room. From the kitchen she watched him sideways as she filled the kettle and set out cups, her mind lightly considering the relative merits and shortfalls of being with a man who sweated that much – it was such a short ride – or a man as devoted to cleanliness. Which was worse? Again, she couldn't decide. She would try to err on the side of hygiene and be grateful. The first thing he had done, after they'd pulled in the day before and unloaded their bags, was wash the car.

———◆◆◆———

Gretel had found the place on the internet. They had decided against the coast because they agreed that it would be too far, the long-weekend traffic would be congested, they would return tired and cranky, and what would be the point. Lance was doing the driving. It was his car. He would bring his bike because the area was flat and he wanted to keep up the program he'd recently adopted. He was now up to ten ks every morning. Soon he'd be doing fifteen.

Exploring the villa had taken no time. One large room was a kitchen that morphed into a dining/sitting room. The main appliances, a stainless steel wall oven unit and a huge plasma TV, seemed like two antagonists, facing each other off over a field of cream berber. The bedroom was small. Though it must have been closed up against the summer heat, the villa was warm and the bedroom hot and stuffy. Gretel had left her bag on the bed and slipped out of her sandals. She pushed the window above the bed as wide open as it would go, wondering about insects later in the night. Off the bedroom was a white on white bathroom with spa. She peeled away her cardigan, soggy under the arms, and left it on the towel rail, splashed water on her face and drank from the tap. Adjacent to the bathroom was a laundry. She inspected the white goods and cleaning products, wondering who would feel compelled to do washing on a weekend holiday.

She was on the verandah with a hand shading her eyes when Lance appeared beside her. His canvas shoes were damp.

'That'll do,' he said. 'I should give it a proper wash, but at least I've got the worst of the dirt off.'

Should she agree that it would do, or that he should give it a proper wash? To be truthful she had not thought the car dirty at all. The drive had been on bitumen, until the last two kilometres. She said nothing.

'Let's unpack, sort out who's going to do what, then have a nap.'

Gretel had only brought a small overnight bag. And as for a nap, she was thinking of heading for the lake. There was a glimpse of it – brittle, metallic – a few hundred metres away through the casuarinas. The water looked blue, grey, silver. Maybe there were canoes for hire.

'A nap? What about we check out the lake?'

'Aren't you tired? I am.'

She risked a joke. 'Naps are for babies. Or pensioners.'

He ignored it and stepped closer. 'Then we can stay up late and watch the stars. We could lie out here all night if you want.' He embraced her, kissed her on the neck. 'Let's lie under the stars.' His voice dropped, pouring directly into her left ear. 'There's no one else here. Let's make love all night under the stars.'

His kisses were sweet and firm. She turned her face to his, met his lips, feeling the familiar, wonderful tug to earth of desire, the desire that ran down her spine and flooded her crotch and made her want to fall, limp and soft and open, yet made her body feel strong and eager at the same time. Her voice dropped too. 'What about right now?' she said, pulling him close. Over his shoulder she glanced across. The lake flashed again and again, a semaphore of wavelets and light, more intense out here in the bush, as if the openness inspired the sun to be bolder, more showy. But he was right, there seemed to be no one else around, there were no signs of life in the other villas. She pulled him closer. With his ex-wife's phone calls and unexpected appearances at his front door, it felt like they were alone together for the first time. But he eased out of her embrace.

'I'm just going to freshen up.'

He had probably meant to say, Come with me, lie with me, let's organise our stuff, have a nap. Take a shower together. Instead he dropped her arms slowly, walked back a step, turned and entered the villa.

'Well, I might just wander over.' Gretel spoke to his back. 'To the lake. Won't be long.'

Lance waved, a half wave, really, his arm dropping again quickly. It could have been a dismissive flick. She imagined he would walk into the bedroom, set his duffle bag on the bed and unpack underwear, shorts and T-shirts into the chest of drawers, before stowing the bag in the wardrobe. He was methodical like that. She would return to find his razor, comb, toothpaste and toothbrush placed in a soldierly row on one side of the shelf. There would be all sorts of unnecessary products and tools, for a weekend away. Nail clippers. Men's moisturiser, whatever that was. He used more products than she. Her bag was not much bigger than a handbag. She had brought a change of clothes, a book and her perfume, which she always carried. Chanel Chance. She did not care for No 5.

━━◆━━

She should not have come in her bare feet. Except the sand, when she reached it, was cool and firm underfoot. She walked carefully to avoid the nut-sized casuarina cones. There were no canoes, despite certain claims on the resort's website, though there was a small timber jetty. She walked along to the end where an aluminium dinghy was tethered. At the end of the jetty the water was still only a few feet deep. The shore was wide and clear. The dinghy could have been left there, but it seemed to her that only to justify its claims of recreational water sports, had the resort owners supplied the jetty. It was little more than a long duckboard. Somewhere to dry your feet before heading back to the villas. She sniffed at the idea of resort. The place consisted of a few villas – perfectly comfortable, she could see that – all well spaced out for privacy, and the lake. Resort to Gretel rather inevitably suggested pools and spas, beauty treatment parlours and sporting activities, like windsurfing or scuba diving. And bars, several of them, including one by the pool. With palm trees and lithe waiters bearing tall drinks sporting coloured umbrellas. The place was advertised on the dating site where she and Lance had met. His profile had been up for three months when she sent the first kiss.

The water was so clear, so still, she could see down to the bottom. Farther out, the reeds thinned and across the lake there seemed to be a small disc of an island. It might have been a huge mat of waterlilies. She shaded her eyes but couldn't really tell; birds were landing there and taking off, herons or gulls, she didn't know what. She was not good with bird species.

———◆—◆———

She didn't know why she returned to the site. Of course, they had both deleted their profiles after the third date. She hadn't told Lance that she still checked it now and then. Only a couple of times, late at night after he had fallen asleep and she was unable to settle down in his place. She padded through his flat without turning on the lights and opened his laptop in the kitchen where he always left it, in between the landline and the toasted sandwich maker. Once she had been reading through the profiles to find that of a previous disaster, the man who called himself Take A Chance On Me! Who turned out to be called Ken. Wide awake, she read through the entire profile. He hadn't changed a single detail, not even his age. He was still claiming to be thirty-seven. He was still after a casual relationship. Right from the start Ken had made it clear to Gretel that they might be in a relationship, but would not be girlfriend and boyfriend. The first time he had initiated intimacy was on his sofa in an otherwise bare and chilly room of his house, while his recent partner (not girlfriend) was away, following their break-up. This Gretel learned soon afterwards was a lie. The partner was only overseas for work, returning within three months. And in any case, on her next visit when she peered into the bathroom cabinet and spotted the half-used box of Meds, the lipsticks and bottles of face products, it was clear that, semantics aside, this was a relationship of a serious sort.

Ken brushed aside her initial questions. Underneath his jokes and good humour and breezy demeanour, even regarding his own name, was a hard and serious devotion to the pursuit of his own interests and pleasures. Kissing, for instance, was not something that interested him.

On his sofa, an ugly thing, Ken delighted to practise contortionist sex, bending over its arms, or draped along its side, or kneeling before it, but Gretel found its peacock blue brocade cold and slippery and unsexy.

The room contained not even a painting or book-shelf that she could gaze at to take her mind off the tedium of his mechanical thrusts and regular groans, which was what sex with Ken quickly amounted to. She might have assumed it was second-hand, except it was matched by two wing chairs in opposite corners of the room, and besides, Ken had expressed disdain for anything second-hand: cars, clothes, antiques.

After the first few weeks she looked beyond the nights out at boutique hotels that served antipasto and oysters, beyond the flowers, the cards, and began to notice what hope, optimism and perhaps generosity had suppressed. That his teeth were rather prominent and abutted against her mouth. That when purporting to kiss he seemed unable to do anything else but bump his mouth against hers. And yet all the time he teased and joked about her kisses as if she were the one doing the wrong thing. She suffered in Ken's awkward embraces that focused on kisses that never quite worked out.

Too quickly, making love with Ken became a series of small torments. While he would not kiss her, joking all the while that she was no good at it, he approached her nipples in a methodical way. He sucked as if he were trying to extract marrow from a bone. First one, then the other. Plain, straightforward, earnest sucking, in which his brows would furrow in concentration. There was no art and therefore no arousal for Gretel. After he finished with one nipple, he would raise his head, offer a dutiful smile, then set to work on the other. Worse, on one of these occasions when his head was just below her face, she noticed the distinct spread of a thinning patch of hair that she was sure had not been quite so large or spare a month or so before. Distraction from nipple-chewing was welcome. Intimations of his imminent baldness not so.

And the flowers. Always of the one kind. Oriental lilies, which he'd given her the first time and for which she'd been polite and grateful, even though their thick night-time scent was one she found overpowering. He could not be persuaded that she liked any others. In Ken's view women liked flowers. Women loved receiving gifts of flowers, perfume and wine. These were the romantic symptoms, and he was not deviating from that view. So it went for food. The first time at dinner she ordered oysters on a whim, and thereafter he always ordered a dozen each. She had not much cared for them. The taste was passable, the texture revolting. She could not understand how he savoured them. He had little rituals involving lemon, salt, a chunk of bread.

And then, not so long afterwards, he had admitted his relationship with the partner was probably more serious than he had at first implied. That the partner was probably something more like a wife. It turned out they had been together for over twenty years. She did actually live in the house, this strange austere chilly place that contained no books, ornaments, papers, mementoes, and would be returning to it. Her favourite flower was the oriental lily. When Ken revealed this, Gretel's heart dropped another notch. She wondered how she could have been such a complete fool. She wished she had been a more confident kisser from the start as it might have exposed his own incompetence and severed their relationship early, before she noticed that it was all going to be unwanted flowers going slimy in their vases and blind sucking at her breasts. Not to mention another woman overseas, soon to return.

Gretel sat on the jetty, kicking her feet in the water to watch the sand swirl then settle. Tiny curious fish brushed her toes. The water was cold but the sun was getting hot on her neck. She should return to the villa and get the sunscreen, see what Lance was up to. She kicked her feet again, raising another cloud off the bottom. It all came down to the kiss. If she had understood how crucial that was, if experience had helped her see how bad Ken's kissing really was, the relationship, and the fallout that haunted her for many months, may all have been avoided. She had believed she was unkissable. A bad kisser. An unworthy kissee. Take A Chance On Me! She should have paid more attention to Ken's introductory line, to that exclamation mark. Punctuation invariably concealed insecurities.

For a long time, Gretel had hesitated to look at the dating site and only included her profile again after many months and careful editing. Lance's face in his picture had been partially in shadow, but his mouth looked safe, soft. When they first met, in the protective ambiguity of a cafe slash bar (suggest a bar, she'd learned, you could be labelled a drinker; suggest a cafe, you were being insultingly cautious), she had inspected his mouth closer. When he first kissed her, he was gentle and confident. It was a kiss that gave her hope, and one that she knew inspired her to do better, to reciprocate with warmth. Perhaps, she now thought, standing up and shaking the water from her feet, she had invested too much in that kiss. Still, it had given her a nasty pleasure to come across the profile of Take A Chance On Me!, to know that despite all his swaggering good humour and his oysters and champagne approach to romance, Ken was still looking for a partner not girlfriend, while she was enjoying quality kissing with another man.

⬤◆⬤

She returned to find Lance asleep, the washing machine humming. Looking through her things, she was surprised to find he had unpacked for her, the little she had brought. She slipped off all her clothes, twisted the sarong around her before going to the kitchen. She took the lid off the esky. He had forgotten to transfer the food to the fridge. She put one bottle of wine in the freezer, the rest in the fridge, then hunted through the cupboards for glasses, plates and knives, setting out crackers on the bench, expecting he would wake soon enough. But it was another half-hour before he came out and she was just taking the wine out of the freezer.

'Good nap?'

'Perfect.'

They took their drinks out to the verandah and watched the sky above the lake deepen in the late afternoon light. There were two stiff chairs and a tiny table on the verandah. The towel around his waist gaped as he leaned back, eyes closed against the last of sun. She placed her glass on the table and moved over to him, parted her legs and slid down onto his lap. 'Kiss me,' she murmured, pushing aside the towel. After a few seconds she vaguely registered that he remained unaroused beneath her, but his kisses were firm and moist and she stayed there on his lap while he cupped her buttocks and pressed his mouth over her face, her neck.

'What's wrong?' she murmured.

'Nothing, nothing at all. Just a bit tired.'

Tired?

'Come on.' He pulled her up and inside and by the time they reached the bed he was hard enough for her.

⊱—◆—⊰

Afterwards, he insisted on getting up and turning on the shower jets. 'Come and join me,' he sang out as she stretched back with the pillow tucked in hard under her neck, her arms above her head. But she wanted to remain where she was, sheeny with her own sweat, slippery in the groin. She knew she smelled of pheromone-rich salty sweat, and she quite liked the smell. She walked out to the verandah and retrieved her wine, taking it back into the bed, which was splendidly disarrayed. She pulled a sheet up to her knees and sipped thoughtfully.

'Aren't you coming in?'

'No.' His heart had not really been in it. As if it was all anticlimactic. She wondered about the washed underpants and shorts in the laundry. She heard the stream of water soften. He would be standing with his whole head right under it, holding his breath and rubbing around his ears in the way he did. 'I'm right. Just relaxing here,' she added, in case that sounded too terse. But perhaps, with his head under the water, he didn't hear. With his ears folded forward. For some annoying reason, she thought of Ken. She could smell something sweet, a smell like oriental lilies.

Back at Lance's flat – usually his rather than hers, with its inconvenient bathroom off the kitchen – they'd stumbled from bed to shower and continued their love-making, her back pressed against the tiles as the water flooded over their heads. Or they'd slept afterwards and he'd showered as soon as he woke. But until now it hadn't occurred to Gretel that he felt the act of sex made him grubby.

※

Now Gretel was trying to eat her roll as slowly as possible, nibbling pieces as she glanced through the life-style section of the Sunday newspaper he'd bought.

'I knew we wouldn't be hungry,' said Lance, pouring another orange juice.

Knew? Or just assumed, Gretel thought. Although they had eaten well last night. Her appetite had surprised her. She was famished after sex, a walk as night fell, then the second bottle of wine. They'd eaten most of the salmon and a large portion of the barbecued chicken she'd hoped would last the weekend.

'Usually,' Lance said, 'for breakfast I eat gluten-free muesli and soy milk. Low fat.'

She'd noticed healthy products in his kitchen. Organic almonds. Linseeds. Cloudy apple juice, almost as expensive as wine. She wrinkled her nose.

'I don't like that much. Especially soy milk.'

He sniffed. 'Yeah, no, well it fills me up. And keeps me regular.' She noticed he'd slapped a great wedge of butter, salted, non-organic, onto his roll. Opposite, the lake looked a dull dark blue. The rain had started at about four that morning, thundering down so swiftly it had woken Gretel, though Lance had remained asleep. She had got out of bed and stood at the door watching the purple solid mass of the early morning, unable to distinguish a single feature through the wall of water. Just as swiftly as it'd begun, it had eased, and she'd sat listening to the gentle pattering rain until she fell asleep again at six or so.

The sky remained a treacherous-looking grey blue, clouds as far as she could see. They still hadn't explored the lake together. Last night they'd walked back along the road, to see if the bitumen resumed after the turnoff to the resort. Lance was keen to find another route to cycle, having pronounced the main road unsuitable. Too many semis, he said, and the shoulders were steep and crumbling. But his plan to rise early to complete his morning ten ks had been foiled by the early rain. It was not that he minded riding in the bad weather, but it was too dangerous, on the main road, and he hadn't thought to bring his fluoro.

'Shall we head off to the lake?'

'Hmm?' Lance raised his head from the sport section.

She pushed her chair back, intending to signal that he should clear the plate away, but he now appeared to have a distracted manner. His breathing was becoming audible. He wiped his mouth and tossed the serviette down, picked at his teeth and shuffled through the gutted newspaper on the table.

'Let's go to the lake? There's a boat we could take, see if that's an island I saw yesterday.'

'Island?' He frowned, picked the business section up then put it down. 'No, I couldn't do that.' Not meeting her eyes, he stood up holding the colour supplement. He was breathing louder, almost whimpering, as he sloped past her and headed for the bathroom.

She stared at the door for a long time, then turned her

back on it. She took the business section that he'd left, then tossed it down again, leaned against the verandah rail. Gretel came from a family where defecation was not a ritual, where people just went and did it, quickly and discreetly, then got on with whatever they were doing. For him, though, there was clearly a routine. She found that egotistical. That he would insist on this, no matter the situation. Regardless of this special holiday, their first. Time passed. She considered cleaning up the breakfast things, decided against it. She considered going for a walk by herself. Ten minutes, fifteen. What was he doing in there? She ventured closer to the door, then stopped, retreated. Out on the verandah was his bike. She hauled it down the steps and hoisted herself onto the saddle, only wobbling slightly as she headed off down the drive.

—◆—

He was watching from the top step, scratching slowly under his shorts, as she returned. His half-smile indicated mild guilt as well as annoyance for her liberties with the Giant Trance. Thirty-speed and dual suspension, it had been a bargain at just under four grand. But still.

'You should have worn the helmet.'

She eased herself off while he held the handlebars steady, surreptitiously looking for signs of injury, then steered it back onto the verandah. She walked to the kitchen for a drink of water. And now she needed to use the bathroom herself. He had slapped the colour supplement onto the bench. As she opened the bathroom door the air was solid and foul, making her stop and involuntarily hold her hand to her face. She could not go in there. She should have hopped off the bike and peed in the bushes somewhere.

He reached for the kettle. 'Coffee?'

'No thanks.'

'Sure?' He fiddled at the sink. 'Something in there you might want to read,' he said. 'Article about a breeding program for numbats.'

As if she would so much as touch it. And what was worse was his indifference. Even in the kitchen the air was tainted. She would like a coffee too, but that would mean drinking it with him. And she was busting. She wandered away into the back garden, pretending to examine the plants. There was a path leading to a set of garden furniture she had not previously noticed, behind a clump of grevilleas in flower. A noisy miner squawked and fluttered amid its leaves.

She could never have that overconfidence. Arrogance. As if. She would scuttle in when he was out on his bike, or asleep even. Defecate quickly and quietly. And if she did make a smell, disguise it with air freshener, or at least run the shower. Something to cleanse the air. No, not even that. She wouldn't shit at all. She'd remain constipated rather than risk flooding the place with the smell of her body's waste. Disgust swelled in her stomach. Her bladder ached. It would still stink in there. There was no one around. She pulled down her shorts and crouched over leaf mulch as the miner watched her with one eye.

——◦—◦——

Inside Lance was fiddling with the sound system. He had found a local station playing retro music and was listening to an ABBA song, something about changing your mind, being the first in line. The lyrics came in static waves out to the garden where she sat with her book. He sang along, delight in his gravelly voice. Gretel had not intended to bring Ken with her, but she now thought of Ken's rapid fire sex, his quick eating and walking, his swift ineffective kisses. Everything he did was fast. He even seemed to sleep quickly, dropping off late, waking early and eagerly to morning sex, then bounding out of bed. She never recalled him hogging the bathroom, or leaving a smell. She sighed. Ken had been a total bastard, and was obviously right now trawling for another victim while his partner – or wife, it was never clear to Gretel – was on another overseas posting, judging by his profile. She closed her book. Lance was a gift from heaven compared to Ken. She would go into him and hug him, show him how much she appreciated him, the weekend, everything. He was dancing around when she appeared at the door and without a trace of self consciousness held out his arms as he sang about doing his very best, baby, about taking a chance, smiling like a pop star.

And then for all his showering over the weekend she became conscious of an odour. A sweetish smell, with undertones of something slightly sour. Decaying. It was the smell of something just past ripe. She caught it when she went into the bedroom for her cardigan. Yet it was so subtle she believed she had imagined it, that first time when they were in the car. But then by the second day it was unmistakable. It was attached to his clothes, the bed, the bath towel he had used and which he had even aired in the sun. It was there in his bag in the wardrobe. It was a smell that seemed permanently in her nostrils. Roaming over his body, tasting his mouth, his neck, the bulge of his belly. She could not escape it. Once, mid-kiss, her stomach rebelled. She pushed him away, gulping air, pretending to be overcome with a fit of coughing to disguise the fact. But she felt it, more than a faint turn of nausea. It was as if her body was rejecting his.

After lunch he decided to see how the Trance coped with the south road, and after the ritual with helmet and sunscreen, headed off with a wave. He would be back in half an hour. She watched him ride off before going to her bag where she had thoughtfully slipped a packet of cigarettes into a concealed side pocket. She poured a glass of white wine and went back to the verandah, taking her time smoking two cigarettes as she watched the lake. She pressed both butts deep into the garden bed below the verandah, took her glass to the kitchen and rinsed it, then went to the bathroom and cleaned her teeth. She took a long shower herself, making sure she used the complimentary bath gel and shampooing her hair twice.

She was rubbing the towel over her hair when she heard his voice. She opened the bathroom door to reply, then realised he was not talking to her. She could see him past the bedroom, hunched over the kitchen bench, his back to her and his phone pressed to his ear. Not right now, he was saying. I'm in a meeting. Yes I know. They don't care about long weekends.

In a meeting? She pushed the door to nearly shut and kept listening. He must have thought she'd gone off for a walk again. There was a laugh. Of course not, he was saying. I'll do it as soon as I can. Yes, they're bastards. Another laugh. I'll be here until late. Let me get back to you tomorrow. What if I come over as soon as I'm free? Yes. Five. Sure.

Gretel realised she was dripping behind the door. She dried herself and shook her wet hair back, then wrenched the door open and slammed it shut again. Bastards indeed.

'Lance.' She walked out into the bedroom, still damp and naked. He seemed to jump. His phone clattered to the floor.

'Oh hi. I thought, I thought . . .'

She walked right past him to the fridge and yanked the door open, 'Lance, we need more wine. I feel like a drink.' There was more than half a bottle left. She took it and tipped out a generous glassful. As he watched she raised the glass and drank steadily. She watched him over the rim.

'Oh, there's um . . . There's plenty of red left,' he said, bending to retrieve the phone, but not bending quite far enough to hide from her the relief that poured across his face.

'But I want white. And that's all there is.'

'Okay.' He put the phone on the shelf beside his helmet. 'Hey. I know. Let's go for a walk into town. We can get more wine. Maybe buy fish and chips for dinner.'

'Hey,' she said. 'Great idea. But aren't you all tired and sweaty from your bike ride?'

She was still standing there leaning against the fridge, entirely naked, wearing nothing but a cynical smile. He pulled his shirt off, undid his shorts and went over to her, took the glass and drank the rest in one go. 'Not that tired,' he said.

———◆———

When he was gently snoring (so gently it was really only strong breathing) she pushed the sheets back and walked out to the living room. Light shone through the large window overlooking the front lawn, the path that led to the lake. The moon had risen, pouring a flood of milky light over the water. A light breeze pulled at the surface, then soothed it again, making it look as flat as a spill of oil on a road, like you could just walk over it to the other side. They still hadn't explored the little island like she had wanted. Tomorrow would be their last day. Gretel shivered, turned away. His phone was still on the shelf. She took it over to the window and scrolled through the call register. Maureen. 3.33 pm. Then yesterday. Maureen 3.29 pm. The day before that Maureen 3.31pm. She didn't bother looking any further, tossed the phone back onto the shelf. It would be every day, though what was so significant about that time, she couldn't tell. The same ex-wife he claimed to be so relieved to be away from. Gretel went to the bedroom and dressed, took her book and went to the living room. Luckily she had brought a fantasy novel with her – they were always long. Ken had loaned her this book, though she'd not felt obliged to return it.

Ken had been frank about his deceptions, in a way. He had rung her to say that his partner was returning the following week and that it would be best if they didn't see each other again. And could he have his salad bowl back, the one he'd brought with tabouli that night, as Patty would wonder about it. Gretel remembered the bathroom-cabinet evidence, but never Ken making furtive phone calls. In fact, she recalled Ken picking up letters from the floor at the front door, barely glancing at the name on the envelopes before tossing them onto the hallstand, making no attempt to conceal them. As if Patty was a former tenant who'd skipped town owing rent. She had to admit, now she thought about it, Ken had never brought Patty into bed with them, never implied a comparison with Gretel. The oysters, the flowers were Ken's generic girlfriend slash partner accoutrements. It was part of the package, when you took a chance on Ken.

She woke as the sun was rising, with her book on her lap. There was the smell, she could swear, of oriental lilies. Or was it that other sickly smell, the faint odour of decay that Lance carried with him?

———◆———

He was at the fridge, throwing little bits of cheese, a wedge of lemon, a half-eaten tub of pesto dip, into the bin. The esky sat upturned on the verandah, draining the last of his vigorous sluicing. Gretel stood outside, thinking. He had already backed the car close up to the villa and placed the bike at the ready, the helmet dangling from its handlebars. He had planned a final ride, she imagined, as what other pretext would take him away from her at the appointed hour? Otherwise, she assumed he would announce his intention to walk down to the manager's office with the keys. Or perhaps he would require a final nap, and disappear to the bedroom with his phone. She looked at her watch. 3.25.

Behind her she heard the clatter of cups, some knives in the sink. The rush of water. The clang of the lid on the kitchen bin. They would have to leave soon.

By the time Lance appeared at the top step she was already mounted on the bike.

'Where are you going?'

But kicking off the stand, she waved a hand behind her as she headed for the lake, riding straight towards the shore, and then in the water, the low smooth water that looked only ankle deep all the way to the little island, and beyond. She was wearing the helmet.

Writing [in] the New Millennium

Professionalising the Creative (11.00 am–12.15 pm Sem. Rm. 3). When someone in the audience asked how long it should take to write a book, all the authors exchanged glances. I expected the answer to be depressingly precise, but not this depressing. Nor this precise. Ten years, said one author, not missing a beat. Six weeks, said the author next on the panel. The first elaborated: ten years from early notes to final draft but another two before publication, so strictly twelve. Her book was a nervous-looking volume of fiction that sounded more like poetry. In the book display it sat disdainfully to one side of the embossed historical novels and the fiction with perky covers and one-syllable titles. *The Lonely Flight of the Soul*. It looked a lot like its author, a lonely soul clad in muted tertiary shades, sitting apart from the rest of the panel. The author who said six weeks went on to explain that he only wrote in the evenings, as his real job was in finance. He held up his book, a fat action thriller well over 120,000 words called *Code Six*.

My evenings were spent in front of the TV. Sometimes after Rosie and Jay settled down for the night and Curtis and I were done throwing clothes in the washing machine or cleaning up the kitchen, there was no point even switching it on. If I ever got to bed with a book, I couldn't seem to stay awake. It took me three years to write my manuscript and it was still less than 30,000 words. I wondered how late the finance guy worked? Six weeks of 120,000 words came to 20,000 words a week, or 2,857.14 words per day. Not so bad if you said it quickly.

But I wondered how many words per hour he wrote. And were all those words good ones?

⌁◆⌁

Hothousing New Talent. Mentoring and Marketing. Furthering Your Manuscript. I chose all the sessions that sounded like they meant business. I wanted action, results. When the assessor confirmed our details for the program, eight of us, all expenses paid, she added a final comment in her email. More like a warning. Our manuscripts had been chosen for their potential, but the rest was up to us. Even if we were to secure a book deal at the end of the conference, we had to understand that afterwards we would be on our own. With a deadline. She recommended we approach agents on the first day. Potential alone would not be enough.

The agents were all very tall. Twice, I lined up to speak to them after sessions (*Managing a Literary Career; Breaking through the Paper Ceiling*) but even seated they towered over me. One of them had severe cheekbones and shorn white hair, under which her skull protruded. I could almost see her thinking how she would rather be back in her office overlooking the water while on the phone to New York finalising a deal for a client, a real author. Instead she was in this small town, which had doubled in size for the week of the conference, talking to people who thought that because they had been told they had potential they were something special. Waiting in line, I overheard her saying something dismissive about potential writers. Potential started to sound less like a quality with inherent power, and more of a handicap. Each time I walked away before reaching the end of the queue.

———◆◆———

At the first session after breakfast, someone said, 'You know the Annals woman is still in her room? She's written a thousand words this morning!'

Oh, the Annals woman. So famous she did not require a name. Like a duke from Shakespearean drama, Norfolk or Gloucester, so powerful that she went by an abbreviation of her estate instead. *The Annals of the Golden Children*. Five or six books, all with two definite articles in their titles, just to make sure. A body of work almost legendary among fans even though she was still so young. Annals dressed like an extra in a fantasy film. She could have been Galadriel's understudy. Everything about her was bountiful: flowing hair, long velvet skirts, the thousands of words. Before breakfast.

Another writer, a bearded vegan from the mountains, said to no one in particular, 'Apparently Trollope wrote three thousand words every morning. Before going to work. And he didn't even have a laptop!' He slipped a banana from the breakfast buffet into the pocket of his coat, which had telltale leather patches at the elbows. He looked like a nib-pen kind of writer.

Annals had a silver laptop. It really did seem made of precious metal. On opening night, when the rest of us were laughing and drinking too much wine, she clutched her laptop close to her chest, talking with head bent to her editor. She departed early in a way that announced, *I am going upstairs to write now; that is what writers do*, while the rest of us quite obviously were not writing. Unless you counted the flirtatious text messages crisscrossing the room. Arts bureaucrats, literary professionals, let loose for a week together. Even I caught on to that.

And writers. A writers' conference is full of them. Why such an obvious thing took so long to strike me, I didn't know. There were books and people to sell them, but no readers. We were all writers. Dozens of people attending each session. Here to learn writerly things. I was so eager. A great sheet of blotting paper ready to soak up everything about the writing life. And yet all the writers, the ones with books on display, seemed a different species. Everything they told us was contradictory. Write no more than three drafts, otherwise you overdo it. At least ten drafts. Twenty. Write with your eyes shut and let the words flow. Don't censor yourself. Learn how to self-edit. Don't even *try* and edit yourself. Be ruthless. Cut, cut, cut. I began to suspect they were all telling lies. The thin nervous author and the mountains poet whispered over skinny soy lattes during the morning coffee break, though on stage they seemed to despise each other. Maybe they were conspiring to keep us potential authors out of the scene.

And for a writers' conference there was some very sloppy language around. I studied the program posted up at the information desk. I couldn't knock out thousands of words in a day but I did know my grammar. Why was everything a gerund?

'A what?' Another Potential Writer, next to me.

'Writing the New Millennium. Professionalising everything. All these verbs without subjects. And nouns posing as verbs.' She looked sideways at me and moved away.

⇒•⇐

Streamlining and Storytelling. Approaching Publication. Writing the New Millennium. That was the keynote session: only top-shelf authors participating, we privileged mentees up in the front row, part of our fabulous opportunity. The authors had hardcover editions and overseas agents and Commonwealth Prize shortlistings. The audience questions were vetted beforehand. I dared not offer mine. Writing about, writing in, even writing for the new millennium. But what was *writing* the new millennium? The missing preposition bothered me.

The top-shelf authors were all unsmiling males over sixty. They read from their books in wearied drawls, making comments about dead European writers I'd never read. They wrote historical novels, and somehow we all knew that did not mean Regency dramas or anything with a bodice on the cover. Everything they said was addressed to the corner of the room somewhere past our heads, as if there hovered a better quality audience, a more appreciative and deserving one. The writing life of the new millennium sounded like afternoon tea in the staffroom of a boys' school. I left the session early. The millennium wasn't even new any more.

Back in the bar I knocked back two cold beers before

moving on to red wine. Behind me on the wall was one of the conference posters. After my second drink I took out a felt pen and added the word *in* between Writing and the.

❖

Annals wore her flowing clothes and silver jewellery at breakfast. Looking closer when I fetched my coffee, I saw she was also wearing full make-up. Her hair was sleek. Like a waterfall. An advertisement for hair conditioner. She drank decaffeinated tea and only ate a tiny wholemeal roll and an apple. Her figure was perfect. Her voice calm, well modulated. I knew her study back home would be organised with document trays and proper bookshelves. Her kitchen cupboards would be tidy, her bedsheets always fresh. I didn't need to see photos to know that her husband would have slightly greying hair and project an aura of stern kindness. Actually, I was certain he would resemble Hugo Weaving. And her children, one of each. Sebastian and Aurelia. They would have excellent teeth and school reports.

Even the university where she worked was a magical place, on a hill. Evergreen trees, misty mornings. I expected that on teaching days she also wrote a thousand words before breakfast. Hugo was probably something in design, or advertising. They would pay their bills on time and upgrade their cars every five years and have family holidays at coastal resorts. Curtis and the kids and I holidayed at the coast too. But somehow I couldn't see Annals in a tent, the whole shower-block, burned-sausages thing. Where would she write her morning thousand words for a start?

———◆———

Between sessions, tall young men stalked the grounds, phones clamped to their ears. Impossible to decide if they were successful young authors or successful young publishers, agents or editors. Producers or consumers. It didn't seem to matter. Suits worn nonchalantly with T-shirts. Shaved heads. Ray-Bans. Once, you could pick authors by their straggling hair or unfashionable floral skirts. But here only the bearded mountains poet seemed to be playing the part. Everyone else had a corporate look. These young men with phones were doubtless negotiating deals with New York, Frankfurt, Hollywood. One of them had thick black hair that he pushed back from his forehead, but in petulance, not despair, for surely he was too successful for that. He pulled his phone away, stared at it, then reattached it to his ear while gazing into the distance. As if he were listening to the sound of the sea in a conch shell, the sound of a faraway sea, the Atlantic, or the Nordic. The immense swell, the crashing waves of success and prosperity, the white caps of book sales cresting in triumph before pouring into a bank account.

Another of these men emerged from a doorway as I walked past and we almost bumped. He was looking at the floor while talking on the phone, uttering single words punctuated by brief silences. 'Ambiguous.' Pause. 'Deficient.' Pause. 'Vulpine.' So he was talking to his publisher or agent. 'Accommodate.' Pause. 'Windfall.' Shorter pause. 'Yo-yo.' Or maybe providing answers to crossword-puzzle clues. His voice was soft and the hair on the back of his neck curled endearingly, just like Rosie's when it was damp, but I did not let that fool me. I was sure he was a deeply focused, humourless individual who wrote five pages each day and secured literary fellowships every other year.

❦

Not fast enough at leaving one session, I became trapped in the first row before the next started. *Contemporary Mythical Narrative* (4.00 pm–5.30 pm Sem. Rm. 1). My eyes started closing, though I willed myself to remain awake. Luckily the lectern hid me from most of the panel. The author at the end was reading in a piping monotone from his new novel. The story was all about a woman walking across a windy mountain pass that seemed to go on for miles. He read for twenty minutes and still all she did was brush some grit from her eye. She never got anywhere near the end of the rocky path. The roaring wind did not abate. I was alarmed when I noticed he was only halfway through a very thick volume, and it was while speculating on what might lie ahead in the novel (a speck in the other eye? another mountain after this one?) that I fell asleep.

Afterwards I decided I must make a greater effort. I returned to the book display and selected one of Annals's books from the piles of them under her photograph. Unfortunately I could not read past the second page of *The Annals of the Soothsayer*, which contained the phrase, 'Alamandra swooned at the feet of Alaric' because a) I did not believe that anyone had swooned since 1801, and b) I was already confused by two characters' names commencing with Al.

I was allotted a half-hour, one-on-one session with a Strategic Marketing Consultant. His head was polished to match his shoes. At the start of our session he placed his BlackBerry beside his appointment book and pressed a button firmly. Possibly he was activating a timer.

'And what genre do you write in?'

Genre.

'Umm. Well, it's a sort of children's story.'

'But what genre? Fantasy? Adventure? Crime?'

'Not any, really. Elements of all, I guess. Maybe.'

'Children's or young adult?'

'Oh definitely children's. I mean kids from any age. If they want.'

'We need a specific target audience. What age exactly?'

'Around twelve? Ish? Maybe younger. Eight, nine.
But then teenagers might . . .'

'Children or teens. You don't do both.'

It was the first I'd heard that kids aged eight and thir-
teen weren't allowed to read the same book.

'Look around you,' he said. 'What are you doing here?'

'Well, my manuscript was selected . . .'

'That's not what I mean.' He glanced behind him.
'I mean, look at all the *successful* authors here.' He
emphasised the word in a way that showed contempt
for the handful of writers, like Thin Nervous, whose
book might have been translated into French but whose
sales remained under four figures. These writers were
not even bothering any more to turn up for their book-
signing sessions, whereas Code Six and Annals sat
there signing and smiling every day. Their publicists
slid padded chairs underneath them and stood by with
supplies of bottled water as if book-signing were an
Olympic event. 'These authors understand exactly their
place in the market.'

Author? He meant I really was an author?

'*They* are focused.'

No, clearly he meant I was not.

'Your target audience,' he repeated, closing his
appointment book just as the BlackBerry buzzed. 'You
need to define your target audience.'

<hr />

No one could confirm when and where I was to meet my mentor. Or if she was even there. I carried my manuscript around all week, expecting anytime to start the hours and hours of blissful intensive hands-on work that I had anticipated ever since I'd applied for the program. My manuscript began to have a dog-eared look to it. Then I noticed that few people had manuscripts with them. As if it were impolite, or show-offy, hawking a folder of paper around. Writing the new millennium seemed a very private affair.

At dinner one night I was seated next to PB, an author from Los Angeles who wrote for twenty-somethings.

'What do you have there?' She tapped my folder.

'It's really just a first draft.' This was not true. I must have rewritten it fifty times.

She did not step in to ask what it was about or had I been published, but took a bite of her cheesecake.

'No one here seems to be doing much writing,' I said. Apart from Annals, but I knew better than to mention her to someone called PB. Not with her hot-pink wig and tartan miniskirt.

She laughed. A sudden barking sound like gunshot at daybreak.

'We all do it but don't admit to it. Like picking your nose, or masturbating.' Seeing the shock on my face, she leaned closer. 'Listen kid, writing sucks. Getting your name out, that's what counts. Do you blog?'

Kid? I was at least ten years older!

She got out of her chair. 'Are you going to the WordSlam?' But it was not an invitation.

➤◆◄

Writing the new millennium was clearly for a different kind of writer. I wanted sessions on the problems that bothered me, such as choosing names for characters and keeping my desk tidy. Or advice on posture and diet. And I wanted to know how to inoculate myself against the contagiousness of style that I once read about. I didn't want to be told that writing sucks. I hoped my mentor was not like PB, with her interactive texts and Californian advice.

Not only was my mentor unable to answer these questions, she looked at me as if I were a species of vermin. Finally, on the last day, I had found her seated at the back of a small room smoking a cigarette out of the window.

She told me to sit and pushed some forms at me.

'Publishers. Conference committee. They're after details,' she said.

'More details?'

She shrugged. I had already filled in forms and answered questionnaires when I was selected. When my manuscript was selected. She shrugged again, saying she was just a freelancer, funded by the conference trust and the local council, just doing what they asked. I signed the forms and pushed them back. I wondered how much she was paid to sit here on the last afternoon and blow smoke in my face. The mentors were meant to be professional writers and editors. I asked if she had written books too, if she was an author.

'Freelancer,' she said ambiguously.

Somehow I already knew that she would ignore my folder too.

———◆———

When I got back home on the Sunday night I threw my suitcase into the corner of the bedroom and headed for the spare room with my notes.

'I'll have to be set up properly in here,' I called out to Curtis in the kitchen. 'Your friends won't be able to stay the night any more. And the kids' toys will have to go back in their room.' I kicked a plastic dinosaur out the door and tossed three stuffed animals onto the bed. Then I took them and the other toys off the bed. I needed it to set out all my notes and drafts. I was dismantling the Thomas the Tank Engine train set that took up half the floor when Rosie walked in, sucking a finger.

'Sorry, petal. All this has to go. Clean sweep. Mummy's gotta write.'

'So you got the book deal?' Curtis appeared in the doorway.

'Yeah. Well, I signed something.' I pulled Rosie's finger out of her mouth.

———◆———

Over the next few weeks I learned that the greatest impediment to writing was not the children, not the TV, not even the lure of the refrigerator, but the telephone. The phone calls anywhere between three and eight-thirty, from telemarketers, consumer researchers and someone offering me a free holiday if I attended their investment seminar. I couldn't unplug the phone and I couldn't ignore it. Sometimes I did ignore it. But after five or six rings I would give in, then after I'd growled into the phone and returned to my desk, forget what I was going to write. If Jay had been a few years older I'd have asked him to take messages. Curtis had not a clue what I was going through.

'You try being creative at home,' I told him. 'You try pulling an entire story together and keeping the household running. And that bloody phone. What do we need one for anyway?'

But I knew why. The third week back, still no contact.

'Haven't you already written it? Isn't that manuscript what they contracted?'

The ignorance of some people. 'Duh. As if I won't be pressured for the next one. Gotta have that ready when they want it. Besides,' I gestured at the dog-eared folder, 'this needs a complete rewrite.'

⸺◆⸺

One afternoon I was staring at the blank space on the screen where I had just deleted two paragraphs. They had to go but then I panicked at the sight of this big hole that needed filling. My head felt as empty as the page before me. If I stared at it long enough maybe the words would bore through to the screen from my pupils.

When the phone rang, for once I was grateful. Though I quickly regretted agreeing to take part in the survey.

'How much of your weekly income is spent on take-away food?'

Instead of answering, I asked, 'What are you reading right now?'

'Pardon?'

'What book are you reading? You are reading one, aren't you?'

She mentioned a title I had never heard of. The author's name sounded fake. Edwina Montgomery. Either that or she'd died in 1939.

'Name her other titles,' I demanded.

'*Return to Galaxy Red. Journey to the Edge of Time. The Starship Propheticus*,' she said. 'Science fiction.'

'Speculative fiction,' I hissed into the phone. That much I'd learned from the conference.

What I did not learn from the conference was why so many of these authors were stuck in the old millenniums. All those books about medieval travellers, the taming of dragons, the quests for sacred swords and magic stones and shimmering portals that transported unlikely heroes to other worlds... What did this have to do with the new millennium? When someone mentioned adult fantasy I examined these titles in the book display and, no, they were not sealed and black with R-rating stickers, though I couldn't help imagining leather bras and purple glow-in-the-dark dildos. They were fat and colourful, the covers embossed in gold. The blurbs mentioned battles, lost jewels and magic talismans. Fiery hearts and pure minds and kingdoms and keys and ravens. I wondered what the difference was between adult fantasy and children's. I flipped through each one, scanning the storylines. No sex. Chaste embraces. Kisses on rings or hands, when warlords met or wise men bestowed blessings. Adult fantasy seemed very innocent.

<hr />

I became obsessed with organising my time. I spent so much time planning how I would organise my days, I did not have time to write. I was stuck between ten (or twelve) years and six weeks. I alternately despised both Thin Nervous and Code Six, but then I knew that Thin Nervous had won two literary awards while Code Six had sold over 80,000 copies of his book.

In ten years Thin Nervous had devoted herself to writing 26,000 words. (While at the book display I had counted them – it was easier than reading them.) That was exactly fifty words a week. But fifty words a week divided into 7.12 words each day, and how could you write a fraction of a word? And she must have written half or quarter sentences since some of her sentences were much longer than that. At what point did you divide words into fractions?

As for Code Six, I imagined him sitting there with the clock set like Trollope and laughing at us all while running off just under three thousand words every evening after dinner. Probably all before eleven pm, the bastard. Of course being in finance he wouldn't have to muck around with the washing-up or the kitchen floors after dinner; he could just disappear into his study. But I still wanted to know how he did it. Six weeks. Faulkner wrote *As I Lay Dying* in six weeks, but then he cheated. One of his chapters was only five words long. *My mother is a fish*. If only I could write chapters like that and win the Nobel Prize.

The phone rang. There was the familiar lag and crackle before a voice said, 'Good morning, madam, how are you?' but it was not a Bombay accent.

'It's afternoon.'

'Oh sorry, ma'am. How are you this afternoon?'

'Who is calling please?'

'I am calling from Mordern.'

'Where?'

'Mordern. Have you heard of Mordern, ma'am?'

'No. Where is it?' It sounded like a place in a fantasy saga. Perhaps Annals created it. Or Code Six. I didn't mind, I would have liked to go there.

But Mordern was not a place, it was a company that made roller-shutter blinds and I said not interested thanks and placed the phone down as the guy was asking me to reconsider.

———◆◆———

How hard could it be? They were only words, after all. Not anything difficult like microbes or atomic particles. And it was not like developing a vaccine for testicular cancer or isolating the gene that causes Down syndrome. I was not meant to solve any of Fermat's remaining theorems or even understand them. Writing a thesis on the Brahmagupta–Fibonacci identity or completing the Gold Coast Triathlon or interviewing Tom Cruise or discovering a way to reverse baldness – all those things were *really* hard.

What about those people who engraved pictures on grains of rice, or built entire sailing ships inside bottles? If they could do that, then I could write a second children's story of under 30,000 words by the end of the year.

———◆◆———

'What book are *you* reading?' I demanded of the person who called to sell me tickets in an art-union lottery.

'Tom Clancy's *The Archimedes Effect*,' he said as if it were right beside him.

Even so, I was a step ahead. 'Incorrect. Are you aware that Tom Clancy did not write this book? That his name is a brand for the Net Force series?'

'Ah . . . no.'

'And that the real authors of this novel are writing under sublicensing agreements?'

'Really?'

'Yes. Their names are Steve Perry and Larry Segriff.'

'Oh, okay.'

'Can I help you with anything else today?'

'Er, no.'

'Thank you for calling,' I said before I hung up.

———◆———

I began to see my target audience. They were lashed to a frame by the ankles and wrists, while my story arrowed its way right through a bullseye painted on their chest. Shoot, shoot, shoot. I reached my target audience again and again, until they slumped on the frame, blood leaking down to pool at their feet.

———◆———

You are not a writer, the convenor of *Professionalising the Creative* had said, if you don't write every single day of your life. If you don't wake up and write your dreams or make notes or plan your day's work. I ensured that I had a notebook and sharp pencil beside the bed. When I woke up I grabbed them – but before I fixed my glasses and stopped yawning, Jay raced in and jumped on the bed, and my dream vanished like water out of a bathtub.

━━━◆◆◆━━━

PB was right. Writing sucks. Words were sly, mendacious, untrustworthy, treacherous, dirty, rotten scheming BASTARDS OF THINGS! I hated them more than anything. I wrote and wrote and those slippery words, those stinking lousy mongrel BASTARDS, disappeared from the page sideways, upwards, anyways. Anything but stay in place on the line, forming nice tidy sentences, one after the other. Pinning them down on the computer screen was like trying to pick up mercury with chopsticks. They rolled and slid away from me whenever I got close. I yelled at the screen. 'I hate you I hate you I hate you I hate you!' Why couldn't I write my story with numbers instead?

'I hate words so much!' I told them one night, slamming the keyboard up and down on the desk. Rosie was doing well with books up until that point. I grabbed *The Very Hungry Caterpillar* from her hands and tossed it aside. 'Forget it, they'll only turn around and betray you when you're older! Look at me, all these words around and do you think I can get a single one to make any sense?'

She started to cry. Curtis hissed at me, 'Grow up, why don't you! You're only trying to write, for god's sake, not trying to solve the riddle of the fucking phoenix.'

'But I have a deadline,' I wailed as he slammed the door to the kids' room in my face.

'Whatever.'

'And it's sphinx,' I called through the door. 'It's the riddle of the sphinx.'

Thank you for attending the Writing the Millennium Conference. Please note the conditions for the submission of manuscripts:

The date of final submission is not negotiable.

Manuscripts received after this date will not be considered.

Manuscripts must be hard copy and not emailed.

Please indicate by return email if you will be complying with these conditions.

———◆———

No, it didn't sound like a contract. Curtis used the same email address. I printed the email out, then deleted it, then hid the printed email between the pages of a second-hand copy of *Gone with the Wind*.

———◆———

'No distractions!' I announced. 'No distractions until I'm finished my final draft.' I listed all the things

I wouldn't do: the ironing, picking up toys, making beds, changing the sheets unless it was absolutely essential. Within a week I refined my list: no more washing, shopping, cooking. I looked in the cupboards. There was plenty of tinned food, cereal, instant noodles, packets of biscuits. We had enough food to last for months. Millions of people in other countries lived off barley soup and plain rice; so could we.

One evening Curtis came home to find Jay feeding Rosie peanut butter on stale mini toasts while I gazed at the computer screen and scratched at my dandruff.

'I'm going to the supermarket for fresh food,' he said, picking Rosie up as if she needed an emergency infusion of green vegetables. As an afterthought he asked if I needed anything.

'Yes,' I said, deleting the ninth sentence in the last half-hour. 'I need adjectives. Bring me some nice fresh adjectives.'

He shut the door.

'No, make that verbs,' I called out.

⟞⟐⟝

I had a deadline.

'You make it sound like something bad,' said Curtis, he heard it so much.

But it *was* bad. How could something called *deadline* be good? Pages and pages of prose, and what for but a deadline. As if their fate was to be killed, victims of some distant war. All those words, tens of thousands of them. The infantry of prose, the front line. How could I have hated them so much? Poor little soldiers, lying flat and lifeless on the line, their letters dripping off the pages, clotting and staining everything beneath. I would have felt more sorry for them if I hadn't been so worried about my manuscript. Maybe those dead lines could join my target audience, shot through the heart, left to bleed out there somewhere, under the pitiless sun. In the mud. On the beach.

'What an imagination,' he said.

'Thanks.'

'It's not a compliment.'

<hr />

One day Annals materialised beside me at the wash-basins in the women's toilets. We rinsed and shook our hands in unison. She leaned over the basin to inspect her perfect face in front of the mirror. Her hair fell forward in a silent swoosh then rippled over her shoulders and down her back when she stood straight again. The water wound down the plughole, as if reluctant to leave her.

<hr />

Please note the following additional conditions:

Authors whose work is accepted will be contacted by telephone.

We are unable to provide feedback to unsuccessful authors.

The editorial team's decision will be final.

No correspondence will be entered into.

———◆———

Curtis would never think to open the pages of *Gone with the Wind*.

The Pirate Map

He set off in the morning but the journey had begun several days before, in Drew Saltman's accountant's office.

He would need a W-7, she had explained. And once he had his ITIN then he'd need to fill out the W-8BEN, but first he'd have to obtain his certificate of residency.

'Certificate of residency? Won't my passport do?' Drew Saltman had said.

'Absolutely not. This is only for the USA IRS, remember. And you will probably have to get several certificates while you're at it. Make it a dozen.'

'I could photocopy them.'

'No. They all have to be certified by the ATO.'

It had the complexity of algebra but none of its logic.

Not that algebra was his strong point. And not that he would get any sympathy from Mrs Zhang in that respect.

'And don't forget your TFN and your ABN,' she said. 'You do have a TFN, don't you?' Though it was rhetorical. It always was. She turned to her filing drawer before he could reply.

The weight of these acronyms alone. Documents with mystifying serial numbers, as if they were motor vehicles or household appliances.

'Couldn't I just pay the withholding tax instead?'

Mrs Zhang had looked at Drew as if he'd just confessed to bestiality.

And then there was the time involved. He was itching to get back to his studio. It was getting cold in the mountains, and he'd already delayed stacking the load of timber for the pot-bellied stove.

'Just go to the ATO. Believe me, it will be worth it in the end,' she said.

⸻◆⸻

He took the early train from Woodford and arrived at Central Station before nine am. He could have changed trains but had already decided to walk the few blocks down. Mrs Zhang had given him a clue. A photocopy of a fax of a recent copy of the document he was expected to obtain. The top left-hand corner was partly obscured by a pre-copy fold, but in tiny lettering there was the

Sydney GPO box number of the Australian Tax Office, and the name of a street. The number of the street was obscured, but it was an excellent start. He would simply have to walk along this street and find the right building. It would beat loitering around the GPO boxes waiting to follow the person who collected the mail back to their source. In the train he had taken out his handy wallet card 'Contacting the ATO' and examined it again, but there were only virtual addresses, phone numbers and website links. Contacting the ATO in person, he decided, could be an adventure. And it had been a while since he'd visited the city.

⸻◆⸻

Drew Saltman walked up and down the street, once each way, before settling on a process of elimination, but when he decided on the place it seemed obvious. There was no sign, number or nameplate, but on the footpath were smokers draped in lanyards, representing government office workers the country over. They stared at him with the skittish collective suspicion of the endangered species, undecided whether he was foe or friend, whether to tough it out as one or break ranks and bolt for cover. He paused for a microsecond, contemplating a comradely cigarette himself, although he had given up a year ago. In fact it was outside Mrs Zhang's Emu Plains office that he had smoked his last, pushing the butt deep into the pine-chipped border garden of the little business estate on the edge of town where she had elected to work. The other tenants were a small printery, a cleaning agency, a nut roaster and packager, and several indeterminate businesses that could have been cardboard packaging or cocaine supply. When Drew had asked why here, Mrs Zhang had pointed out the obvious advantages of more space and lower over-heads. Cheaper than the CBD, she had assured him. And her clients came from all over the place anyway, they didn't need a central location.

Did Emu Plains even have a CBD? Drew had doubted it. His butt was still there, unless she had picked it out and binned it. Mrs Zhang was meticulous like that, which was why she was his accountant. It went with her failure to invite him to call her Georgina, and her persistence in calling him Drew, as if he were somehow subservient to her and she were paying him to perform a routine task, not the other way around.

It didn't matter that his sculptures were exhibited the world over, and were being sold right now, in galleries in San Francisco, in Philadelphia – in Miami, of all places – the whole reason he needed his Certificate of Residency and had to organise the ITIN urgently, before the USA IRS scooped a great hole in his fees like a hungry bulldozer. It would always be like this. He worked with his hands and got his clothes dirty; his workplace was a Nissen shed. Mrs Zhang was a clean trim accountant in an office. It was she who had given him the 'Contacting the ATO' card. She had picked it out of a clear plastic box on her desk and handed it over like a strip of prescription sedatives. Use it sparingly, was the implication, there won't be any more.

The smokers' stares followed him into the building. The entrance was a tight empty space, grey glass and grey steel, yet nothing seemed to reflect, his shadow captured and absorbed as he walked through the glass doorway, as if he had entered a dimension where light and shade flattened into one. The automatic door slid back behind him with a disturbing electric hum. Ahead of him was an escalator, and as he stepped onto it he registered how clean it was, how shiny, how unlike a public escalator. The ones at Central Station had been sticky underfoot, dull with a paste of commuter grit and industrial grease, and had thrown a draught of foetid air onto his face with such hostile force it was as if CityRail were, for some perverse occult reason, both punishing him for entering its domain and forbidding him go back outside. He had felt filthy as he'd stepped out into Eddy Avenue, glad to expel from his lungs the pungent station air that still inexplicably smelled of coal dust, eighty years after the introduction of the electric train engine.

Now he felt trapped again, in a sterile airlock. Above him he could not see where the escalator ended. There were no other doorways. As it silently glided up he glanced back at the door he had entered. Would it reopen to let him out? The tinted glass allowed him a shaded view of the herd of smokers, a few of them now breaking away from the pack, grinding butts under their feet and eyeing the entrance with distinct dismay. He placed his hand on the escalator's glossy belt, already feeling intrusive. At the top there was a row of security turnstiles, and more glass. He tripped off the escalator and looked around. There was still no sign, but now, a couple of people walking through the turnstiles, waving ID cards over the electric scanners. Grocery items, checking themselves in and out. Two people, tobacco-scented, brushed past him from behind. To his left was a wall, more dark tinted glass, to the right a polished stainless steel counter and two guards dressed in grey. Nowhere else to go, except for the escalator down.

He approached and placed a hand on the counter. One of the guards stood and watched his hand. He took it off the counter and put it in his pocket. As they each watched, a faint misty impression evaporated.

Drew Saltman cleared his throat. 'Is this the ATO?'

Both guards were female. The seated one had hair the shade of Dijon mustard. After several long seconds the one standing behind her, portly and short, like a mug of beer, hinted it might be, without actually speaking.

'But there's no sign,' he said.

'That's right.'

'Why not?'

Neither blinked. The portly one placed both hands on her belt, above her gun. Drew smiled, feeling the millisecond his lips stretched that it might have been a mistake. Impassive, bland, might have been better.

'Security,' she finally said.

'So how do you enter?' At this, Dijon mustard stood up – she too wore a gun – and they both stared at him with unclothed suspicion.

'You don't.'

He attempted to explain the nature of his quest – it was beginning to resemble something mighty and epic – 'And so my accountant said I needed to obtain the certificate in person from the ATO. That's here, right? Even though there's no sign.' He said this with a final shot at levity but as soon as he'd arched an ironic eyebrow and looked around for the non-existent sign and smiled, he knew it was a mistake. Inwardly, he was cursing Mrs Zhang. And his handprint was on the counter. Fingerprints.

Whether the two heard or comprehended his explanation was impossible to ascertain. Portly, sticking a tongue in one side of her mouth, barely broke eye contact to glance at the photocopy of the document, one of Mrs Zhang's other clients' copy of the Certificate of Residency, which he unfolded in front of her. It was now very creased. She glanced at his face – still smiling, too nervous, would he never learn? – then at her colleague, then pushed it back.

'Can't help you with that.' She posed with her hands on her belt again, the left one a whisker away from the holster.

'Well. How do I get in then?' He gestured past the turnstiles. 'Someone in there must be able to help me?'

Another big mistake. Dijon and Portly drew breath and shook their heads in unison.

'Can't. Be. Done,' Dijon finally said.

'Not at this office,' Portly added. 'Public not admitted here.'

Any amusement Drew Saltman felt in the situation vanished. He had got up earlier than usual. He had spent two hours on the train. Breakfast had been a CityRail doughnut, not even fresh, and a weak, luke-warm coffee. He deserved better.

'Look, I've been told to come to the ATO to get this form.' He waved it now, like a crumpled flag of surrender. 'This is the ATO. You've more or less admitted to that. What am I meant to do?'

Staff, meanwhile, were walking back and forth through the entrance having waved their security cards over the turnstiles. In fact it seemed very busy, a peak period, though it was not yet morning tea time. Some of them glanced at him. He watched them. All of them ATO employees, none of them lesser mortals such as himself, abject members of the mere public. Ordinary taxpayers, the rest of the population. How dare these guards with their grindstone stomachs and badly tinted hair treat him like this. He was a taxpayer, therefore the tax office was funded by him; they should be serving him, not treating him like toenail fungus. Even the smokers here, universal pariahs that they generally were, were higher on the pecking order, waving their passes and gliding through to the inner sanctum.

Some of this he was framing mentally, to renew his protest, when Portly said, 'There's another office.'

'Oh.' Drew almost smiled. 'Good. Where?' He folded the document and slipped it into his pocket.

'Around the corner.' She removed her hand from her holster to wave in a large semicircle, in the direction of the rest of the city, taking in Liverpool Street and the commencement of the eastern suburbs, around all of Circular Quay, and Darling Harbour, back through Chinatown, to here where they stood, the epicentre. That was a large corner. He asked for a street name.

'Lang Street. Not far.'

Had he heard of Lang Street? He thought not. Around the corner, he knew reasonably well. Pitt, Liverpool, George Streets. In the other direction, Campbell, even little Cunningham Street nearby, back to George, beyond that Sussex. No Lang Street. Perhaps it was in Chinatown, a warren of street names he'd never fully learned. Mrs Zhang would be pleased.

'Where, exactly, is Lang Street?'

Again without breaking eye contact – how did she do that? – she produced a photocopied map and flicked it across the bullet-proof counter with her forefinger.

He picked it up. It was only an A4 sheet of white copy paper, 80 GSM, but the map was so remarkable that he would keep it, as proof of an experience so strange he might have invented it; one that, had he not already suspected it, confirmed that he had embarked on much more than a mere quest for a one-page document and was instead on an epic journey, the significance of which would probably remain opaque for years to come. Not until he was an old man perhaps, settled by the fire in his mountainside home, with a pipe and a bottle of whisky by his side, would he fully understand the nature of this journey, and explain it to yawning bug-eyed grandchildren. He would be like an old pirate, an ancient mariner, a fount of fabulous tales of far-off lands. Or a creature from fairytale perhaps. He would be Bilbo Baggins, enchanting little hobbits with tales of fire-breathing dragons and hoards of treasure. The map was just a hand-drawn sketch, presumably by an employee of the ATO, but it was or would be as valuable as the Magna Carta.

Open-mouthed, he gazed at it in childlike astonishment. True, it was not yellowed and bloodstained, but in other respects it was exactly like a pirate's map, semi-literate but imaginatively illustrated. Few of Sydney's main streets were spelled correctly. But who cared for spelling when on the high seas to saucy adventure!

'Ah, here we are,' he said, pointing to a spot endearingly labelled *GOLBOURNE ST*. Portly almost looked proud. Drew's frank admiration inspired a spark of helpfulness for she leaned over and pointed where, just like buried treasure, X marked the spot. Lang Street. According to the map it was four blocks away. The map included a sketch of a pointy object labelled *WESTIFIELD TOWER CENTER POIN*, and next to *GROSVERNOR ST* were recognisable images of the Harbour Bridge and the Opera House. Not quite Ken Done or Martin Sharp, but clean, clear images all the same. Presumably the theory was that if the misspelled names misdirected him, these landmarks would reorient him.

Clutching the precious map, he thanked the guards, but they had already turned their backs on him. He descended the clean steel escalators and exited, the doors hissing smoothly open and then shut behind him. The air was pungent with street smells. The smokers had gone and the moisture laid by the early morning rain was now rising in visible wisps from the footpath, as if deciding to join the rest of the warm day after all. Leaving *GOLBOURNE ST*, he would go around the corner, down George Street, turn left at the Harbour Bridge, take ten paces south past the enormous fig and presumably reach another vast and unnamed building, an outpost of the empire that was the ATO.

It was not that easy. If he walked, he would miss his next appointment with a designer in Surry Hills. He hailed a cab.

'Lang Street,' he said clearly and slowly as he always did in Sydney cabs.

'Why?' the driver said, swivelling around.

Drew Saltman thought for a moment. Would he divulge the location of what was evidently a great secret? Would he surrender this easily his hard-won information?

'There's nothing there,' the driver continued while Drew wrestled with his conscience.

'Yes there is. The tax office.' He couldn't help himself. He was incorrigibly charitable. The driver shrugged and sped off down George, one hand on the wheel, shouldering the cab past buses and scattering pedestrians while Drew reassessed his moral position. Driver probably didn't even pay tax anyway.

He was coughed out at the smallest street in the city. Opposite was a park, a very Sydney park with the usual Port Jackson figs and a representative pine – Norfolk Island, he thought – flanked by a long neat row of motor scooters. To the left was a large building, no windows, no street access, a sign saying *Suncorp Group*, but no sun. The cloud cover was now dense, such was the remarkable changeability of the city's weather this time of the year. He walked around the entire small block, a triangle, and found no trace of any premises, came to rest opposite a flight of pebblecrete steps so steep it was impossible to see what lay at the top. He consulted the map again, tucked it in his pocket and swore. He was standing right beside the first of the row of motorcycles, many of them Vespas, pale green, cream and red. He felt severely tempted to tip the first one over and watch the rest tumble down the sloping street like shiny dominoes. He crossed the road and commenced up the stairs, where at least from the top he might obtain a better view.

However, at the top was an astonishing sight. A glass doorway and a sign proclaiming *Australian Taxation Office* and featuring the national coat of arms. Drew Saltman smiled. And the sun came out again. He smiled wider. The native animals of the coat of arms had never seemed more friendly. How he loved the kangaroo, the emu. What benign creatures they were. They blessed him above the doorway as, sun-kissed, he wiped his feet on the mat, and stepped through into a large and nearly empty room. Before him was a row of vacant waiting chairs, to the left a bank of computers, mostly unattended. There were no guards. And no other customers. From a small reception desk someone smiled back at him. Still smiling, Drew approached with the limp unfolded photocopy of Mrs Zhang's other client's certificate of residency.

Almost reluctant to speak – he would break the spell, surely – he spread the page out on the reception desk and asked, 'Am I at the right place? The public office of the ATO?'

'That's right. Can I help you?'

Can I help you? He sighed with pleasure.

'Yes, I need to obtain a document. One of these, a certificate of residency.'

'Okay.'

'I can get one here?' Drew felt his body tense. It was starting to sound a little too easy.

'Sure can.'

'Well, that's wonderful.' He looked around again. There were four other employees in sight. 'You know, it seems very quiet here, for a government office.'

'Yeah.' The receptionist leaned closer and lowered his voice. 'That's because no one knows where we are!'

Drew stiffened. The man's frank glee was unnerving.

Standing straight again, he spoke louder. 'Just take this ticket and sit over there. You'll be called soon by our next available customer service officer.' He pointed to the row of empty seats opposite the customer service officers.

Drew Saltman took his ticket and sat. The receptionist, still smiling, pressed a button on his desk. The other four employees, waiting by their computers, stared at Drew. He wondered which of them was the next available customer service officer. The receptionist gave him a reassuring nod. The customer service officers waited. Drew felt like an actor in an improvised play. Some offbeat street theatre that conscripted innocent and good-humoured passers-by.

During the reverential pause, the receptionist and the first customer service officer exchanged glances and raised eyebrows. Surreptitiously, in case there were concealed cameras waiting to humiliate him, Drew looked around to confirm that he really was the only customer, the only person in a queue. Which made it therefore not a queue.

———◆———

It had been a disaster, that night out.

Sitting in the row of otherwise vacant chairs staring out through the glass doors into the sunshine of Lang Street, he could see the tops of the fig trees, above them the cold blue sky plastered over with chubby clouds, the sort that contained cherubs with long golden trumpets in Christmas cards of his youth.

It was before Mrs Zhang had moved offices and they had wound up a meeting well after six pm. He had extended an offer for a drink at the nearby bar as a courtesy, expecting she would refuse. He had already mentally downed a solitary schooner of Coopers and was on the 7.22 pm back to Woodford when she surprised him by agreeing. Perhaps that had flustered him, led him to taking her elbow a little more eagerly than he should, or taking it at all, as he steered her down the street and across the road to Harry's Bar, but when they were seated at the window with her gin and tonic and his beer, he may have been looking rather too smug.

Normally she responded to his jokes with a tight smile, the sort that said, yes I find that amusing but watch yourself. He appreciated this sense of humour. So few of his friends liked the dry wit. His ex-wife had, he'd discovered too late, no sense of humour at all. But Mrs Zhang. She had a way of watching him sideways and allowing her mouth to flicker. Or tremble.

Perhaps it was the second schooner. Or the third. But at some point he realised Mrs Zhang was still mashing the lemon of her first drink with a straw. While he was asking questions about a husband. Or lover. Or maybe he'd just said boyfriend. And she'd said something about living alone *and* going home to a man, which was beyond confusing. The man might have been her father. He was sure the Mrs was ambiguous. Whatever. She had risen quickly, grabbed her coat and bag and walked off before he'd barely realised. On the train home he'd tossed his mobile phone back and forth in his hands, before finally pocketing it. And then the next morning when he went to ring, replaced the receiver. Whatever he had said – or maybe had *failed* to say, that was also a possibility – he would only make it worse. She was so proper. She still hadn't asked him to call her Georgina. He would not ring her. It would remain professional, as it should. And besides, it was only a companionable drink. It was not like he'd asked her for sex.

His ticket number was called out. Number 32. Had there already been thirty-one customers through the premises this morning, all subjected to the same bizarre courtesy? Perhaps in a moment someone would call 'STOP!' and the director would come over and shake his hand, slap him on the back, thank him for being such a good sport and hand over free tickets to the screening. He approached the four customerless customer service officers a few metres away with the feeling that if this were not a staged performance, it was then possibly some kind of occult ceremony into which he had stumbled. Either way, it was not the public service as he had known it, all four decades of his life. The first customer service officer waved him closer to his desk and Drew sat down again.

'Can I get one of these, a certificate of residency, please?'

'Pardon?'

Drew Saltman had to ask twice more before Parmod (his name was on a lapel tag, no surname, just like in the supermarket checkouts) waved the receptionist over. Perhaps the entire office was a sort of training outfit, thought Drew, as the receptionist and Parmod conferred behind the computer screen.

'Ah.' Something clicked for Parmod. 'Certainly. You give details please.' His navigational skills of the ATO website were also apparently minimal, for he pushed the keyboard aside and handed Drew a tiny yellow Post-it block and a pen.

Conscious he was perhaps deviating from the script, Drew summoned the receptionist back over himself.

'Are you sure about this? I write my details on this?' He waved the Post-it block. 'And it gets processed?'

'That's right. Just your name and address.'

Not even his TFN? Or his ABN? All the acronyms and their numbers he'd carried around like a mouthful of marbles?

They both assured him the little yellow sticker was sufficient to contain all his details. The minuscule note would be the official and comprehensive record of the details that would generate, via registered post in ten working days, the document he needed. The certificate of residency. Twelve copies.

Was he keeping a straight face as he thanked them and walked to the door? The whole thing was so unreal that it was beyond ordinary humour, though the irony was palpable. He was in a Pirandello play, trapped between reality and illusion. He was a character from the chilly fantasies of Kafka. He was Josef K, he was Gregor Samsa. He scuttled out the door.

⬥

At least, he *thought* he'd not asked her for sex. But maybe there were profound cultural differences here, codes he was incapable of knowing. Perhaps his hand had brushed across her lower back in a way that in Shanghai signified, I think you're a loose woman. Or he had held her arm too long, tantamount to a marriage proposal. How would he know? He was just a boy from the mountains who'd gone to TAFE and found he had a talent for sculpture.

He had never phoned her after that night. Since then he had only made the most necessary of communications until the appointment in her office at Emu Plains a few days before. Meanwhile he ascertained from another client, someone he knew from the barber's, that there was a man, in the form of an aged parent. At the appointment she had not betrayed a flicker of either contempt or disappointment. Yet he noticed her lips were garnished with gloss, rosier than usual. And her hand, when she pushed across the little 'Contacting the ATO' card, had painted nails. And when he caught himself registering these things, he told himself nothing was new, only that he was noticing things about her for the first time. He allowed himself to recall that at Harry's Bar she had made a brief phone call, which could have been solicitous, daughterly. She wore no ring. Had she ever? Now he had no idea. One drink. Or two. But how did a well-intentioned drink bring him undone like this? He was baffled by his own actions, ones that he'd assumed were correct all his life and yet were also all wrong. Clearly asking a woman who was also one's accountant who was also Chinese whose marital status was undetermined out for a drink was a minefield.

Was she even Chinese? There was another assumption. Would he not learn? He was forty. He made timber and metal sculptures that were sold the world over, that sold so well he was obliged to wrestle with the ATO, here in Lang Street, the unknown crucible of international transactions. And yet he was an ignorant klutz, harbouring desires for a woman he knew nothing about. She might have been Malaysian. Or Australian. Maybe she was born there, in Emu Plains, or St Marys, and he was a crass fool unable to shake off prejudices and assumptions as ingrained as his fingerprints.

But she was a genius with figures. There was that in his favour. She had taken his shoeboxes of receipts and bank statements – what a cliché he was – and smoothed over six years' worth of unlodged returns, placated the ATO, obtained a refund, of all things, and charged him less than his dentist.

Outside, he decided to forget the appointment with the Surry Hills designer. He would ring Mrs Zhang. He would ring her right now. Ebullient with the success of his mission, he would ring her and put any misunderstanding behind them and arrange to meet her after work. He could walk down to the Quay and get the train from there. He went down the pebblecrete steps and over to the lone park bench.

Taking out his phone he punched the numbers quickly, before he changed his mind again. He would only drink soda water this time. The phone rang five times then went to the answer machine. He punched stop, then rang her mobile number. When the voice-mail message came he took a breath to speak, then killed the call.

Fuck it. He chewed his lip, glared at the Vespas opposite. Stared back at the ATO at the top of the steps like a shrine on a ziggurat. What sacrifices had been made there in the name of federal fiscal authority? What human blood spilled, and consumed? Metaphorically speaking. He felt exhausted actually, despite his triumph. The Post-it would survive, wouldn't it? It wouldn't get stuck on a corner of a desk somewhere, or attach itself to some random document to be folded and filed forever?

He stared at his phone then pressed the envelope symbol. *Success at the ATO!* he typed, relying on the exclamation mark's marvellous capacity for breezy self-deprecation along with its reminder not to take its user too seriously.

Drew Saltman was halfway along the Quay when the phone chirped. He stopped in the crowd to read it. *That fast?* He could almost see her smiling, in that lip-flickering way of hers. She had known all along. He laughed out loud. People passing looked at him. *Dinner tonight on me*, he typed, and pressed send.

And like in a fantasy story, the Post-it note fluttered through the ATO, a magical yellow bird ultimately transforming into the document that arrived in his letterbox two weeks later. It was only a certificate of residency but it did indeed seem like something from a pirate's treasure trove. Twelve copies. He placed eleven in an envelope to give to Georgina straight away, and filed the last one in a plastic sleeve in a folder, right next to the copy of the pirate map.

The Moon Will Do

By the fifth letter, she thinks, What the hell, what do I have to lose anyway? In fact, she agrees completely with David Rhodes who says he had nothing to lose and that he couldn't stop himself thinking: What if it actually works? It's the fifth in as many months. Someone might be telling her something, and besides, what if it actually works?

Complete these six steps as FAST as possible. SPEED is EVERYTHING.

She is careful not to leave the letter on the kitchen bench for the kids to scribble on, or to collect coffee marks like Olympic rings, or worse, for Margie to spot. Instead she places it in her bag and takes it to work, then brings it home again, then hides it under the Reminder of Penalty notice (a lie, they never sent her the original notice), the AGL bill, the Telstra bill and the FastBuy catalogue because she might buy that skirt. Then she returns it to her bag for work because she realises she'll need to photocopy it there but she doesn't leave it on her desk in case someone takes it while she's not there. And then she panics because for two whole days she cannot find it, and then when she remembers where she's put it, it's ten pm. And she's at the hospital waiting for the last of Jackson's Ventolin to go through the respirator. She is sure it said something strict about speed.

By Sunday evening she has found the letter. She had placed it between the letter of demand from Friend & Holmes Solicitors and under the photocopied pages from the newsletter that contains the invitation to the charity match between the Western Wildfires third division and the Vagabonds. But they won't be going to that.

The letters and notices are all white photocopies, no wonder they all look the same. Rereading the letter she wonders if it's already too late, as more than a week has passed and she still has not acted. But she has made a decision, surely that counts?

Follow the simple step by step plan *EXACTLY* as it is set out and within 60 days your life will be transformed.

The letter is four pages long and contains a lot of detailed information so she rereads it carefully twice more. The whole plan is clear: she has to send some money off to an unknown person in a spirit of generosity, and then photocopy the letter and send them out to two hundred more people, thus keeping the chain going. And enlarging the possibilities for others to make their fortune too.

The first step is clear enough, however if she is to be efficient she can see at once that the real first step is to buy lots of paper. David Rhodes doesn't say you can't use your employer's paper, even though the whole tone of his letter is very moral. He points out that he does not stand to receive any financial gain from her and he sincerely respects her decision if her decision is to let this opportunity pass. He concludes with a reminder that life is short. He does not sound to her like a person who would condone the unauthorised use of an employer's photocopier. Apart from that is the fact that she would never get the chance at work with Ron or some busybody wanting to know why she needed two hundred copies of something. On the other hand she can see that copying the letter up at the newsagent is going to present a lot of problems. There are always people in there, regular queues for the copier. And that copier is not very reliable. It is quite faint, and the letter insists the copies have to be legible. Margie is always in that newsagent too. It was Margie who told her that the copier was no good because she was doing fifty invitations to Ted's sixty-fifth last summer and the print was too faint for the bright orange paper she'd chosen for the invites. At the time Dawn thought pale blue would have been better anyway. It was Ted, after all. And he was already so sick. Not that his wife shouldn't have been wanting to celebrate something before it was too late, but Dawn didn't say that.

She decides that compromise is okay and that the spirit of the thing is what really counts and that although she will follow the plan exactly and send off the ten dollars as quickly as she can, using the work copier will be all right if she uses her own paper. Even the little post office shop has copier paper, so after work the next day she gets two packets. She doesn't understand why the doorway into this shop is so narrow. Maybe Australia Post is trying to discourage people with strollers, fat people or the disabled. Or everyone.

She gets the $5.95 Post brand and realises while she is there she should get the stamps as well, but two hundred stamps is a big commitment, one she knows she'll have to make soon (SPEED is EVERYTHING) but not today. She also pays the AGL bill and the Telstra bill. When she gets home the post has arrived, bringing the council rates. She'll pay that next time. That night when the kids are in bed she is ready for step one.

STEP 1: IMMEDIATELY send a $10 note to the person listed No. 1 on the list at the end of this letter. Do this with a smile on your face because 'as ye sow, so shall ye reap'.

With a smile on her face she goes to her purse. There is only a ten-dollar note. Clearly this is meant to be, so she does not hesitate in taking it out. Still smiling, she smooths the crease across Mary Gilmore's face and turns back the corner where it is bent over the windmill.

Wrap your $10 note tightly inside a brief handwritten note containing your name, address (including post-code) and this short statement – 'Please accept this $10 gift.'

On her desk she has a special notepad, and there is only one page left in this, obviously another sign. The notepad is from Alice Springs and has a dot design along the bottom of the pages. The person listed No. 1 lives in the Northern Territory. Another sign that she is keeping faith with David Rhodes's convictions.

It is an undeniable law that we must first give in order to receive. Your turn will come. After you have sent a complete stranger $10 in the post, something very eerie happens. It gives you the indescribable, overwhelming sense of certainty, belief and conviction in the system.

She writes the brief note.

David Rhodes instructs her to include her name and address but does not say to write anything else. She adds *Dear P. Hickson* and at the end writes *Yours sincerely*. She hopes she is not breaking the spell here but she feels that she should not send the letter without these small formalities. Luckily, there is one postage stamp in the box of paperclips on the desk.

The postbox is ten houses up and when she walks back she makes sure she still has the smile on her face. It is true that something very eerie has happened, it happened when a) she discovered that the ten-dollar note was the only note left in her purse, and b) she realised her Aboriginal design notepaper was destined for a citizen of the Northern Territory. However, she has to admit to not feeling an indescribable sense of certainty, belief and conviction in the system. She does not feel overwhelmed at all, only tired and looking forward to bed. But when she gets back she finds a casserole in a Pyrex dish at the front door. That woman, she thinks, is amazing. She must have been looking out to see if Dawn left the house, which had been for all of five minutes. Tomorrow as soon as she gets home Margie will be wanting to know what she was doing out after ten pm, and if she was posting a letter then she would have done that for her and Dawn wouldn't have had to leave the kids alone. Across the road all her lights are out, no doubt she's pretending to be asleep in bed.

> STEP 2: After you have posted you [sic] $10 note, delete the name and address of the person who is No. 1 on the list, move all the names and addresses up one position and enter your name and address which will now become No. 5 on the new list.

She wonders if she should correct the typographical error before she goes any further. She wonders how many people will notice. Everything else about the letter calls for precision, so it bothers her that David Rhodes has made this mistake. But she can't see how to correct it by hand and the only way would be to retype the whole page and then that would mean retyping the whole letter, all four pages, because then the new page would stand out. Although the letter is readable enough it already has that much-copied fuzzy look to it. People would think that if someone had retyped one whole page then why wouldn't they be bothered to retype the entire letter, and how slack that was. Anyway, she doesn't know what font David Rhodes has used.

She leaves the letter as it is. She types her list of five names with herself at No. 5. The font is different but that doesn't matter as the original list is different from the rest of the letter so she reckons that everyone else is doing the same thing and that reassures her. By now it's way past eleven and when she goes to bed she finds Jackson has sleepwalked into hers again. How can a kid who weighs less than a bag of rice become so heavy when he's asleep? She gives up trying to move him and flops into bed beside him.

STEP 3: Photocopy 200 (minimum) copies of this letter.

———⬥◦⬥———

It proves easier than she has thought. Thursday mornings at work are quiet because Ron comes late as he says it's his turn to take his son to school, except he always looks paler than usual and she knows Wednesdays are his squash round and drinks with the boys afterwards nights, and it doesn't take a genius to work it out. And Anne and Maria have meetings. They love meetings. So the place is virtually hers until morning tea. It does not even take up an entire packet of paper because she realises she can copy the letter on two sides and thus use half. Ron is stingy but loves technology and if they ask for a five-dollar raise he goes purple but when Anne put in for a copier upgrade just before the end of the financial year he was sweet. She copies 203, two extra just in case, and one to keep. She is stuffing the last of the copies in her bag when the others arrive from Meeting Room # 2 next floor up, still discussing the agenda. The Central Administrative Service is to be relocated by next February. Morning tea is to be fifteen minutes instead of twenty. And they will no longer have Rollerballs 0.5 mm EXPs in red, black, blue and green; instead they'll be getting Stabilo Liner 808Ms in just red and blue, which come in at forty-five cents per unit cheaper, representing a huge saving when you factor in all the usage. Anne tells her not to be fooled by the fancy name, Stabilos are just glorified biros, plus the caps never stay on.

When she gets home Margie has the kids bathed and Jackson's medicine measured out all ready to administer. Lacey has completed her list of Ten African Nations and already coloured in half the map which Margie traced from her old Reader's Digest atlas. Which is kind of her. Dawn suspects it is very out of date, but the teacher has said no printing maps off the internet. The casserole is on the stove heating. Lamb and potato. They will eat it but only with lots of tomato sauce. Margie could have brought it over with her this afternoon but she says nothing about it sitting at the front door last night. Jackson had a bad day at kindy, she tells Dawn, in a way that implies she's meant to have asked by now. Some kids pushed him, though it might have been an accident, but he started wheezing and has Dawn thought about getting him to do swimming, she read an article in a magazine just that morning about how swimming's supposed to be good for it.

No, Dawn hasn't thought about it and she won't, seeing as it's the middle of winter, and yes she knows the local pool's heated but it's the getting in and out isn't it? Margie has obviously forgotten about the bronchitis last winter plus the two months of never-ending coughing, but then why would she, it wasn't her up every night. Dawn tries to be grateful their grandmother is only over the road and that Ted's passing means she needs an interest and has the time and everything. Except she's not grateful Ted's passed away, in fact she had a soft spot for the old bugger. They enjoyed a mutual private suspicion of Margie.

STEP 4: Pick out 200 names and addresses from your telephone directory. You can also source addresses covering the whole of Australia by going on line at www.whitepagescom.au. DO NOT order a mailing list. You MUST obtain your own names and addresses. Remember a good list will yield a good result.

———◆◆◆———

It seems to take the entire weekend. First she buys the envelopes, which at $2.99 for a packet of one hundred are incredibly cheap. Another good sign. Back home she decides she will indeed source addresses covering the whole of Australia. After consulting the White Pages she realises she must think further before writing out the envelopes. For instance there are lots of Trans

and Nguyens in the Sydney White Pages. Plus Lees
and Chins and Lams and Suns. And Moons. She does
not want to alienate the Asian communities, in fact she
is sure they would embrace enthusiastically the idea of
such a free-spirited enterprise, however she is struck
with the prospect that she may be mailing to households
with only basic English. Or entire non-English-reading
households. Would they be placed to appreciate the
subtle importance of instructions like, Do this with a
smile on your face because, 'as ye sow, so shall ye reap'?
Would non-English readers know what ye means?
Maybe next time she can get one of Lacey's school-
friends to translate the gist of the letter and she can mail
it to all the Nguyens in the phone book. That seems like
a compromise but one made in the generous and open-
minded spirit of David Rhodes's letter.

At www.whitepages.com.au, she has to select a name
and then choose by city, area or suburb depending on
the size of the population. That way she will get, say, all
the Thomsons in Eagle Vale, Queensland. But she only
chooses places she's heard of, in case they're too small.
If she posted letters to all the Thomsons in a place with
only a population of three hundred and fifty that would
be counterproductive. They might all be related and
think they were being targeted.

She chooses her names carefully. Mainly Anglo
names, and it is surprisingly hard to think of surnames
apart from obvious ones like Smith or Lee, but after

consideration she decides that every letter-mailer would go for Smith, and Lee has the ethnic disadvantage, which she will address next time round. On the floor next to the computer is the pile of paperbacks that Margie brings from time to time after they go through her friends at the community centre, in case Dawn wants to read them. They are all so thick and she has never started one, but the authors inspire good names. She selects Keyes, Roberts, Patterson. Easy names, not too long – they all have to be handwritten – conservative white names, or at least she imagines so. Using one of the blue Rollerballs she's taken from work and is squirrelling away before there are only Stabilos, she writes out about thirty or forty envelopes using names like Turner, Keyes, Mitchell, White and Patterson from various places around the State. Then she decides her efforts must represent every State, however she excludes WA since David Rhodes is from WA and there's a good chance that people there will be sick of getting his letters. She makes a special effort with Tasmania, which everyone forgets. This takes her forever, partly because it's so boring and partly because she has to keep getting up because the DVD player is mucking up and she has to hold the button down to skip back and Jackson wants to see his favourite bit of *Spiderman* about a hundred times. Then she has to go out anyway to get Lacey from the netball gala day and then when they return the kids are hungry. She goes to heat up the leftover spaghetti but they say no, they want a snack not dinner, which means chips and biscuits and stuff, which she gives them because then it's peace and quiet until the end of *Spiderman*, so long as Lacey gets to watch *Legally Blonde 2*, after which it will be dinner time properly.

But by then she will have finished her list. For fun and variety because it's extremely boring – frankly she'd rather be weeding or tidying the linen cupboard – she chooses place names that interest her. Names that suggest something pleasant. Ferntree Gully. Emerald. Paradise. Places that sound full of promise, though she hopes they're not retirement communities as she doesn't imagine pensioners going for this sort of scheme. Where would they get access to a good photocopier for a start? Closer to home she chooses Fairfield, Merrylands and Prospect. She has never really thought about these names, and now she thinks if she lived in a place called Fairfield she might like it. Except she knows what it's like. It's getting dark and the day's been overcast and she likes the sound of these names, they warm her, they fill her with a small amount of cheer. She chooses nice-sounding or even amusing street names too, if only for the pleasure of writing them out. Evergreen Ramble. John Dory Avenue. Honeysuckle Street. Resolution Street. Ithaca Road.

Remember, a good list will always yield a good response.

She does not choose more than three names the same in the one suburb. Families tend to cluster together. Nor does she choose more than two names in the one street, since they might be friendly neighbours and feel there is a conspiracy afoot. When there are still at least one hundred envelopes to go, she is struck with another good idea. If the White Pages lists two residents at the one address, for example EB and SJ Goodall, then she addresses it to the latter on the basis that this will be the wife in the household and thus the one on the lower income, or on none. Thus more likely to regard the scheme with a sympathetic eye. She imagines Mrs SJ Goodall, who would naturally collect the mail in the household, saying nothing to her husband but quietly going about sending out her ten dollars just as Dawn has, copying her two hundred (minimum) letters and mailing them out as she is, then surprising EB two months later with wads of cash. She would pay off the house, they would have a holiday. Just as Dawn will. She will buy Jackson his own respirator so they can go anywhere they like and not have to be within close range of a hospital just in case, then they will get passports and go away. She has not told the kids this yet but they have discussed holidays generally. Lacey wants to go to Bali and Jackson wants to visit a planet, preferably Mars, but the moon will do.

She has not decided what she will do with all the money but she knows that Ron and his pale face and even Anne and Maria and their committees and meetings could all get stuffed. Plus she will get the house painted.

By dinnertime she is confident she has an excellent list and will thus obtain a good result. The kids have finished their movies but the TV is still on. They eat with their plates on their laps again, besides she has taken over the dining table with her envelopes. There is a re-run of that Jamie Oliver show where he tries to teach schoolkids to eat better. He is holding up a bunch of asparagus, they think it's onion. They have never tasted a strawberry, and don't want to.

STEP 5: Fold the photocopied letters neatly to fit into a DL envelope, seal them up and stamp them all. IMPORTANT: Do not fold the letter more than twice.

Why? Is there a magic difference between two and three folds? The folding and putting them in envelopes takes her so much longer than she imagined, more than three hours. She is very glad that she was not required to do this with a smile on her face. After ten minutes the kids are bored so she keeps doing it in front of the TV while they watch Jamie's kids going on strike by refusing to eat the chicken drumsticks in spicy tomato sauce and green salad. One of the kids announces he's never eaten salad in his life and is not about to and where are the turkey twizzlers and chips that he has for dinner every day? She wonders when Lacey and Jackson last ate salad, but she doesn't expect them to eat cold food in winter.

As she works through the piles she stops wondering why she is not allowed to fold the letters more than twice and starts to be glad instead, as it takes so long. Both kids fall asleep on the lounge as *NCIS* is starting, which is good as she doesn't think they should watch it with all the corpses. By the end her back is killing her and the dishes still haven't been done, but she takes them into the sink just in case Margie decides to drop by early in the morning. She leaves Lacey with a blanket over her, but Jackson really does weigh next to nothing so she takes him to his bed.

STEP 6: Copy your 200 names and addresses onto your sealed envelopes and drop them off at the post office. SPEED is EVERYTHING.

There are definite flaws in these steps. She does not think she will have ruined her chances of success by adapting these steps for efficiency. Why copy out two hundred addresses (Step 4) and then copy them again (Step 6) onto the envelopes? No disrespect to David Rhodes, but she decides this is a total waste of time. Also, getting bulk order postage as he advises is not worth the trouble and definitely no cheaper. The next night she brings home her two hundred stamps and it doesn't take that much time. She takes half the envelopes up to the postbox. Early the next morning, before the kids wake, she takes the remainder up in a plastic bag, and when she comes back she finds a plate of cookies, peanut choc chip, Jackson's favourite, and a bag of marshmallows, which would be for Lacey. Margie always treats the kids fairly, so she can't complain. But it proves her theory. Luckily last night she had the dishes rinsed in the sink so if Margie had come in she'd not have been able to witness a lapse.

Remember your life will be transformed! I am very proud to be able to say I have fulfilled my duty to my children by securing their future in an uncertain world.

The first phone call comes the very next night. Right on six pm, when all the market researchers call, she is taking the hash browns from the freezer when a woman asks her who she's speaking to. Just as Dawn realises it is not a market researcher or the Guide Dogs Association the woman demands to know why she's received this letter from someone she's never heard of, and is she out of her mind and how much damn money has she spent on this scam? Oh, and where did she get her name and address from anyway?

As if Dawn is some kind of con artist. Scam? There is nothing underhanded about getting names and addresses from the White Pages, is there? The caller says it's a form of spam and she'll be reporting Dawn to Trade Practices. Her heart is beating a bit faster by now; first that guy who drove into her car then reckoned it was her fault, now this. Could she really be in trouble? She hadn't counted on phone calls. Maybe she should have sent all her letters interstate where getting her phone number would have been too much trouble.

Within 60 days you can expect to be receiving over $70,000 in cash!

———◆———

The next letter comes the following week. This time it has a five-cent piece sticky-taped to the top. And it is very neatly presented, clearly the work of a person who has retyped the whole letter because there are none of the grey freckles and lines that were in hers, the telltale signs of pages copied again and again.

By now she is kicking herself. First the phone calls, then the five-cent piece. As soon as she spots it she realises what a brilliant idea it is. Why didn't she wait to send her letters out? If she had, she would have easily been able to stickytape five-cent pieces to hers as well. She has a huge jar of coins, which the bank has rejected. It's got rid of that change-counting machine and won't take kids' moneyboxes unless the change is all counted and placed in the correct denominations in little plastic bags and she doesn't have time for that.

She is ashamed. This letter is so neat. Its five-cent coin is shiny, like new. The author has added a line at the start saying it symbolises all the wealth she will enjoy once she follows the six steps to success. To think she has sent out such shabby letters by comparison. People will think she doesn't care. And if she has received so many letters, then others will have too. They will not follow her letter, they'll follow one like this. They will not ensure the circle of prosperity she has sent on continues unbroken. Her circle will be breached forever. They will trash her letter.

Jackson wants to know why there's five cents on the letter. She prises it off and gives it to him for his moneybox, but he doesn't want it, he is only collecting fifty-cent pieces and not the ordinary ones either, only the commemorative ones. Margie gives these to him when she finds them in her change. The five-cent coin is sticky so she replaces it on the letter.

That night Jamie is showing the schoolkids what chicken nuggets are really made from: ground-up chicken carcases, skin and fat. The schoolkids shudder and squeal and declare they'll never eat chicken nuggets again. Jackson nestles into her side and tucks his head in her armpit, just a chicken carcase himself, all bones with a bit of skin stretched over, and she asks him if he'll ever eat them again too. Yes, he says, and she knows she will give them to him, she'll give him whatever he wants to eat.

Lacey announces she is never eating chicken again, in fact she has given up meat as of yesterday, and hadn't her mother noticed she picked out all the filling from her pie? Dawn reminds her about that fundraising sausage sizzle she's going to after netball on Saturday, which she's already paid for. Lacey rolls her eyes, then says she can just eat the bread and the sauce without the sausage, they always burn them anyway. What, Dawn wonders, would be the point of wasting food and fundraising money, then she realises the point is fundraising, so there is no point.

The five-cent piece letter sits on the table for a week, reproaching her. Either she acts right now and sends out another two hundred letters, or she trashes it and forgets about the whole enterprise. Can she afford another two hundred, not to mention the time? She places it in the folder with the other letters, then places the folder in the document tray along with the final letter of demand from Friend & Holmes. They are saying their client holds her responsible for the incident six weeks ago when there was a collision on the corner of Buffalo Road and Simmonds Street. This time there is a quote attached, $1,895.

She should respond to this letter. She is sure it was their client who drove into her. She is tempted to write, Your client is a rude, aggressive young man who is also a liar. Instead she invites them to come around and inspect her vehicle which is gouged all down one side by his van. Jackson cried when he hopped out of his van and started yelling at them.

TESTIMONIALS FROM PROGRAM PARTICI-PANTS: 'After two months I had received $71,970 and it is still arriving. We have paid off the house and all our credit cards and had a wonderful holiday.' Mrs C Collins, Brisbane.

She thinks about turning on the computer and looking through the White Pages for a Mrs C Collins in Brisbane. If she tracks her down perhaps she will tell Dawn if that's really true.

The re-runs of *Jamie's School Dinners* are over but Lacey has entered that diet-conscious stage of teenage life Dawn has heard about. She insists on watching *Jamie's Simple & Healthy*, which is live. He says yeah and innit and darling a lot, and dashes around the set for half an hour while five guests from the audience, including a boy who looks younger than Jackson, stand there holding a spoon or dipping a finger into a bowl. Then he produces a plate of yellow pasta strips with garlic, lemon and extra virgin oil. Everyone oohs and claps. Lacey wants to try it and asks if Dawn will buy her a pasta maker. She says you can get the same result with bought pasta, plus she'd never eat something dripping in olive oil, but Lacey insists it has to be fresh, really fresh. Dawn wonders if she's also entering that stage where they become vegan or only drink Diet Coke. That used to happen when she was about sixteen but it's different these days. Eleven would not be impossible to start holding strong views about exploiting cows and bees, and rejecting supermarket quality pasta. She reminds Lacey she hates garlic too and she pulls a face. She is still sore about the netball thing, especially because Dawn said in front of her friends at the gala day that she couldn't afford the fare to New Zealand. She has nothing against kids going off to play against other nations, but privately she feels that eleven is too young and the team manager should not have agreed, Trans-Pacific Netball Club Annual Play-off or not. She did not want to sound like an unsupportive parent, but it's the Wildfires, not Test cricket. And Lacey is only in the third division. She tells herself that when her $70,000 starts rolling in she will buy a pasta maker. She will go to David Jones and buy her the best electric one.

She should have attached those five-cent pieces. She could have gone one better and attached ten-cent pieces, there are enough of them in the jar too. Ten cents by two hundred letters is twenty dollars, and what's an extra twenty dollars to a woman who's going to make thousands, tens of thousands? She examines the five-cent coin letter again. Maybe she couldn't have put five- or ten-cent coins on hers because the letter definitely states DO NOT change any of these steps even slightly. Would taping coins on count as changing the steps? She is still considering this when the phone rings again but it's not another angry recipient of one of her letters, it's the angry young man himself who yells at her, Aren't ya gunna reply to me lawyer's letter, bitch? and then tells her he'll see her in court if he has to, then hangs up before she can reply. If she could have, she would have said that when she makes her tens of thousands she won't have to deal with insects like him, she'll be getting her legal advisor or insurance representative to handle it, and he will indeed be no more nuisance than a housefly. But no, she wouldn't tell him about the scheme, he's not that type, not deserving. She congratulates herself that she's not sent any letters to Hamids, Friends, Holmes or any name connected with him so there's no chance of him or his relatives or his lawyers getting a chance of what she's got.

The next letter comes in a recycled envelope with a scrap of lined notepaper stickytaped over the window. The scrap is cut crookedly, and right up against the pink margin is her name, surname first, then initial, in biro block letters, the whole thing looking like a child's done it. She is aghast at the evidence of such cheapskates. If someone would go the trouble of collecting two hundred (at least) recycled envelopes, then surely they would buy proper labels, which are a few dollars a roll at the two-dollar shops, and write the names neatly.

She would not bother responding to a letter that's been issued with such obvious lack of care and definitely not in the spirit of generosity, as David Rhodes advises. She drops it into the bin straight away, knowing that M Cody of 6B Jenner Street Kilgore (NSW) will not receive a single letter with ten dollars inside it and a note wishing him or her good fortune. She doesn't need to read it to know it will be a blurred photocopy containing more typographical errors than the one David Rhodes sent her.

Even now as I write this story for you I find it hard to come to terms with the fact that, like most people, I've worked hard and struggled all my life just to get by, then something so ridiculously simple drops into my lap and turns my life around immediately.

Apparently Jamie just got lucky when a TV producer noticed his boyish charm and convincing patter behind the counter. Now look at him, bouncing around a stage larger than her house with an audience of hundreds and five guests all overcome by the fact he has produced a rocket and pear salad in minutes before their eyes. Go on, he says to the guy meant to be crushing red, green and white peppercorns onto crusted veal, give it a good ol whack there, yeah thassit, whack it like that, don be afraid. The guy brings the mallet down once or twice with a look on his face as if the veal's going to leap up and bite him back, while Jamie grabs the Bamix from a woman and plunges it deep into the jug of chopped onion and tomato she's meant to be pureeing.

Lacey is rapt because Jamie wears jeans and rides a motorbike and Dawn can tell she's even rethinking the meat thing, but all she says is, You know he's got another cookbook out? And she feels like replying, Yeah and you know I could cook veal in peppercorns and dance about in the kitchen pureeing cold soup too, but as if you and Jackson'd eat it, but relations are still strained because of the netball trip.

TESTIMONIALS FROM PROGRAM PARTICI-PANTS: 'I have received many letters over the years similar to this one and although I am sceptical by nature, there was something different about yours, which has been proven by the wonderful results. Thank you David Rhodes forever.' Mr L Cavanaugh, Adelaide.

The next letter, she is pleased to see, is beneath contempt.

THIS IS NOT A SCAM OR ILLEGAL
DO NOT THROW THIS IS THE BIN
READ IT FULY
THIN ABOUT IT FOR A FEW DAYS
FILE IN PENDING.

Although it starts the usual way, My name is David Rhodes and in September 2000 I lost my job, it is clear that David Rhodes has had nothing to do with this letter. She is sure that if he knew of the poor quality of chain letters now in circulation bearing his name he would be horrified. He would not want his reputation associated with letters featuring errors in the second line, or ones that claim, This is legitimate business opportunity and perfectly legal.

And when she looks at the list of five names and addresses at the end of the letter she suspects it is a joke, except why would you waste money on a joke like this? The last name listed, the name of the sender, is IT Works with a post box address somewhere in South Australia. If she were David Rhodes and she knew people were mocking his scheme like this she would be truly disappointed in humanity. She is more sad than annoyed, as she is sure there would be people responding to that letter in genuine good faith and that is unfair. Not everyone picks up errors like that, but not everyone is like her and used to compiling weekly business reports and proofreading marketing strategy initiatives where inattention to detail has cost some people their jobs.

The next evening when she gets home Margie has placed the mail on the kitchen bench, right next to the latest letter which she forgot to throw away. Which she would have read, though as if Dawn would take any notice of something so badly spelled. She hopes Margie doesn't think she's keeping it for a reason. There's also a letter with a Spanish stamp, along with one from the local Holden dealer inviting her to their end of year sale (FINANCE CAN BE ARRANGED!), the Medicare receipt and a bank statement. She notices the date on the statement. It is more than sixty days since she has sent her letters out. Her ten-dollar notes should be arriving pretty soon now.

LOTERIAS Y APUESTAS DEL ESTADO
FROM: THE DESK OF THE VICE PRESIDENT
INTERNATIONAL PROMOTIONS PRIZE
AWARD DEPT.
RE: AWARD NOTIFICATION, FINAL
NOTICE.
Dear Sir/Madam
We are pleasured to inform you today of the release of the result of EL GORDO DE LA PRIMITIVA LOTTERY MIDDLE OF THE YEAR HIGH STAKE INTERNATIONAL PROGRAM.
Your name and lucky ticket numbers 14–26–27–40–43–58 have WON Lottery number 0016/3592/12, second division.

The letter goes on to say she has won €785,510.00 (Seven Hundred and Eighty-Five Thousand, Five Hundred and Ten Euros) from a total cash prize of over five million euros. She is congratulated. To claim her winnings she only has to contact an agent called Don Ricardo Sanchez by the end of August. She is to quote the reference number and the code at the bottom of the letter, and all her bank account details to ensure speedy payment. And again, congratulations. There is a form for her to fill in all her personal details and bank account number, which she can scan and email back if she prefers. Ordinary mail will do, but she must remember to hurry.

She doesn't know any Spanish but she would say there's a typo or two in there for sure. She places the letter and the form on the bench, where Margie spots it on her way to the sink with the kids' dirty bowls. Then she glances at Dawn and away again and raises her eyebrows and they both snicker knowingly, both thinking, As if.

Harder than Your Husband

The reasons people act the way they do never fail to fascinate me. Even when there is a clear line between cause and effect, it still intrigues me, the choices they make. That is, as if there are no choices. As if they have dropped into the groove of a disc and they must follow it around and around until it stops.

I manage a pastry factory, a medium-sized business in the vicinity of Wetherill Park. We employ about twenty people, mostly on the factory floor. I know nothing about pastry, but I have a good head for administration and marketing, while the owner of the factory, Mario, spends all his time in the kitchens. The only time he comes into the office is to hold a new product under my nose. When I show him forms that need to be signed and statements that should be read, he just laughs. 'Try this,' he'll say. It will be something buttery and crumbly, or rich with cream. Lately he has been experimenting with white chocolate and almond milk ganache.

Some time ago I advertised in the local paper and online through several agencies for a part-time bookkeeper and accounts clerk to cope with the modest but steady growth of the business. After nearly thirty applications I interviewed six women. Only women applied for the job. For some reason all the interviewees were overweight. By the last I began to worry whether the successful applicant may encounter problems working in an environment inimical to good health and general wellbeing. Mario, perhaps due to the fact that he is constantly on his feet, is pole-thin. I myself have no problem with weight, and though several of the factory workers are overweight, clearly this does not constitute a problem for them. Most seem uncaring of the fact, and if they continue to eat the pastries and other products they handle, they do so more from curiosity. I have noticed that after a week or two, for the factory workers, the novelty of working in this place is replaced by revulsion, then indifference.

This factory, I should explain, only manufactures sweet pastries and cakes. We supply a range of cafes and restaurants all over the city, and several cake shops in the district.

The final interviewee, however, was only slightly overweight, in fact I would not say overweight at all unless I were very unkind and the type who focused critically upon a woman's hips and thighs. Cheryl came with impressive references. Her most recent job, six months previously, was as the office manager for the spare parts division of a large car company. After that she had given up full-time work to concentrate on getting her house in order – quite literally – before deciding whether to keep it or sell it. Cheryl was also about to be married. She wanted a part-time job only, in order to spend more time with her new husband, and to be able to assist in his car detailing business.

I could tell straight away that she was highly efficient and a well-motivated worker, someone who would be able to work without supervision if necessary, which it was, seeing as I had started to spend a lot of time away promoting our products and securing new markets. We were looking to expand interstate and lately I had been in Melbourne and Perth. Our products travel well. Mario's cousin is a designer and has created some clever packaging, especially for the most fragile pastries, the lemon curd tarts and the macaroons. Mario, needless to say, is indifferent to these plans.

After okaying my decision with Mario, who barely paused in folding rice flour through his meringue mix – another experiment with setting and durability – I returned to the office upstairs and rang Cheryl's referees, who all gave me glowing reports. I then rang to tell her that she had secured the job. This was a Friday. I spent the rest of the day ringing or emailing all the other unsuccessful applicants. Awkward and painful though it is, I prefer to telephone if I can, although many of my calls went straight to voicemail and I had to leave messages. At the end of it I felt as if I had attended a dozen funerals in a row. They say there is no unemployment crisis. But that does not account for the number of unsuccessful applicants who began to cry, and the two women who abused me.

On the day Cheryl arrived for work I noted that she had a new hairstyle, perhaps to celebrate. At the interview her hair, though neat, was faded and frizzy. Now she had been streaked and smoothed, though the effect was to make her seem older. Or perhaps it threw her face into more relief. She was still wearing the same spectacles. Hers featured those photochromatic transition lenses, which in my view are unflattering. They never really seem to make the transition from tinted to clear lenses. Cheryl worked hard, as I expected, quickly picking up the somewhat clunky bookkeeping system and setting to work to clear the backlog of accounts. She did not take long to convince me to invest in a new version of MYOB. I did not bother running that past Mario. By morning tea she was already on the phone to debtors and by the time she left that afternoon had secured promises that three accounts would be settled by the next day.

But at lunchtime I felt obliged to offer some social chitchat. I asked a couple of questions about her forthcoming wedding, and her future husband. I asked how long she had known him, or something like that, and she surprised me by replying with a question of her own.

'Do you have a vacuum cleaner?' she said.

I considered asking why she was interested, but instead said that I did, and then she asked how much I had paid for it. I was not entirely sure, but I thought it was a couple of hundred dollars.

At that she almost sneered. 'My husband's got a Speed Queen,' she said. 'He paid fifteen hundred dollars for it. That's the kind of man Dennis is. That's the kind of man I'm marrying.' She managed to express all this with a mixture of contempt, for me, for my cheap vacuum cleaner, for all cheap vacuum cleaners and all the kinds of men who buy them; as well as pride, for her vacuum cleaner, for Dennis, for the quality of his love.

'He's still paying it off, actually.' There was even more pride in her voice. For the kind of man, I assumed, who would commit himself financially like that, for a small domestic appliance. This, was the implication, was a man worth having.

I detected an anomaly here. Cheryl called Dennis her husband when the marriage was yet to take place. It was to be in several weeks' time, on a Saturday afternoon, in the Dancing Bear Garden Court and Taverna in Greystanes. Fifty guests. This, however, is common among people, especially in the western suburbs. The word partner is restricted to business relationships. I myself have a wife, not partner. By this time, I ascertained, Cheryl and Dennis had been living together for two years.

The rest of the lunch break, that first day, proved to be a steep learning curve for me. I realised that Cheryl and I only seemed to be of the same culture, the same society, the same linguistic group. In fact I would have felt more at ease with a naked Amazonian exchanging nods and grunts instead of English words. She gave me all the fine details of her expensive appliance, a thorough description of its myriad virtues, and I learned that spending anything less than fifteen hundred dollars on a vacuum cleaner constituted not only grave uxorious shortcomings but also possibly moral failure.

At some stage I explained that I only thought my – our – vacuum cleaner cost a few hundred. It might have been more. And when Cheryl pressed the point, I told her I was almost certain it also did dust mites, although I could not be one hundred per cent sure about the upholstery attachment, because we never used it.

'Never use it?' she said. 'What do you clean your lounge with?'

'Oh, we just give it a wipe over with leather cleaner now and then.'

'So it's leather,' she said. Then, after a pause, 'Ours is crushed velour.'

She went back to the pile of accounts on her desk. I noticed the dust on my computer screen, the grimy desktop. Underfoot the carpet was grey from crumbs and sugar. Mario never cared when he brought things up trailing icing sugar or dripping caramel. His industrial boots were dusted white, and crunched wherever he walked. I did my best but sugar in a carpet is a magnet for dirt. In the five years I had worked here I had never noticed, until now, after just this one conversation with Cheryl. I even felt unclean in my shirt. Perhaps she would insist on fresher office conditions. Perhaps she would bring in the Speed Queen. Or perhaps she would not stay in the position.

When I recounted the conversation that night to my wife, she reminded me that our vacuum cleaner had cost three hundred and ninety-nine dollars, and that I had bought it several years ago on a wedding anniversary. She had kicked the old one which had just expired in a blast of dust and declared that if I were any kind of a husband I would buy her a new one. In fact, if I expected the marriage to continue at all, I would go straight away. She had been only partly joking.

How could I have forgotten that? It had been a Saturday afternoon, and instead of going out for that anniversary, our tenth, we were having friends to dinner, which was why my wife was stressed. I left her to start preparing the paella and, taking the dead vacuum cleaner, I drove to the nearest Godfreys where I paid cash for a sturdy and voracious Wertheim, discounted by fifteen per cent with my trade-in. And no, I recalled, it did not do dust mites, but at the time of this story it was still sucking hungrily.

The next day, however, it seemed that my telling Cheryl all this, and therefore proving I was not quite such a lamentable example of a husband, was an irrelevance. And I caught myself, just before I mentioned the anniversary Wertheim, wondering why I wanted to prove this to someone I barely knew. In any case Cheryl did not seem so interested in a conversation about cleaning standards the next day, nor on any of the other three days each week when she worked. It was as if now she had proven something she could then move on to the next theme.

It turned out that Dennis's Speed Queen was more in the way of an engagement ring. The real gift cementing their union took the form of a second-hand but very much restored red Holden Commodore V8 with mag wheels, aprons, skirts and quadraphonic sound. Over the weeks following Cheryl's arrival at the factory and her wedding, I came to appreciate the importance of things like mag wheels and aprons, but only after learning what they were, because of course in this, as in the matter of domestic appliances, I was also ignorant. I always take the bus to work, leaving the car for my wife, who is a district nurse for the Western Sydney area. At the time she was doing geriatric care, and some days she visited up to six patients in their homes, driving as far away as Narellan or Orchard Hills. Besides the fact that the bus is convenient for me, I have no interest in cars. I bought our Nissan Pulsar from a friend and to this day still have no more idea of the model than that. As a kind of test, I believe, Cheryl asked me how many cylinders, and even though I answered satisfactorily, she stopped talking and concentrated on her computer screen. I felt I had still managed to disappoint her. Something in the set line of her mouth indicated that Dennis would never stoop to catching buses.

But it was my turn, when I learned about the wedding-present Commodore's sound system, particularly about the graphic equaliser and the boot-mounted speakers, to be incredulous because Cheryl had never shown the slightest interest in any form of music. She never mentioned a singer, a group, a song, even a style of music. The only time she listened to the radio was when Alan Jones was on. She listened to him every morning until she arrived at work, where my old portable CD player would often be belting out Tom Waits or Frank Zappa. When she came in at nine am I would turn it down, or off, and switch over to the ABC. The player is also sticky with sugar. She once examined the covers of some of my CDs. She flicked through them all one by one, holding them by the corners – I keep them in a cardboard box beside the printer but they get sticky too – pausing to stare at Frank Zappa's swarthy features for a bit longer than the rest, before replacing them and returning to her desk without saying a word.

However, I am digressing. By the end of the first month I knew an enormous amount about cars, Holden Commodores in particular, much more than I ever realised there was to know, and certainly far more than I ever wanted to know. By the end of the second month the marriage was unravelling, quickly. On reflection, this was understandable in context, though not exactly inevitable, which is why I and everyone else at the factory were so surprised to learn of the demise of this new union.

Dennis, it appeared, did not tolerate women driving. I shall qualify that. When Cheryl drove her old but reliable Mazda to work, that was quite okay, quite within the bounds. Apart from the fact that she had owned it long before ever meeting Dennis, it was just a Mazda, of an unremarkable colour and with narrow wheels, unworthy of any expense beyond the absolutely necessary, and certainly not a candidate for the sort of devotion accorded the Commodore.

The Commodore, on the other hand, was a shrine on wheels. And these wheels happened to be very new, black and unmarked. Early one morning not long after Dennis had presented his bride with this gleaming symbol of his love, Cheryl had left him, still asleep, taken the key and started the ignition. She only intended to drive to the 7-Eleven for a loaf of bread and two packs of cigarettes. She got as far as the letterbox when Dennis came lurching half awake down the driveway, screaming obscenities. He was wearing a singlet and teddy-bear patterned boxers. Thanks to Cheryl's obsession with details I also know that the singlet was mesh and that Dennis's chest hair stuck out of it in an unflattering way. Also that this chest hair was greying.

I understood that strong words were exchanged on both sides, that neighbours to their right and left and over the road were involved, giving rise to the ventilation of a range of other grievances. These were mostly to do with unwelcome noises generated by V8 engines with inadequate mufflers, for Dennis owned a number of Commodores, in various states of restoration. Late-night revving, in their drive, in the street, was alleged. Which Cheryl, despite her issues with Dennis, insisted to me was outrageously untrue. But all that is off the track of the main story.

It transpired that Cheryl was under the impression that the Commodore so lovingly presented as a nuptial gift was hers to drive. But Dennis, equally bewildered, was stunned beyond belief that a woman would actually dare to drive such a machine. He faced her down in the driveway yelling, in his teddy-bear boxers, until she finally turned the ignition off. She got out of the car and he went up and wrenched the key from her hand.

Still yelling, though she was right beside him, he threw at her all the work he had performed on it. The many nights in the garage under the fluorescent lights. The layers of Turtle Wax. The fake-fur upholstery, which he had ordered specially and had made up locally, at huge expense, and not some shit factory job from China. And many other factors.

As a man, he would only consider driving it on rare occasions. As a couple, they would only take it out to, say, a Commodore Car Club function or maybe the annual CommRally, in Camden. While Dennis continued to yell the neighbours dispersed, the situation being too confrontational even for them. He had called her names – stupid sheila, fucking idiot, and worse – until, enraged and exasperated, he was depleted of all words and he stamped, barefooted, back into the house. She followed him to the bedroom as he flung on track pants and runners and as he walked back out the front door towards the Commodore parked in the driveway. At the letterbox Cheryl uttered the unforgivable words.

'Then what's it *for*, Dennis? If it's not to drive?'

Now speechless, Dennis shook his head, slipped into the driver's seat and slammed the door, but not too hard. He started up the ignition, which growled rather than purred. What was it for? The question, or at least the answer, was so monumentally obvious he had never had to confront it before, not even to himself. What was.

it for? He slipped it into gear and stuck his head out the window.

'A stupid woman wouldn't appreciate. Couldn't appreciate. Obviously. I thought you were different, but.' Then he drove into the garage and slid the roller door shut behind himself and the car.

———◆———

It was an existential question I pondered myself after Cheryl had finished telling me all the details of this incident and retired behind her computer screen where her face became unreadable. She had a way of peering through her transition lenses as if just by effort of her considerable personality she could force them to darken even though we were inside and the light remained unchanged. What was the Commodore for? Any Commodore, for that matter, at least any like the ones he fixed up, with their pink or blue fluorescent lights radiating out from underneath, with their stereo systems fixed so that even if you were underneath tinkering with the exhaust system you needn't miss out on the effect, with their duco so brilliant you could shave in the reflection, and with all the little things like their sheepskin-padded armrests or the customised his 'n' hers fold-down travel trays and coffee cup holders.

This existential issue apparently also preoccupied Dennis for days afterwards, as, according the Cheryl, he did little else but mutter and shake his head. He left the new marital bed and shifted into the double garage, which was just as comfortable, if not more, than the house, since he spent so much time there that, years before, he had fitted it out with all the conveniences. It was warm, dry and equipped with facilities like a toilet, telephone and fridge. It even had carpet, which the Commodores never soiled, for their tyres were always washed and wiped dry after their occasional outings. Naturally they never dripped oil.

Soon afterwards Cheryl stopped driving her Mazda to work and was dropped off by Dennis, then picked up again in the afternoon. He drove one of the lesser Commodores, or ones he had not finished making over, and would park in the factory driveway with the ignition running. If Cheryl did not appear within several seconds, he would sound the horn. These came in a variety of tunes, all of them tuneless. The one I remember most was that of La Cucaracha, played fast and flat. The factory workers, also leaving then, would jump in the air, startled by the sudden blast of synthetic trumpet right in their ears. Cheryl would glance out the window, then at me, before grabbing her handbag and stomping down the stairs.

This seemed to go on for weeks. Cheryl remained as hardworking though much less talkative. To me at least. From being efficient and personable when dealing with our creditors she became voluble, at times even strident. I was not fully aware of this myself, not until one day when Mario appeared with a tray of crème brûlée tarts, still smelling deliciously of singed sugar, to hear her berating the owner of a coffee shop in Surry Hills who owed three months' worth of orders.

'Do you think I give a stuff about your rising rent?' she was saying and Mario raised his eyebrows, left the tarts on my desk and quickly retreated. He abhorred commerce. It was what people like me were for, so that he could cook and avoid people who owed or even paid him money. When Cheryl slammed the phone down it seemed her mouth was set straighter. Dennis tooted from below. She pulled her mouth into shape and left.

One day I had the old CD player ready at the window and as soon as he opened the driver's window I pressed the start button. I was not subtle. Frank Zappa and all his instrumental syncopation blasted into the factory yard before I let him have the chorus at full volume, the part about being harder than your husband, harder than your husband . . .

The next afternoon, Dennis arrived early. This time he got out of the car and stood on the nature strip. He was wearing track pants and trainers, not cheap – Nike or Adidas – and a tight polo shirt, also with its signature tick emblem. He lit a cigarette and tucked the packet into his track pants pocket, then smoked steadily, staring up at the factory office window through his sunglasses. I noticed he was stocky. Almost, but not quite, fat. It was as if his skin was only just holding the rest of his body in, that if he breathed differently, harder or faster, it would all start to subside. I thought of that body in its mesh singlet and teddy-bear boxers. The anger. He threw his cigarette butt into the dwarf grevillea. When Cheryl joined him he took her by the wrist and pushed her inside the car, all the while staring up at me through the window.

They continued to live separated under the same roof, she told me. He was very comfortable there in the double garage. To make room for himself he would rotate the cars, keeping just one at a time inside while the others were lined up in the driveway like a string of racehorses waiting to be exercised. He shut himself in there and turned up the volume of his sound system and refused to come out, though she continued to cook meals for him which he would sometimes take, slamming the internal garage door behind him. They spoke only when necessary. I did not ask what music he listened to, alone in his garage. When she told me that he often had the engine running as he tinkered and polished, she stared at me, her lenses inscrutable.

'He likes to listen to the sound of the engine running,' she said.

<hr />

I was not surprised when Dennis ceased to bring and fetch Cheryl to and from work. Nor even to learn that she had found him early one morning, slumped over the open boot, the engine that he had tuned so perfectly still growling harmoniously after running all night.

But I will say I was surprised when the police arrived one morning a day or two later. It was just after she started work and she had arrived, as she always did, right on nine. Their boots crunched over a mess of meringues that had been dropped the day before and not been properly cleaned up. As they led her away, she turned to me and said, 'He was very pink, you know, when I found him. He didn't look dead at all', as if that made a difference.

Airlock

The first appointment is not until 9.30 but I like to give myself plenty of time, so it is just gone 8.30 when I turn into the driveway. I drive all the way to the end and around the corner to park behind the house. Beside the shed and the bins there is nothing else on the concrete slab, just a washing line. Which is never used. I have a steering lock, which I always attach before getting out and locking the car itself. Out here, kids are prone to come through the back lane and up the side. It is a short cut to the station.

The washing line wheels uncertainly in the breeze, a few centimetres above my head but I duck anyway to get past it. The handle is stuck, otherwise I would wind it further up. I unlock the security door then the wooden door, which leads directly into the back waiting room. I shut and lock the security door behind me. If the weather is pleasant I leave the wooden door open, and I can see the clients before they see me. The security door presents them with a blank face. They peer at it, trying to see the figure behind it, but I know I barely form a shadow to their squinting eyes.

It must take the department ages to find these places. So many conditions. Close to public transport, and a medical facility just in case. A police LAC within five minutes' reach. Central enough to both parties. No garden, to minimise upkeep. Quiet neighbours, or preferably none. A driveway all the way down the side of the house. Not so large as to be wasting space. But not small either. A lockable side gate. And two separate entries, front and back, security doors on each. Of course the department can take care of the latter requirements, and in some cases they install window shutters and CCTV systems too. But the other conditions are not so easy to satisfy.

The place is brick but still traps the heat, or the cold if it's winter. It feels hot inside already, and since I cannot open the doors and windows to let in the breeze, the first thing I do is go to the middle room and turn the air conditioner on. The rest of the house does not matter. The second thing I do is switch the kettle on in the kitchen, which is off the waiting room. I might not have a cup of tea straight away, but I like the sound of the water humming into life. I stow my bag in the lockable cupboard beside the unused stove, and place my folders in the tray that is the only thing on the bench aside from the kettle. There is a special bay for my laptop, which I attach to a lock and then plug in.

Everything else that is needed, and this is not much, is in the cupboards. There is still fresh milk in the fridge and all the cups are clean and dried and put away. I did this yesterday before I left. After I check through the appointments list and then leaf through the Lewis folder, I walk through the middle room to the front of the house. I check the front door is locked, and the security door. I stand at the door to face the front room. The lights have to be on, as the blinds are down and the curtains drawn. Some of these places have those security shutters, like blank eyelids, forever shut against the street. But not this house. I am meant to keep the blinds down but sometimes the airless, sunless spaces close in on me. I raise the blind an inch to allow a band of sunlight to cut into the room, but still pull the curtains shut. No one should notice. I am glad there are no security cameras either. I am lucky that my clients are classed minimal risk. Not that I do anything compromising, however the thought of someone watching me drinking my tea, or standing at the back door looking at the bare yard as I wait, would be unnerving.

The front room has oatmeal-coloured carpet and walls, a light brown, two-seated sofa, a small coffee table and some magazines. *Women's Weekly. New Idea. National Geographic.* Most of them outdated, some by more than a year. I will bring in some recent ones, I sometimes think, and then I remember that no one will care, no one ever reads them. The fathers sit there, arms crossed, staring at nothing. The mothers, the few who come, tap at their phones. There are some posters. Anti-smoking. Breastfeeding. Say No To Domestic Violence. It could be the waiting room of a doctor, except one who sees few patients.

I walk down the hall again to double-check the back waiting room. Everything is in place here, I know. But still. Three lounge chairs, matching though in different shades, with the look of Ikea about them, though they are more probably Fantastic Furniture, because the department has an arrangement there. A small side table with another stack of magazines. Nothing else. They always look around for an ashtray, even the ones who have been coming for a long time, and I always shake my head and point them out the back door. I have brought in several pot plants but only one of them survives – a small prayer plant, which I water carefully and move around so it gets neither too much nor too little sunlight. I check it now before returning to the second room. The middle room. Sealed from each end of the house like an airlock in a submarine. First I check each door shuts and locks properly. When I first worked here the number of different keys was ridiculous. I asked for a locksmith to rationalise them. Now the one key opens and locks all the doors, the front and back doors, and the mesh security doors and the two connecting doors to the middle room. I have separate keys for the gate and the cupboards.

In the middle room I also check the window is shut and bolted, the blind down. It is getting cool in here by now. I switch the air conditioner to low, unlock the cupboards and begin setting out the books and paper, the crayons and board games, the jigsaw puzzles and packs of playing cards, Happy Families, Uno, the fishing game, and tubs of Play-Doh. There are no electronic games. These are regarded as counterproductive. This room is quite cheery. It is painted banana yellow, and the carpet is blue. There are two beanbags, adult and child-sized, two easy chairs and two smaller chairs at the low table where I set up the colouring-in books. Someone has attached an alphabet frieze at head height all the way around the room, and if you think to turn the lights off, dinosaur stickers glow in the dark on one of the walls. But no one, as far as I am aware, turns off the lights.

———◆·◆———

Winston arrives several minutes before 9.30 but this time it is not with his mother. An older woman propels him into the back room after rattling at the mesh door.

'Nikki couldn't make it today,' she says, coughing. She falls into the lounge chair and bangs her chest, then gropes in her bag for a handful of tissues. When she stops coughing she adds, 'Job interview. She had to leave before seven to get there.' She starts coughing again.

Winston glances at me before going over to her side and saying, 'You okay, Nan?'

I lock the mesh door again behind them, leaving the other open. It is not right. They are meant to phone or email at least twenty-four hours beforehand if arrangements are to be changed. Winston knows this, though perhaps the grandmother does not. But something in his glance tells me not to make a fuss. He is very knowing, for a nine-year-old. And still quite small. Besides, I have to go to the front room. The father generally arrives first. He is probably at the front door now and indeed I only just have time to show the grandmother where to sign the register before I hear the discreet buzz. I leave them there and close and lock the back room door to the hallway.

Winston's father is always on time, to the minute. He does not drive. I imagine him taking the train then walking from the station, which takes seven minutes, and timing the entire trip so that he arrives early. Perhaps he sits in the park around the corner, the tiny one that is sandwiched between two houses, just an empty block no one wanted to build on. It is called Francis Spears Playground and I cannot imagine that Francis Spears must have been held in any great regard by the local council. There is one bench seat opposite the one swing. The grass is scuffed thin. I imagine Winston's father sitting there checking his watch until he walks up the road to ring the front doorbell.

Or perhaps he takes the bus, which would deposit him at the local shops, two blocks back on the main road. This would require more planning, since the buses here are notoriously unreliable, and a much longer walk. But whatever he does, every fortnight he is here, ringing the doorbell exactly when the clock reaches 9.30.

As soon as I open the door he walks inside and goes straight into the front room. He is not hostile. He never acknowledges my existence. And why should he? Despite this I always say, 'Good morning, Mr Lewis. Please wait here and I will call you shortly.' Sometimes when I speak he sniffs, or moves his mouth or crosses his arms or something to signify he knows the drill, but he never looks me in the eye.

As for Winston, he has lost the haunted look he had when he first started coming. I will not say he was frightened. But certainly he was apprehensive, and the very first time refused to come in until I promised to stay outside the door where he could hear me. I had to close the door, I explained that to him. 'But I will be right there,' I said, pointing to it. 'I will bring my chair up to the door and if you need me I will come straight in.'

And I did. Not all children would be reassured like that, I thought as I sat there trying hard to block out the sounds of their conversations, if it could be termed that, but also to keep alert for any hint the boy might be distressed. It seemed to me then to be a terrible breach, to listen in, despite the crimes of the father. It still does. I feel that for all they have done, for me to hear even the routine conversations, about what happened at school, or what they will do come the holidays, or what their best friend's new toy is, let alone the whispered endearments, or the half-uttered apologies – all the more eloquent for their strangled delivery – to be a violation of their intimacy so profound that I should be the one under duress, not they. It still does seem like that to me.

Now, however, there is no need for that sort of vigilance. Winston will have his forty minutes with the convicted rapist and manslaughterer who is his father, and I will sit out in the back room with his grandmother.

Her name, she tells me, is Gloria. The cough has subsided. She is looking around the room and I can read every thought all over her face. She wants to make some comment about the basic facilities, but isn't sure if that would constitute a personal insult to me or not. I would not care. I have worked here for three years but feel no affinity with the place. The look on her face also says, what kind of person has to come to a place like this? It's only a fleeting look but I've seen it on every face in this room. The kind of person like your daughter, I would say if I could, and your ex-son-in-law. People who can't stop hating each other for a single hour for the sake of their own children. I offer tea.

'Coffee, please.' Unfortunately there is only instant. However, none of the clients seem to mind. I get the impression they would prefer real coffee but feel unable to ask, as if already they are receiving far too much.

When I place it on the table Gloria leans forward and says, 'I told her not to do it, you know. I knew he was no good, I felt it right from the start. Before the littlie had even turned one, he was abusing her.' She sniffs and applies her tissues before settling back in the chair with her coffee. 'Never surprised me to hear what he did. Just glad it wasn't Nikki.' She brings the cup to her lips then pauses. 'Disgusting that he got parole so early. Just disgusting.' She shakes her head before sipping.

Gloria is apparently unaware of the codes here. There are many rules and regulations, but the most important ones remain unwritten. And we do not need to articulate them, the clients and I. Of their situations, I do not enquire, and rarely do they offer. I am not a confidant, a therapist, a friend, an anything. I am here to unlock and lock doors, to tick off forms, to watch the clock, and everything I do reminds them of how they failed, even if they feel they are in the right – and they all do – and they resent me for that. The worst thing, I have learned, is that coming here means they have a witness to all that shame. The junkies, the serial offenders, the prostitutes who have had their kids taken by DOCS five, ten times – even Traynor Lewis in there right now, who has been on parole for six months – they might have robbed at gunpoint or killed rival gangsters or stolen from their best friends and family to feed a habit, but the one thing that eats at them is the loss of their children.

Forty minutes is a long time to sit by the brick wall of someone else's resentment. I often find I need to spend that time in the kitchen, which is possibly why it is so very clean. Sometimes I go out the back door, though not far as I am required to stay on the premises at all times. Sometimes I wish I smoked as it would give some small shape to my moments out on the concrete slab, watching the washing line slowly circle in the breeze like a skeleton. Someone has placed an old biscuit tin filled with sand by the shed door. Half the butts do not make it that far.

<hr />

'Another fifteen minutes,' I tell Gloria, taking her empty cup. 'Would you like a second coffee?'

She shakes her head.

From the kitchen I hear her moving about, slapping a magazine down on the table, then she is coughing again before she comes to the doorway.

'It's a bloody joke. Do you know how long it takes to get here? Took me two trains, then that walk. With my knees.'

'I know,' I say, turning around from the sink. 'But that's the limit. Forty minutes each visit. There's nothing I can do about it.'

She coughs again, not wanting to appear to be an advocate for *more* time. And then, as if it's all my fault, while looking me in the eye, says, 'Nobody gives a stuff about people like us. He –' she jerks her head towards the middle room '– shouldn't have the right to see the boy, after what he's done.'

'Well. The family court decided.'

'As if Winston needs that.' She goes back to the chair.

But I disagree. I have seen the boy's face transformed when he walks back out from the middle room. At first, months ago, it was a sort of blank dull look, not the fearful, hunted one I expect his mother was hoping for. And now is it something much more. Not pleasure. I would not say that. But a look of calm satisfaction. His face says, I have been acknowledged here, by my father. For exactly forty minutes I have been the object of his attention. I have seen that look on other faces too, and I cannot deny it has its importance.

Besides, as Gloria mutters and squirms, making a big deal of repacking her handbag and putting on her jacket, I am here, this place exists, because both parents failed Winston, not just his father. I know that Nikki repeatedly ignored court orders for access, leaving Traynor Lewis waiting long afternoons every fortnight, in the McDonalds' carparks, or at gates of playgrounds while she took the child to distant friends. Gloria would not know what I have in the file. While Traynor was in jail Nikki took Winston interstate, and then moved house three times before the court tracked her down again. That file tells me of the father's dogged attempts to see the son who was just a baby when the mother first left. It describes his violence. It details the first AVO, when Winston was only two weeks. The second. Her application to have his name removed from the birth certificate. The ninth AVO, when from desperation she claimed he had picked her upside down and slammed her head into the ground, whereas the only injuries the police recorded were a bruise on her wrist, and grass stains on her white jeans. Which would suggest all the other AVOs are also lies, except I know they cannot be. There is a list of all the Christmas and birthday presents he sent, another of the cards and presents she posted back. Photos of the smashed window of his ute. Of her broken mobile phones, three. I have read all the stories, two narratives, two parts that are the same and yet separate, like a Siamese twin that hates itself as it draws life from a single pulsing heart.

This is why both parties resent me.

Gloria sniffs loudly as, exactly when the forty minutes are up, I go to unlock the door to the hallway. And when I unlock the door to the middle room I can hear her straining to listen, desperate for evidence this is all so damaging for her grandson. However, Winston is holding a hand out to his father. I know that there are also embraces, as I've seen the shadows of movement as Traynor Lewis draws back, stiff, the second I enter the room. But they have reached the handshake stage, that much is clear.

Winston, clever child, composes his face as he turns to his grandmother waiting at the hallway door. It is as innocent as a new penny.

At the back door, I am poised with my keys when Gloria turns around and says to me, 'What kind of person does a job like this?' though not quite loudly enough for Winston to hear.

⟡

Even though I know the rest of the cases for the day I go through the files one more time. I am lucky because there are fewer visits today. Some days, not many, the appointments come one after the other. At first the department scheduled them with no breaks, and I was running up and down the hall unlocking then locking doors endlessly, it seemed. I would make their teas and listen to the sobs and sometimes their abuse until, before half the day was done, I was exhausted. Now there are decent stretches of time, some of them all mine after I've tidied and checked off the files. I make my own tea and sit for a minute. What kind of a person does a job like this? No one has ever asked me that before, outright. A methodical one. Someone with time, and patience.

I take out my purse and dig for the photo that I keep turned face down in the little clear window section. He would be fourteen now. I put it away as I hear the side gate rattle. It is nearly 10.45.

Chantal and her mother are both quiet. Megan Pavlich never speaks to me unless she has to, and I don't think Chantal has ever glanced at me, let alone opened her mouth. She looks down at her ballet slipper shoes while holding my hand as I take her into the hall, then runs to her father when I unlock the door to the middle room and all I can see is his face, unexpectedly illuminated by the most generous set of teeth when he smiles. He picks her up as carefully as spun glass. I think her mother dresses her in those sorts of clothes deliberately. Nevertheless he holds her close, folding the ridiculous net fairy skirts against his black T-shirt, and I see him nudge her face with his mouth before I close the door.

Megan Pavlich gazes at me as if I have caused what she suspects is too much affection being demonstrated there in the room next to us. She would like it to be airless of all emotion, at least. Preferably intense with fear so that she could brandish the distress of her child in the department's face and never have to deal with her ex-husband again, even through the medium of my presence. Only once, on the first visit, did she ask me how long she had to keep bringing Chantal here and was deeply unsatisfied when I indicated this would be up to her and Chantal's father.

'Call him a *father*?' was all she said before turning her back and grabbing a *New Idea*.

Chantal has uncooperatively refused to be upset by her visits, and indeed, in the six weeks she's been coming, seems to arrive looking forward to them. When they leave – not a single word to me from Megan Pavlich – I hear her chattering about the next visit. She is holding a fluffy purple rabbit. All gifts are meant to be checked by me and recorded in the register, but when I return to the middle room to escort Ben Pavlich out the front door, the memory of his lit-up face stops me from mentioning it. He does not, of course, smile at me.

I keep my phone on discreet, letting any calls vibrate if I cannot answer them. Few call. Most of the department work is via email. Yesterday, before I returned from escorting a client out through the front room, I stayed and tidied up. A scrap of a foil pack, though not anything illicit, as far as I could tell. An empty plastic Coke bottle. The wisp of a cigarette pack string, from a client hastily setting to light up as soon as he was off the premises. When I got back to the kitchen my phone registered a missed call. Reed Macken. Detective Reed Macken. We have almost become friends. Now I look at the phone and consider it. There are ten minutes to the next client. In ten minutes what can Reed Macken say to me considering it's been ten years? If it was urgent he would have rung again, and again, possibly even texted me. I turn the phone off. It will not be urgent. It cannot be. And the next client will require all my senses tuned.

Bathsheba – she has insisted on the one name as if it's a formal title – saunters into the front room, several minutes late. But it never matters as her children and their father are always late too. Half the time Bathsheba does not arrive at all, but when she does it is with an intensity that seems to be intended to compensate.

'Can't wait to see my little darlings today,' she says, her rasping voice loud, as if for an audience. But as soon as she's inside the door she collapses into the lounge chair and draws her knees up, hugging them tight. Her arms are skinnier than ever, and it looks like she has two new tattoos on her upper arms, roses with thorns and hearts and chains, similar to all the rest. Or they could be peonies. She is trying, I can see how hard by the way she clamps her lips with her teeth.

'Would you like a drink of water or something?' I ask. She has come with nothing.

'Coffee. Three sugars,' she says before looking up at me. 'Thanks.'

I make her coffee in a melamine mug, with hot, not boiling, water – we have been trained to take care, for any contingency – and am returning down the hall when the back door rattles. I see them of course, and they can't see me. Two children, and the baby, held by her father, peering through the mesh with the midday light behind them blinding them into silhouettes.

'G'day.' Mick is probably the friendliest client I have. The children, one not much more than a toddler, Bradley, and the eldest, Dolly, who is six, dart into the back room while Mick dumps the baby onto the floor. She's sitting up now, wobbling slightly from the waist and displaying a wet smile before plugging her mouth with a fist.

'Gail here yet?' he says, fishing in his bag.

'It's still Bathsheba,' I say.

He rolls his eyes. 'Whatever. Here you go, Princess.' He takes the fist from Rebecca's mouth and gives her the bottle instead. 'I should change her. What's she like today?' he indicates the front of the house.

'Bad, I think. Better do it later.' Bradley and Dolly hold hands and walk before me while I carry Rebecca, who does smell of wet nappy, though it is not an unpleasant smell, up the hall. Bathsheba is pacing the middle room when I unlock the door and it reeks of cigarettes, though I cannot see how she could possibly have been smoking. For this visit, I am required to wait outside the door the whole time. And Mick stands just outside the house, on the back slab, smoking and running his hands over his stubbly head.

As I expect, the visit doesn't run to forty minutes. I try not to listen but I hear Bathsheba's voice barking through a volley of topics. How's kindy. Didjya see

Gran'ma. Bradley's three nearly! No way. Cute T-shirt. I forgot your lollies. Do ya like my rose. How's kindy. Oh yeah I said that. Soon she calls out, then knocks on the door and when I open it I see how much she is shaking. She gathers the older two in her skinny arms and kisses their heads then picks up the baby, by now sodden, and hands her to me. Rebecca starts to wail. Bathsheba practically runs to the front door, and I have to give Rebecca to Dolly and leave them in the hall to let her out.

She is like a sudden wind that rises and drops so fast there is only a flurry of dead leaves to show it existed. The children look so deflated as I lead them into the back room, I fetch some Poppers from the kitchen. There are also lollies for situations like this. Mick looks on as I offer the two older ones the bag of jelly snakes. I join him at the back door while Dolly and Bradley select their favourite colours.

'They're not even all mine, you know.'

'I know.' It's in the file of course. Three biological fathers, the last, Rebecca's, apparently a client.

He wipes his hand over his face, then tucks his cigarettes back into his shirt pocket.

After they leave it's as if they have taken the last of the oxygen with them. I am exhausted but there are two more appointments later in the afternoon. I spend my time writing up the notes of Bathsheba's visit, as her parole officer will be wanting them soon, and the department case worker. Bathsheba has left her children in parks, shopping centres and cars, and once on the doorstep of a neighbour. She has gone to Mick's place, off her face, in the middle of the night and begged and demanded and threatened to see them, several times. She has forged notes of authority to take Dolly home from school. Once she was apprehended at Central Station trying to take them north on the train. This was before the last baby. And when Rebecca was born, premature, addicted, she left the hospital and disappeared for six weeks. Mick went to the hospital and held the baby through all the anguished days of her withdrawal. I know she still has trouble feeding and sleeping.

———◆———

The final client has one child. Maria Bruner almost creeps through the back door and I cannot blame her. Her son's father disturbs even me. What he and Nicholas, who is five, say to each other I have no idea. Nicholas Bruner senior slides into the front room more like it is an appointment with his security manager than a meeting with his son. He is a thin tight streak of pure menace in a silver-grey suit. He drives a black Lexus which he parks right at the door. Someone is always waiting in the car but the tinted windows give no clue as to who. Maria has large brown eyes and ash-blonde hair. She is like a gazelle. It seems that Nicholas senior treated her like prey too. But his legal connections, which he exploited to try to retain custody of the boy, after trying to relieve her of the family home and all her possessions, have all recently vanished in the light of certain investigations, pending prosecutions. The court for once has seen the side of justice and Nicholas Bruner senior is permitted to see his boy only once a month.

Maria regards me as something of a saint. The first visit, she sat stiffly in her chair, facing the door through which her son went.

'He will be fine,' I reassured her again and again. 'Nothing can happen here. It's a safe place for children.'

She relaxed when I brought her a cup of tea, though did not drink it. It was clearly the longest forty minutes of her life and when I unlocked the hall door again and brought Nicholas through, it was as if I had delivered him from the brink of hell.

Today she has brought me a soap in a box wrapped in white tissue paper and bound in gold string. I can smell its fragrance, damask rose, through the wrapping.

'You shouldn't bring me gifts.' It is not very gracious, I know. I lift the box to my nose. 'It smells beautiful. Thank you.' Last time she brought me a Terry's Chocolate Orange.

When she leaves, one arm tight around her son's shoulders, she looks almost content.

The last thing I do for the day is return to the middle room. There is so little evidence of the children and their parents who have been in here all day. A lid of Play-Doh lies on the floor. Two sheets of drawing paper have been used. I tidy the pencils and crayons, wipe the table clean. The fishing game, the jigsaw puzzles, Happy Families can stay out until next time. Everything is locked and tidied. I take the laptop from the kitchen and switch my phone back to general. I will return Reed Macken's call later, maybe tonight. There is nothing he could possibly be wanting to tell me, nothing that I haven't already known since my boy was taken by his own father, to god knows where.

Out the back, as usual, Mick's butts litter the concrete slab. I put my bag down and sweep them up with the broom from the shed, ducking the washing line as it circles in the breeze. As I unlock the car door, for some reason Gloria's question is still circling in my head and it is not really clear why this bothers me because I know the answer, I have known it for years: the sort of person who does this job is one who has time, endless time, in which to hope.

Letter to George Clooney

Dear George

I was in the supermarket when I decided I had to write. Checkout six, one of only two open. Apart from the express lane of course, but then I had more than twelve items. Checkout six features a stand of magazines so that people can read something while they wait. Or the covers of something. I myself don't pick up the copies of *Who Weekly* or *Woman's Day*, though not out of a sense of superiority (because I do have that sense, believe me), but usually because I am overloaded and juggling the bags and baskets and the purse, the phone and the extra large pack of toilet tissue or the three for the price of two tinned tomatoes because I can't help buying in bulk. So I just look at the covers, which lately always feature fat celebrities in bikinis or thin celebrities in bikinis. The thin ones are accused of being too thin and the fat ones . . . Well, you get the idea.

I was waiting for the woman in front who only had two jars of instant coffee (I was also holding a bulky kilo packet of coffee beans) and thinking simultaneously, *instant coffee* and *why didn't she go to the express lane?* when I realised that all these celebrities were people I had never heard of, literally never, and I pride myself on taking more than a passing interest in popular culture. And the urge to write to you was so strong that, having manoeuvred my way this far along the checkout, I was tempted to toss the load right there and walk out and go straight to my desk. I've done that before, at the checkout. Once when it was torturously slow and the clock seemed to be leaping toward three-thirty and I only had five minutes to get through. To race out the door and make the few blocks downtown to pick up my child who would be finishing up school any second, while the man two places in front's card had a problem and the woman directly behind him had a pyramid of bags containing, I could see with growing horror, one capsicum here, two zucchini there, a handful of baby spinach leaves, three bananas, a pineapple, a cos lettuce, a parsnip, a single lime for goodness sake (why bother?). And I could see all the weighing and scanning and swiping ahead of me and the argument over the fact that the pineapples were on special or the operator asking were these Braeburns or Fuji apples and then, the ultimate horror, me noticing the operator wearing one of those large cheerful-coloured badges that make one simply wilt: *I Am In Training To Serve You Better*.

I lost it, George, that time. I'm afraid I simply dumped the lot and pushed through and raced out and along the street and if I doubted my haste and impatience then the sight of Essa's six-year-old face brightening like a pansy when I arrived at the school gate with my chest rasping was worth it. I have told her many times she will never be alone and I'm keeping my word if it kills me.

There was no urgency this time. My letter to you could wait. I had a good half-hour until the first of my clients arrived, and my office was only across the road and up a bit, conveniently situated in the community centre, which is next to the library. Presuming my next client would arrive. Many of them are still nervous. They think that anyone in authority is potentially going to steal their children and gouge their eyes out. Imagine! A million miles away from Farchana or Geneina. Why would they think that? And I am not even an authority.

Still, I fiddled in the checkout queue, impatient, restless. I am never equipped for these excursions. You would think I'd have learned by now. After all, I've done the shopping plenty of times. I estimate I've gone to the supermarket at least twice a week for the last three years. But I still haven't learned to bring enough bags, take a trolley, bring a book for when there's a slow queue. Other people have no problems: they read the magazines, they make calls, they play games on their phones or check their Facebook pages. I just stand there, thinking. Wasting my time. Why are the celebrities always in bikinis? Is it always summer and are people always at the beach in celebrity land?

And there you were. Sporting a beard now, I see. Of course I've seen your face on magazines before, and everywhere else – the TV, the movies. Only last month I saw your new film at the local cinema. Yes, we get the latest releases here, even though it's a small building with retro posters and unreconstructed choc-tops (I've learned about choc-tops now, and pavlova, and thongs, just as I learned about Bondi Beach and Vegemite before I arrived) and your face was on a poster out the front. The first time I saw your face on a magazine – and it is hard to believe that this is so – I didn't realise it was you.

My clients need not be so suspicious. It is true that until the airport in Cairo most of us had never met, but they should have had no reason to distrust me. I had seen those eyes sliding away before, especially from the men. The look that says they know what has been done. Perhaps it is the fact that Essa is somewhat lighter and finer boned. The narrowness of her nose. Perhaps it is that I am alone with her, while they are mostly mothers with three, five children, some with aunts and sisters, even if they have no husbands. This was a family program, and I slipped in with my command of English and my simple good luck. If luck is the word for it, considering my only friend had disappeared and my daughter would always be without grandparents, aunts, anyone but me. Perhaps it is that word always gets around, even in a refugee camp of over ten thousand people. Perhaps it is just that the story is always the same story. I should remember that, for it is the truth and has been for many years.

I waited for ten minutes but, as I suspected, the client, Mrs Abeche, did not appear. I went to the door of my office and looked up and down the street, wrapping my coat closer for warmth. I will never get used to the cold in this place, though the wind was especially sharp today. Mrs Abeche is very busy these days. She has four children, all at school now, and she and her mother intend selling pickled chillies and chutneys, and every time I feel a little down I think of her, not a word of English until recently, and how I even had to reassure her that the stove would work without her placing lit kindling in the oven. Mrs Abeche has now bought several new saucepans and boxes of jars. She would like me to write some flyers so her oldest boy can take them around to all the stores.

After a cup of tea I thought about returning to the supermarket and getting some chilli powder and turmeric, some peanuts and green beans, and then I decided not. There would not be any point because Essa would refuse to eat a curry and it was Friday in any case. She would remember that I had promised her pizza. When would that novelty fade?

Let me tell you about my supermarket, though I'm not telling you anything you don't know. Or am I? Sometimes I wonder about this. You strike me as the sort of man who would do his own grocery shopping, at least some of the time, and know how to find his way from frozen fish (not that you would buy any) to kitchen utensils or personal care products. But perhaps I am ill informed. Prone to make assumptions. Near your home at Los Angeles, or more likely the one on Lake Como, there would be a supermarket, the equivalent of our town's IGA, with its preprepared gourmet food section and its organic vegetable display and the carefully placed Asian cuisine shelves, integrated within the sauces and the pickled and preserved goods, but still segregated, when you think about it – tinned coconut milk, laksa paste, prawn crackers and palm sugar and wasabi sauce all stacked next to each other. There would be the Turkish food, the Middle Eastern section. Perhaps the nostalgic English section with its HobNobs and pork crackling. Even in our small IGA there is a Mexican section. And nearly an entire aisle of Italian food. You might have noticed there is never a section for African cuisine. It may be that the very idea is some form of joke, a kind of culinary oxymoron, amongst grocery retailers. Perhaps I should ask the manager here, Brett. We're on quite good terms now.

Sometimes in the supermarket I buy nothing much. It is enough to roam with my string bag (old habits, George) and gaze at the labels. I might pick up an avocado and press to test its ripeness, or sniff the base of a pineapple to gauge the level of its sweetness, but really I am just pretending and sometimes I return home with only a loaf of bread and the milk. The first time, I could buy nothing. I was unprepared for the abundance. You might laugh at this (I've heard about your Thanksgiving dinner deep fried turkeys, your mounds of lobsters and the amazing towering fruit displays at your parties). But believe me, it was abundant. I walked into the premises on Pioneer Street and smelled the fresh baked goods in Bread and Cakes that is situated as you go in. Which is really very illogical, for this is followed by the fruit and vegetable section, and if you take the route imposed by the supermarket designers, you end up loading your tinned beans and tomato paste and bottles of mineral water on top of your strawberries and hamburger buns. That is very stupid. So wasteful. I should ask Brett about this too.

The first day, I closed my eyes and breathed in the smells, but I couldn't keep walking around pretending I would be buying. Soap powder, cloves (or maybe star anise?) and the distinct smell of overripe rockmelon.

Coffee and dog food, that dry roasty smell despite the packaging. I could smell all this although the air conditioning seemed intended to suck all life out of the air. The cold smell of the meat display, just a whiff of fat. And the bread. Doughnuts. Ciabatta. Helga's Traditional White Sliced. You do detect these things even though for years your nostrils may have been filled with nothing but dust. I felt very stupid and no doubt I looked it to the other shoppers and the checkout staff, who that day, I recall, were both In Training To Serve Me Better, for they stared at me as I very slowly edged my way through all eight aisles, turning my head this way and that, gazing at the variety, the extent, the abundance, which so overwhelmed me I could buy nothing. I could only look, then leave.

That's not quite true. On my way out I spotted a small yellow toy duck, on a key chain. It was attached to some kids' magazine at the checkout. Essa was still young enough then and she reached out for it and grabbed it and didn't want to let it go, so I bought it, and threw away the magazine, and she clutched the duck tight to her chest. She still has it, attached to her schoolbag. The girl at the checkout made a point of looking into my empty string bag even though I would have thought it quite evident it was empty. Why then had I brought it, she was obviously thinking. I placed Essa down to open my new purse and pay for the duck toy – it was four dollars ninety-nine, I remember it exactly as I groped around for the final four cents until I realised they didn't exist – and wondered myself. We had already been provided with the basics. I was really just testing myself. And why did I fail the test? I don't know, George, I really don't know. It wasn't as simple as the idea that if I were to fill my string bag with sweet potatoes, cherry tomatoes and grapes, frozen chicken drumsticks and tubs of flavoured yoghurts and orange juice from a dizzying choice of pulp-free, unsweetened, organic or regular, I would be guilty for those back home who I knew were still starving. There is not the slightest scrap of logic in that, and I knew besides that I'd had my mouthful of dirt for long enough, so had Essa, and I had every right to stuff my bag until it bulged with the most expensive chevre in ash or the punnets of raspberries I had spotted, and the King Island triple cream to go with them. If food is earned, I've prepaid, for an entire lifetime. Still, I couldn't even buy us a tin of baked beans or a couple of bananas.

So no, it was not a moral dilemma. It was just so visually, sensually, overwhelming. I needed to put my toe in the water first. When I returned, I remember standing in front of the shelves of hair shampoos and conditioners with a smile stamped on my face. I examined a tub of pink shimmering Hair Repair Leave-In Treatment, with protein and silk extracts. It actually seemed possible. I would have believed it contained ground diamonds, liquid gold, anything. By the third or fourth visit I stopped only looking and started to buy. Back at our flat the bar fridge in those first few days held half a dozen eggs, the most of a litre of milk, a container of something called Flora which I took to be butter, a packet of sliced cheese and a soup pack of vegetables (three carrots, two sticks of celery, an onion, two potatoes, a sprig of parsley and a beef stock cube), while on the kitchen bench sat a plastic bowl of apples and oranges. The cupboard held a box of Weetbix, a packet of raw sugar, a jar of honey and another of peanut butter, tins of tomatoes and apricots. There was a sliced loaf on the bench. Sausages in the tiny freezer. It was more food than I could remember having in one place for a long time. I could make it last us forever.

Essa at that stage was eating pretty much nothing but sweetened boiled rice, but I persuaded her with that white bread and honey. You know how children are – or perhaps you don't – their food fads. There is a kid in Essa's class who only eats peanut butter sandwiches. And as for Vegemite, I knew about this substance before I arrived because I did my homework, but you have probably never heard of it. You spread it over your toast. It is salty, curiously palatable. Essa took one sniff and practically vomited. Her friend Tabitha also rejects it, though I suspect that is more to do with her mother's views on diet because the local children seem to like it very much, and amongst people there is an affection for the brand that I can't quite pin down.

I still keep a jar in the cupboard and have managed to persuade my compatriots, who understandably are given to overindulge in everything, that they only need to take a tiny scrape. The ones who want to integrate. Some of them of course have no such desire to become so local.

Tabitha actually now eats a few other things, all of which her mother doubts for nutritional value. Tabitha and Essa have become friends, which is to say they sit together after school in front of the TV, and in these circumstances a shared bowl of something sweet or salty is the glue that keeps a friendship together. Occasionally they circle around each other's rooms. Essa's is full of dolls and plastic toys. The people here were very generous in that respect. She is rather disdainful of the dolls and Tabitha has gone home a few times with some spoils. Tabitha also eats potato chips, which I served one afternoon as a treat, and she will drink chocolate milk which I produced to celebrate the arrival of her new baby brother, just recently. I had told Tabitha's mother she was welcome to stay after school, if that helped. Kylie agreed but made a point of frowning as she did so. I suspect it is the chips. There are views among some people regarding junk food and naturally I tend not to be so conscious of what children should or shouldn't eat. I made a mental note to have a plate of celery and carrot sticks next time Kylie comes to fetch her daughter.

There was yet another health check the day after we arrived and the paediatrician did raise her eyebrows when I mentioned this staple of Essa's diet. How long, she wanted to know, had she been eating only white rice, sweet and mushy at that. But I wouldn't feel guilty. She ate a lemon chiffon pudding on the flight, I told her. And she loved the Coke. The bubbles made her gasp then burp then laugh. We were probably over the middle of the Indian Ocean at the time and the passengers were sleeping, the cabin darkened, but I laughed too because it was the first time Essa had laughed since we left the camp, when we lost Safiya.

The paediatrician frowned. Actually she did a lot of communicating with her eyebrows, up and down, up and down, but there were many other parents with more than one child, whole families to process, while the interpreter the department had sent was struggling with an unexpected regional dialect. The community centre was so full that day the queue roped out the door and down the road into Pioneer Street, where the locals stood around outside the pub, the bakery, the IGA, the bank, their glances arrowing back and forth across the street. So she let us go. I had actually been breastfeeding Essa up to the time we reached Cairo, not that I told her this. The doctor in the clinic there had advised me to stop. You have no milk, he said, and the child will be too dependent. And there will be other food from now on, he assured me. You won't have to worry about that.

He was completely correct and by the time the long wait for the flight and then the long flight itself and the next long wait and the last flight were finally over and Essa and I too exhausted to move, she seemed to have forgotten about the breast anyway. We were installed in our row of flats in the block beside the railway line, and I have never worried about food since. Or rather I was worried, as you can see, so worried by the sheer abundance and choice that for a while I stuck to tinned beans or bread, though I believe I am over that now.

It was a process line that day in Cairo too, though my impression of that may have been slightly skewed by the fact that the authorities had fitted out a former cheese factory for the refugee clinic. And I was beyond fatigue. Every time I closed my eyes I saw Safiya, open-mouthed, held back by two soldiers at the camp gate as I was pushed onto the transport out of there. We always thought we would leave together, but in the end, even though I had nothing, she had less.

The cheese factory smelled musty, but at least there was no dust. Essa was clinging tightly to me by this stage. We were sent to a screened-off section with a laminex table and a doctor with a green stethoscope around his neck. Did I need an interpreter? Definitely not. Did I prefer to be assessed by one of the women doctors? No, I didn't care. Did I require specialist consultation, such as a gynaecologist? You don't want to go there, I thought, but instead I said no and suggested an orthopaedic surgeon might be more useful. Though my arms, I must admit, look reasonably straight now. Safiya did a good job. And I've fleshed out a little these last couple of years. If I'm not careful I'll start resembling those jolly mammas, all rolling buttocks and tight cheeks. It is not only Essa who likes sweet things. I have developed a taste for three teaspoons of sugar in my tea. Cream biscuits, iced doughnuts. Kylie would be horrified if she knew. I have already heard her discussing how she made her own sugar-, salt-, gluten-, dairy-free rusks for Tabitha when she was a baby, and it remains to be seen what she will cut out of the next one's infant diet. I cover my porridge with brown sugar, like a crust, having already cooked it with salt and milk. And then I add cream but sometimes I carve a chunk of butter – I buy butter now, I ditched the Flora, you would too – and melt that over the top. I eat it very slowly, licking my spoon clean between every mouthful. In Farchana, after Oxfam pulled out and the supplies all but vanished, people ate their porridge – more of a gruel, made from dusty millet – almost before it hit the tin plates. Once I saw the aid worker slip and lose his grip. The aluminium saucepan went flying and before the guards could aim their guns a swarm of children had fallen to the ground and licked up every drop.

The supermarket in my previous place of residence consisted of wooden trestles spread with empty hessian sacks and bearing some bags of rice and tins of powdered milk, along with a pile of maize cobs. That would be on a good day. On a very good day there would also be dried dates and Maggi instant noodles. Chicken flavour. And once I spotted cartons and cartons of Chinese cigarettes, stacked high. No matches, however. But most days the supermarket, manned by a yawning boy who fanned the flies from his face with his G3, held rusty empty tins, which, if you peered into them, seemed to contain the remains of a white powder that could have been anything from detergent to cocaine, but was probably flour.

One day in Geneina, or Mille, or maybe it was Farchana – excuse the confusion: they are much the same, these places, except for the volume of people, say twenty thousand, or ten, give or take – one day there was another visiting delegation. This was a regular thing. Overseas dignitaries, spokespeople for aid organisations, celebrities such as yourself, or the head of pointy-ended UN humanitarian groups, and there are many so forgive me if I don't recall exactly whom. I think it was Farchana now, and there's a reason I remember but I'll get to that. That day the supermarket consisted of ten trestle tables covered in green palm leaves and featuring tins full of white powder, ones with labels – Nestlé Milk Formula, Protein Enriched – plus piles of sweet potatoes, only slightly withered, branches of green bananas, dried fish, candles, matches (but no cigarettes this time), condoms, cooking oil and many sacks of rice and lentils. Nearby the water jerry cans were stacked high. And the guard had quadrupled. Also developed muscles. And beards. The boy with the G3 was nowhere to be seen and the guards, wearing camos under their jalabiyas, smiled as the visiting dignitaries were escorted out of the jeep. There were a few handshakes. More smiles. One of the plumper babies was brought forward, his mother shy underneath her shawl. The rest of the camp had been warned off the day before and was cowering behind their mud bricks or cardboard.

We had set off early that morning to collect grass and sticks, rather hopefully termed firewood and fuel, but it was the only way people could make a few cents. For the women, it was the only source of income barring their bodies, but those women were pariahs in the camps – there is a respectable hierarchy even among the poorest of the poor – and they lived in a corner none of us ventured near. We were five, and we had walked for hours to find the denser grass that attracted an extra cent a pound, carrying string bags and sticks. One of the women had a baby, another was seven months pregnant. I also took my backpack and even then was scanning the ground for pieces of pottery that I might recognise, since Farchana was said to be within a sultanate that

covered many miles in the sixteenth century, a pros-
perous and civilised trading junction. On the way here
I had failed Professor Kass and, despite all that had
happened, I was still a budding student of something, if
not history. Indeed it was the one thing the ordeal so far,
the long journey, the pain, the hunger and the humilia-
tion could not remove from me: my education.

We had travelled farther than usual, rested for some
hours in the heat of the afternoon beside a well with a
trickle of water, and the others were preparing a small
meal, baking flatbread on a fire while I was poking
around with my stick along the watercourse, when two
trucks appeared on the tracks nearby. Our sticks were
of no use at all, and I tried to use my backpack as a
shield but the man who advanced on me ripped it off,
rummaged through its laughable contents, tossed everything on the ground, then ripped off my toab, revealing
my cargo pants, then, even more enraged, ripped them
off too. He called his companions over. They left Safiya,
whom they'd pushed back into the fire so that her hair
singed permanently against her scalp; they left Aisha,
the pregnant woman whose baby they ritually punched
as they fucked her; they left the woman whose toab they
covered in oil from the back of one of the trucks, then
lit, then rolled in dirt, all the while laughing; and they
left the woman whose baby they had dropped on the
road while she sat blinded by tears. They all clustered
around me, pawing through my backpack and showing

their teeth through their beards. It was the cargo pants, the tattered magazine in my backpack, or both, why they called me, Whore, American whore, even as I moaned, No, no, I am of this country too.

It was totally dark by the time they left. They had burned all the grass and sticks we had spent the day gathering, and stripped our clothes into rags so we huddled together all night for warmth, Safiya and I holding each other close as we had for a long time before. And still huddled we all limped back towards the camp at first light.

We stopped in sight of the southern fence and clustered under a tree. The shame of our nakedness was suddenly more unbearable than the baby we had buried and our dead companion we had had to leave, her stomach split like a watermelon and beaten to a pulp and gathering flies by the second. I volunteered, holding my filthy backpack before me. When the first soldier at the gate saw me he put his G3 on the ground and placed his hands over his eyes. He called me over in a soft voice and with his eyes still shut began to unwind his turban. There are five of us, I said. Excuse me, I mean four. His companions turned their backs and also unwound their turbans. I wrapped his turban around my body and beckoned the other women over and handed them the cloth from the soldiers, who all stood facing the fence until we were covered. The cloth of my soldier's turban was very soft.

It is a funny thing, George, that whenever I think of all the atrocities that have been performed, I can feel almost nothing except for a brick-like hardness, but when I recall this small act of decency I soften in my chest and cry for the kindness.

Your name, the soldier enquired? Aisha, I told him. And your companions? Aisha, I pointed at Safiya. And Aisha. And here too was Aisha, all four of us. If we were Aisha there was a small chance our shame would not be hurled at us some time later, though we would never escape completely the jeers and hisses, and the taint would return to us like the smell of decaying flesh that once captured in the nostrils never seems to fade. He gave us each a ticket from within his hut and with it we entered the camp and passed the two other checkpoints and eventually found our places in the rows upon rows of cardboard and mud huts. Past the supermarket, where the dignitaries' jeep was just leaving. That is how I remember it was Farchana. Where if your name was that of the Prophet's favourite wife there was a chance you might be protected, to a point.

<hr />

You would not think there'd be much use for archaeology in Darfur but Nyala University held a chair in Sudanese history and prehistory and due to the efforts of one professor, a large collection of artefacts had been amassed, dating back past the fifteenth century.

And academics have this endearing, almost childlike capacity for resistance to political or other pressure. They almost wilfully carry on delivering lectures while bullets might be whizzing past the windows of their classrooms. They still expect their students to arrive for their tutorial sessions even as they are being dragged through the streets with their wrists tied with wire and their shirts off, the gravel scraping their backs red raw as they scream for mercy and beg for their mothers.

Professor Kass was one of these innocents. He was still poring over his boxes and papers the day the first of many bombs were dropped from the Antonov-26 planes that began circling the region. Painted a bright UN white these planes indeed looked benign for a while. But they came and went with no real logic and so it was easy to see how someone like Professor Kass could over the years bunker down when necessary but basically spend his time methodically brushing dirt from a fragment of clay pot or burnishing a gold anklet, circa 1530. He had a sense of honour and the Arab Cultural Foundation had given him a grant to study artefacts from the Keira dynasty of the Sahel region and the grant would be spent accordingly, war or no war. Indeed Professor Kass was one of those who clung firmer to the habits of scholarship as the civilised world as we knew it crumbled. It was as if he were a moral shield in the face of so much barbarity. Plus, there was no great reason at that time to think we were in danger.

None of us had the slightest idea of what was in store. The war was confined. It was complex and bloody but the conflict was between the herders and the farmers, far off in the northwest, or so we thought.

Professor Kass had known my parents, and it was mainly on their account that I had returned to Nyala to pay him a visit. Indeed he knew them far longer and better than I, the accidental, late and only child of their marriage. They were, he and others had told me, devoted to each other, though I was first too young and then too far away to see. Professor Kass had organised the funeral, and I suppose he had paid out of his own pocket, though I felt the Church Missionary Society should have taken care of all that. So I had a sense of obligation, that last visit in Nyala. I was planning to apply for a postgraduate position in London – journalism, I was considering – but then he persuaded me to accompany him on a final field trip. And I did have the time, and I was interested enough. In Khartoum I'd taken an undergraduate class in archaeology and even thought it might be fun. He had the departmental jeep and engaged a driver, so we set off for Geneina while the weather still held. In the rainy season it would be impossible, though the drought had taken care of that for many years.

I remember the afternoon we left, later than intended, for the professor was a ditherer and had already kept me waiting in the courtyard outside his office while he shuffled through papers and answered emails. I can see his face tilted upwards at the screen, his moon-sized glasses slipping, as he laboriously poked at the keys with one finger. I wandered away to the student co-op shop and bought us a bottle of water each. At the counter there was a stack of cheap notebooks, plus a stand of magazines. I bought a new notebook and the latest *Time*, though it was already months old, which I would read when I got the chance. By the time I got back to the jeep the professor was at the window talking to the driver. There you are, he said. Let's be off.

There was not a great call for amateur historians of north African culture of the sixteenth century anyway, either there or here in rural Victoria. However, speaking three languages landed me a position in the community centre, though translation is not quite the word for what I do. The other day a Mr el-Shataya (six children, wife or wives killed or dead) wanted me to explain the intricacies of the Australian taxation system prior to his lodging a request for an ABN. Mr el-Shataya, I confided, I doubt even the ATO itself understands its own workings. He did not offer so much as the flicker of a smile. As far as he is concerned I was never married to the father of my child and I have no right to make jokes or understand anything more complex than stewing goat or cultivating tomatoes and chillies. But I give him all credit.

He is enterprising. He wants to run his own business. He has already purchased a new lawnmower and has commenced driving lessons. Negotiating through me, I should add. For which he is doubly, triply, resentful. Mr el-Shataya will learn English, he will figure out the ATO, and Centrelink, and Medicare, and the local parents' committee of his children's school, and then have nothing more to do with me.

Anyway, he is right. Most definitely did I remain unmarried to the man who fathered Essa. Mr el-Shataya and his friends suspect me of everything and they would be right. In the camps it is only whores and abeed who bear fatherless children. Anything else would be an admission no one can afford to make. After I sorted out his papers, downloaded and printed the correct forms from the ATO website, filled them in for him, pointed to the three places where he needed to sign, scanned them, emailed them back to the ATO, and handed him the originals in a fresh buff cardboard folder, and after he left again without thanking me, only pulling his orange jalabiya a little tighter and holding his head a little higher, I felt rather diminished. I locked the office and went out, over the road to the IGA. It would soon be time to fetch Essa and I would get something special for our dinner. I chose some chicken pieces and a jar of Mother Patel's Butter Chicken sauce, something I had never tried before, and went to select tomatoes and cucumbers for a salad. At the end of Fruit and Veg the manager was heaping onto a table a pile of corn cobs, all wrapped in their bright green skins. Special today, Miri, he told me. Market fresh, three for a dollar. I looked closely at them. They did indeed look very fresh. I picked one up. The cornsilk was soft and moist, the colour of a baby mouse. The kernels inside would be sweet and plump. No thank you, Brett, I said. Not today.

◆

The jeep had veered sharply to the left and the driver overcorrected, taking us to the other side of the road, where we came to a stop in a shallow ditch. Blowout, sir, he informed Professor Kass after he got out and inspected the tyres. He estimated we had less than ten minutes before we would reach the next town. The map revealed numerous villages all around and I knew the map was unreliable – or rather, the map was innocent enough, it was the landscape that had changed – but the camel herders had scoured through and burned this village, that village, leaving others in between apparently at random and yet not: they had their reasons. But that had been a while back and the place was quiet. No reports of fighting for many months and not even the professor would have taken us there had there been a risk, grant or no grant. We decided to walk rather than wait, since the driver showed no signs of being willing or able to change the tyre. And even to my unmechanical eye, the wheel looked damaged. The driver sat leaning against the jeep and I wound a toab over my khaki shirt and pants, hoisted my backpack and we set off. There was nothing to show for the trip already and Professor Kass was chewing over the frustration of that when a band of people appeared on the road ahead, walking towards us quickly. Women, children, babies. A few donkeys. Old men. Only old men. We saluted them and some acknowledged the professor but mostly they avoided our gaze. Eyes down. And we kept walking.

What might have been ten minutes in the jeep might have been two hours by foot. But what might have been was never to eventuate as another knot of people appeared, then another, and I began to notice that they were all scared. Even the donkeys were abject, but then donkeys generally are. It was only beginning to dawn on me how clear the signs were of trouble ahead when I also noticed the light was fading. Professor, I said, I think we should turn back. He looked at his watch, looked at the sky. We drank some water, then he agreed. I was not sure at what stage panic set in or even what it was that cemented the brick of fear into place in my chest, but by the time we had trotted back some kilometres towards the jeep and the driver we had left behind, I felt a dread like nothing I had ever felt before.

The screams tore the late afternoon sky. Alongside the road, just where we had broken down in the jeep, were men with their throats cut. The long beard of one had been neatly sliced off too. It was lying on his chest as he lay there, flies already clustering. Beside the jeep I could see the driver still sitting, his head to one side, his chest flooded, red. Babies were crying, donkeys shrilled and honked in that way they have. Women were running or huddled, weeping, moaning. Men with flashing teeth amid their beards. Knives. Dust. Lots of dust, making the afternoon darker. There must have been wind.

They were camel herders, these men, but they had no camels with them now, only trucks the colour of the desert from where they'd come, and on the back were belt-fed machine guns, enough to mow down an army. But the machine guns were silent. Instead the men were slicing with machete-like knives and at the very second I registered it was only men and children lying dead the professor was whisked from beside me and tossed in the same ditch where our jeep had failed us, blood pouring like a stream from his throat into the thirsty ground.

They took all the women and we left. I don't know what happened to the children, the babies, the ones who had not been killed. I was tied to two others and we were dragged into the back of a truck which belted along the road towards the township the professor and I had been headed for. The trucks slammed to a stop in the main street, where already there was chaos. Fires, men running, waving burning torches and rifles. Shooting, screaming. Crying. A few buildings were still standing. A small church. The remains of a post office. A general store, with posters out the front still flapping in the wind advertising publications. *Africa Today* and *OK!* magazine. The air was putrid. Later, the next day, I would know why.

George, you don't want to hear the next bit, but you need to know. And I need to tell you. They tied many of us together, the two women I was already with and several more, our wrists banded like we were paper dolls. I don't know how many men there were either, as I stopped counting after the seventh or eighth. They came at us and pushed us close to the largest fire in the town square, raping systematically from each end of the line as if we were in a factory and they were on a productivity drive. I was somewhere in the middle. The breasts of the woman next to me were weeping milk onto her bare chest. Her baby would have been back on the road in the dusty wind, wailing. Or perhaps not.

It is amazing how quickly some men can fuck. Even more amazing how they can move into a woman regardless of the previous man's semen. Such brotherhood. And since I mention semen there are all the other fluids and excretions, and you may as well know about them. Blood, of course, lots of that. And it seemed even the menstruating women were not avoided as being unclean. Urine, for they pissed over us, many times. One of them pissed onto the woman on the other side of me just as his friend ejaculated, and they both laughed like hyenas. There was shit. People do that when they are terrified. And the tears, they go without saying.

I was waiting my turn, there were men either side of me, and the woman whose breasts were leaking was heaving in grief as the next man fucked her, crying through mouthfuls of ash and dirt that eddied around carried by the dry wind, the wind that tore unrestrained in that place, uncontained by any tree or building. Unfortunately for me it was still light.

There is more, George. And you perhaps should not read the next bit, but I have to write it. Skip to the end if you like, there is something nice there, I promise you.

I was the child of missionaries, sent to school in England. My father was born in Khartoum, of British parents, military people. My mother was a local. They both believed themselves to be British, always. That is the legacy of colonialism, isn't it? My mother was also raised a Christian. And in Abbotsford Anglican Girls' School no one had ever heard of female circumcision, or if we had we would have laughed at the very idea.

George, I was not laughing when the camel herding men got to me, stripped my pants off me, spread my legs and jeered abuse. I was crying, very much so. The first one screamed, This one is unclean! Unclean! They kicked me in the vagina, precisely, many times. I could not move away as three of them held me, one at my head, two at each side. Finally I called out in English,

For the love of God, leave me alone! And this stopped them momentarily.

You are American? English? they wanted to know. No, I sobbed, barely able to speak. I am Sudanese too. But I spoke like a foreigner, they said. I betrayed my country, my religion, calling on the love of God. I protested but they continued, calling to witness the paler colour of my skin, the clothes that betrayed my westernness. They spat on me, and continued kicking, and then one of them advanced with a knife. He cut me free of the other women, but he was not freeing me. Foreigner, he spat, filthy foreign abid, we will make you clean. Two of them stood on my arms to hold me still as he sliced.

<hr />

Later I would see that the bodies – babies, children, men and women – had been drenched in the oil of their own stores, the oil that along with their stacks of maize and sacks of lentils would have seen the townsfolk through the next season. The ones that had not been set alight were thrown into the wells – there were three in the town – and the smell of decay was inescapable. Several heads, black and bloodied, caked in dust, were rolling around the town square, as if they'd been used as footballs.

But meanwhile one of the women had held onto her shawl through all the long night, and had plugged it between my legs as I lay unconscious. When I came to, I discovered her lying very close, holding me still. We were beside the fire which had been fed with smashed doors, chairs and other broken pieces of furniture, and though it flared and then smouldered all night, none of us was warm. By day it was clear the men had gone, on their trucks with their weapons, and all that remained was blood and ashes. Even the sound of sobbing had gone. It was as if the women had lost their voices along with their clothes, their men, their children. My friend – her name was Safiya – helped me to the ruined store where she found water and scraps of cloth that she ripped up to bind my broken arms, which she then crossed over my chest. She brought me my backpack, my filthy clothes, and set me up on the store verandah, while she crept among the debris, the shredded newspapers, the ruined stocks of writing paper, broken pencils, dismembered books and magazines all torn and scattered. The store had escaped burning and she poked through looking for something, anything. A couple of plastic bowls, a grass mat, a packet of paper serviettes.

Is there nothing useful in here? Safiya said, rummaging through my backpack. She dug out the *Time* magazine and held it up with a query on her face. That was when I noticed it was your face on the cover, your eyes looking directly into mine. If that man, I thought, could see me now, what would he think? She pushed my hair back and pressed her lips onto my forehead. Poor child, she murmured, though she was barely older than me. We were all done as little girls, she said.

Did it hurt less then? At the time I could not bear to think. And recalling now the press of her dusty lips on my forehead makes me weep. I realise now that it is not the horrors that are unbearable over the years, but the small kindnesses. One day I might understand why that is so.

She waited until I could walk again. Five days. The other women scoured the ruined town for food and saved some water from the few jars and buckets that had been overlooked. Sacks of sorghum and flour and lentils had been destroyed. The rest that was not taken had been thrown on the fires. They had been thorough, but in the cellar of one house they had overlooked a small store of maize, some of the leaves still intact, though the grains were dried, in readiness for husking. We piled the maize cobs on the store verandah and counted them, enough for each of us, every share equal. Safiya cooked ours in a tin over the coals, but even after boiling they were tough and dry. I can still taste the smoky flavour, feel the gritty kernels against my teeth.

When we limped into the long dusty queue of souls headed for Chad I had less than nothing on my mind. I would have stayed there, beside the road, along with the bundles of dropped sticks and discarded cooking pots and empty sacks and all the things people kept for as long as they could, until it became hopeless, were it not for Safiya. She herded me into the centre of the group, like a newborn baby elephant needing protection from lions. When we reached Geneina at the border, it was like paradise to see the hordes of people, sick and starving though they were. It was bliss to discover people only suffering from HIV, malnutrition and tuberculosis. I could disappear within such crowds and recover. And here Safiya and I would learn to treasure the smallest handful of gritty lentils or the skin of an onion. When they closed off supplies and we could not even beg a bottle of water, we moved on to Farchana where I saw the most abundant supermarket ever. Now do you understand why here I feel a little overwhelmed at times?

———◆———

Kylie's baby is spectacular. His face is pink and yellow, rather mottled. As I admired him I couldn't help thinking of the port wine cheese they sell in Dairy. A touch of jaundice, she said, when she brought him to the school gate the other day. It'll fade soon.

The other mothers were clustering and clucking, and I had a long enough look for the sake of politeness before retreating to speak to Mrs Abeche who expressed dismay at the prospect of a woman out and about just a week after a birth. She turned aside and spoke softly to me from within the depths of her shawl. It did not seem decent to her, let alone even possible, and certainly not desirable – why would you want to leave your house with a new baby when there was no need? A month, I think, was Mrs Abeche's ideal resting period, each birth. But then she did have her mother and mother-in-law to assist, while Kylie seems to shrug off the idea that help is needed. For myself, I was still amazed that she could walk, could get in and out of the car, swing the baby seat into the back. I know I was staring, but she even seemed to be wearing her old jeans.

The school bell went and Essa came and grabbed my hand. Can I go back to Tabitha's place? Please? And Tabitha's little brother is cute. Mrs Lawrence said we could hold him.

She said Mrs Orrence, and I resisted correcting her but placed my hand on her braided head. I should not think of port wine cheddar when Essa's head was like some bruised vegetable when she was born.

I will pick you up at five, I said, nodding to Kylie. I walked back down the street with Mrs Abeche and her two oldest. She was talking about the electric toaster. Her flat, in a former army compound, had somewhat unpredictable electricity. I had only coaxed Mrs Abeche into using the toaster when the supply sparked and crashed, but it turned out that her children had switched on every appliance and overloaded the system. She was now entranced by the way the bread leaped out and landed on the bench, sometimes right on the plate. She was entranced by sliced bread. Come by the community centre tomorrow, I said, and I'll organise an electrician to come and fix it, struggling to find the word for electrician in Dinka. I had to keep reminding myself that until six months ago Mrs Abeche had never handled a house key or used a phone or known of the miracle of endless running water in kitchen sinks and flushing toilets. What she had in the camps would have been the same pit that Safiya held me over time and again. The day we took the Abeches to their new place I showed her around and demonstrated the main amenities. When I watched Mrs Abeche press to flush, then flush again, looking at me, then into the bowl, with the look of simplest sweetest joy on her face, I understood exactly what she felt.

⸻⬧⸻

I thought all my insides were going to pour out and leave me a husk, skin stretched over a frame of bones, except for the hard lump of my baby. Safiya had already had whatever disease it was that kept us heaving into an old tin and running to the pits, and when it finally stopped and I could keep down the boiled water she now spooned into me and lie back on the hessian sacks in our hut and sleep, the pain recommenced, only with a different resonance and direction.

Be grateful, Safiya whispered as I moaned, that the baby is so small, it will be easier for it to get out, you know. How right she was. Essa slid and gasped into the world before too long, her tiny head moulded into a shrivelled eggplant thanks to the scar tissue that gripped both of us so tight. Yet again I was glad Safiya was there, holding out a clean shawl to catch my baby as she broke free of my body, for the tearing pain of that alone made me faint.

❖

George, I have promised you something pleasant and believe me I am getting there, but there is a part of this old and familiar narrative I have not yet explained. I must go back and flesh the story out, as they say. That afternoon we were captured out collecting grass, behind me all the Aishas were wailing. Perhaps I was too. The baby was quiet by then. My attacker rummaged through my bag and tossed out the little I had managed to hold on to all those months. Some aspirins, the packet flattened and the pills crushed anyway, a plastic bottle, my notebook and diary, some pencils. And the *Time* magazine, which by then I had read over and over since there was nothing else to read in the camp. The jeers turned to screeches and yells, then thumps. Who is this infidel, this western man? Why do you keep his picture with you? He must be your lover. You are a whore. And then the word that is the worst of all in my country, abid: slave, black slave.

George, I was only grateful they could not read, since the article concerned your views on our government, its failure to protect our people, and mentioned certain international organisations who denounced the very men who were now attacking us. It mentioned Darfur by name, the people of the Fur who were being systematically raped and starved and displaced and murdered and so comprehensively excised from the map of human history and geography that what remained, for hundreds and hundreds of kilometres, was nothing but circles of ash. There was a picture in the article that showed the curious phenomenon where villages and tiny settlements all over the middle of the country were completely razed, yet nearby other villages, those of the herders, spared. Entire communities reduced to flat black spots, a dozen, thirty, fifty farming families, their homes and stores crushed like antheaps, and yet maybe no more than a kilometre away, other villages or settlements were completely intact. On the satellite map it looked like abstract art, a dot painting. Perfect black circles, perfect brown circles. This was a war like no other, you had said. The systematic destruction of the ethnic farmers was too calculated and too precisely targeted for comprehension. No one was able even to understand it, let alone equipped to stop it, and what was happening in Darfur represented the greatest atrocity of our time.

I was grateful they could not read that for they might have made it worse than it already was and punished me further for the sheer temerity of your involvement in their war, not to mention your denunciation of these very men who turned on their own people and betrayed humanity itself. They threw the magazine down and spat on it and one of them stamped his boot on your face before they commenced on me.

And I should have been grateful that I was only being raped, though at the time all I could think of was how much more my body could take, and whether I would indeed be split in two as it felt, and if those endless thumping penises were ever going to stop, and if it was worse because I had been sliced *clean* those months before, or if rape was always like this. At one point, after the fifth, or sixth, they tossed me over onto my front and as the seventh, eighth, ninth and tenth pumped into me with roars and cheers, my face was pushed into the dirt right next to yours. My tears and snot smeared your face. We ate dirt together. And so when Mr el-Shataya makes his silent accusations about Essa's father I know he knows that she has ten or more fathers or none, and it is why I prefer to believe that her father could only be you.

———◆———

Yesterday, after three clients left me with application forms to complete – one of them needs to obtain a Medicare card – and letters to write – a relative in Brisbane – and a permission note for a child's excursion to the Institute of Science in Canberra, I still had time before I fetched Essa from school. I thought I may as well make use of the community centre's facilities, so I did some research and came across that magazine article where you said that Darfur represented the greatest failure of your life.

George, I promised you there would be good news toward the end of this letter and you must believe me that you did not fail, not me in any case. Every woman in the world wants George Clooney to father her child, or so I have read, and my child is the perfect and inno-cent result of an experience that until now has been too bitter for words but you must understand that every-thing about her brings me joy. Her pansy face. The light in her eyes. The soft plum of her mouth as she sucks the braids brushing her cheeks or eats her white bread and honey sandwich. I did not see their faces as they pumped and kicked and spat and ejaculated enough times to make a million children. I only saw your face, and I see it in her every day, and I want you to know that your involvement in my country was not the great failure that you think and that you were right to have been there, and I shall continue to believe that this was a good thing. I have to.

Yours sincerely

Miriam

Author's Note

An earlier version of 'If You See Something, Say Something' first appeared as 'The Signs' in www. saysomething.org.au (2006) and was also published in *The Big Issue* no 33, edited by Jo Case (14-27 July 2009); 'Writing [in] the New Millenium' was published in *New Australian Stories 2*, edited by Aviva Tuffield (Scribe: 2010); 'The Sleepers in that Quiet Earth' was published in *Best Australian Stories 2011*, edited by Cate Kennedy (Black Inc: 2011).

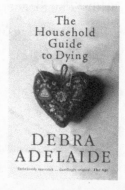